A Milkman,
a Vicar,
and a cat
with attitude

Dai Marshall Green

Publisher : Dai Marshall-Green (Independent Publisher)
Printed : via Kindle Direct Publishing

Book design by Dai Marshall-Green
Cover design by Dai Marshall-Green

ISBN - Paperback: 9798392244577

ISBN - Hardcover : 9798392508013

First Edition : May 2023

For My Family

PREFACE

New Year's Eve 2022, being the party animal that I am, I was on the hunt for some quality reading material to help me unwind and escape the mundane reality of life and fireworks.

I wanted relatable characters, a sprinkle of humour, and a dash of realism to spice things up. And then it hit - I couldn't be the only one craving this kind of story?

As I sat there pondering, I couldn't help but think about all the interesting people and scenarios I've encountered during my day job. From sex swings in the living room to dildos in the kitchen sink, I've seen it all. And let's not forget about the handcuffs still attached to the bed frame! As a professional, I had to maintain my composure, but my mind was going wild with questions and imagination.

So, I thought to myself, why not write a story about it all? And that's how "A Milkman, a Vicar, and a cat with attitude" came to be. It's been an absolute pleasure to put my thoughts and stories onto paper, and I hope you get a kick out of reading it as much as I did to write it.

Yours truly,
Dai x

INTRODUCTION

In *a rush this morning, I threw my everyday undies down for the wash and just put on what was on top in my lingerie drawer. Obviously, I wasn't thinking I'd get the call from mum nor end up here in a 1970's porn scene with two gorgeous (in my eyes), and topless hunks. I've got fencing to do. We've got fencing to do...*

On the plus side, I stand by a bit of advice my grandma gave me years back "Always match upstairs with downstairs in case of an accident. You don't want the doctors to think you can't afford matching underwear my child." The other clothing quote from her being "Never wear white – in case you shit yourself." A lady of wise words.

"Come on guys. Need to get this fencing done."

CONTENTS

ACKNOWLEDGMENTS

I would like to thank all the musical artists, composers, Fix Radio (Your music is what keeps me going throughout my days.) and, of course, any other person/business mentioned in this book as part of the fictitious life of Diana Doors and Co.

I'd also like to acknowledge my family and friends for answering many questions and reading my words without complaint. You are, as always, so very much appreciated.

Thank you all.

1 The Milkman Ad

Maybe he's exhibiting good manners, or maybe he just hasn't noticed I've run out of Veet.

I take a moment to catch my breath and wait, realising that either way, it's not as bad as I remember.

I needed a milkman. An actual, traditional milkman. One of those that delivers the milk at unearthly times of the morning. You know, when the rest of us are still in bed smashing the living daylights out of the snooze button (not our partners).

Yet here I am, splayed out like last month's turkey on the kitchen table wondering if it's just me who ends up in such odd situations.

As I push my stomach down to flatten it, I cannot help but think how "well-marbled" I appear these days – some would say, similar to a quality steak, if they were being polite. Admittedly I've always been an hourglass - nowadays I'm just a slightly easier one to see from a far distance.

Perhaps it would be best if I explained how I arrived at this moment, starting from yesterday.

Sat at my desk, I check my phone screen for what feels like the fiftieth time, or possibly even more, and finally see that Mabel Wainwright has approved my request to join the Malthay village community page. It seemed like an eternity since I had submitted the request, even though it was probably only a couple of hours in reality.

I desperately needed recommendations for a local milkman and was eager to get started on organising my new life; me being "ancient" and single, as my brother, Jack, referred to my present and un-chosen, situation.

Since I had moved to the village between Christmas and the New year, this was my first opportunity to begin settling in and making necessary arrangements. A morning cuppa was crucial for me, and the cat with attitude had a habit of getting cranky if he didn't receive his saucer of milk first thing upon waking.

After taking ages composing my message

"Looking for a milkman in the area - urgent! Please PM me for info." and hitting "send" I now hope to receive some responses by the end of the day, with a few potential candidates to reach out to.

The office remains quiet, and I too, am quietly doing a grand impression of a goldfish in a bowl, in my case, peering through the rippled glass panes, hoping for someone to arrive who either wants to sell a property or is interested in buying Mr Coburn's immense Edwardian home. Since his childhood, he has resided there. His father used the ground floor as a town surgery while his mother worked at the school. The Coburns are well-known among the locals, and it's disheartening to witness the house deteriorating.

In hindsight, adding the property to my books may not have been a wise decision, as it is unlikely to sell quickly.

However, that's just me. I specialise in taking on properties that other agents overlook - the ones that are rich in history or character. These are the properties that emit a musty smell when the front door creaks open once again and have dust playfully dancing in the shafts of sunlight that break through the yellowed window nets when you first enter the room. These are the properties that have a story to tell.

Generally, people sell their homes due to one of four reasons: births, deaths, marriage, or divorce.

As "mere" estate agents, we are often regarded as dishonest and untruthful, which may lead some to believe that this is not a viable, nor wise, career path. However, I am passionate about my work. I love it as a job and put my heart and soul into my small business. I take pride in the fact that neither myself nor my staff (Dylan) have received a negative review on the renowned 'Trusttheagent-ornot.com'

Yet again I check my mobile. And surprise, surprise, nothing there. It's like waiting for a text from your crush who never actually liked you in the first place. This new phone is supposed to be the latest and greatest, but I'm starting to think it's smarter than me. That teenager who sold me on the idea of a phone, equal in size to an actual telephone directory, clearly didn't mention the hours of online video tutorials I'd need, just to figure out how to turn the darn thing on.

Maybe I should log onto "Slapface" and see if anyone's messaged me. Nope, just the sound of crickets.

Since there isn't much activity going on, it is agreed, at an impromptu staff meeting, to have an early lunch. As I step outside, the aroma of damp autumn leaves, abandoned and decomposing in the storm gullies running with the pavement, whacks me full on up the nose, enough to clear any blocked airways - if you happen to have such an inconvenience.

It's the end of the first week of January, and everything still feels incredibly slow. From the weather to the familiar faces of others sluggishly returning to work, everything appears to be in a seasonal slumber with post-Christmas blues added to the mix. The fog not having lifted yet leaves my fringe hanging with small droplets of water from the wet air; I regret not putting on my faithful hat to protect my rather unruly mane of hair.

Turning the corner into the High Street, Dave, the butcher, is serving Mrs Bates, no doubt purchasing tripe for Hedley, her husband. I smile as I duck under the lime tree branches - one of many limes planted to line the high street decades ago - he nods and tips his trilby back in jovial acknowledgement.

The cobbled streets reflect the glow from the modern equivalent of the old gas streetlamps interspersed between the limes; they're not the same as the ones replaced but at least the parish council allowed us something I suppose, and they still maintain the ambience and heritage of the place.

The old bakery, with its twin, bottle glass bay windows and seemingly miniature front door, is only a few hundred yards from the office. The card shop, next door, originally the newsagents, is also owned by the same family now. "Gives the daughter something to do away from the kids" according to Bob, who inherited the business from his father.

"Usual, Diana? Or can I entice you with these strange plant-based steamed bun things? They're not proving popular with the regulars but the through traffic seem quite keen."

"I think you may be on a losing streak trying to get this farming community to give up their daily bovine, ovine, galine and swine, Bob!"

"Only you would describe it like that Diana. Like father, like daughter."

Despite the tempting scent of bacon, I manage to resist and opt for my usual chicken salad sandwich and a can of fizz. After lunch, sat on a memorial bench for the late vicar, I take a leisurely stroll around the block, which involves walking along the rest of the high street and through a narrow twitten between the old Methodist Hall and a towering Ash tree.

If you look closely at the tree's bark, you can spot the faded carved initials "NM x DD forever," which I etched into it with my trusty penknife many years ago.

Continuing on, I arrive at the once bustling Richdore Station, which has been repurposed as a trendy craft beer bar called "Bobcats & Boots," popular among the younger crowd.

The former railway line that runs alongside the station has been converted into a public footpath and cycleway thanks to a local fitness grant initiative. I'm yet to use it. I get enough exercise helping out at the farm.

Besides, I still recall the excitement of the train coming in and how we'd go on school trips to the coast, playing "I Spy" for landmarks along the way, and personally, I much prefer to reminisce of the halcyon days of youth than get on a bike.

I'm greeted back at the office by the top of Dylan's head. "No calls." he informs me and grins, before returning to watching ten second videos on the latest trending app. I have no idea what it's called but he seems to like it.

The afternoon passes with tidying the post-Christmas tat and paraphernalia away, interrupted only by sporadic conversations. And, as the day draws to a close, I start to tidy up my desk, making a mental note of what needs to be done tomorrow. Dylan returns from his deliveries, proudly showing me a handwritten note from one of the vendors thanking us for the personal touch. It's these small gestures that make our job worthwhile, and I feel grateful to work in a community that values them.

With a final check of my emails, I shut down my computer and grab my coat, bidding farewell to Dylan and the empty office. The fog has finally lifted, and the streetlights glow warmly against the darkening sky. I take a deep breath of fresh air, feeling content with the day's work and the familiar surroundings of my hometown.

As I walk back to the car park, passing by the lime trees and cobbled streets, I reflect on the beauty of small-town living, where everyone knows each other's name and life moves at a slower pace. It may not be the most exciting or glamorous place, but to me, it's home.

Back at the cottage I let the pups out. Christa, next door, has kindly been checking in on them. She will be returning to work in the next few months from baby-making leave and I'll need to sort a dog sitter out, but in the meantime she's happy with the arrangement and gives her a bit of peace and quiet from her home life I would imagine.

I reach for my brick sized mobile and see that I have a notification from the Malthay village community page.

It's a response to my request for a milkman, but it's not the enthusiastic "Yes, we'll get right on it!" that I was hoping for. Instead, it's a stiff message from Mabel Wainwright, requesting more information before they can even consider my request.

"We appreciate your request for a milkman. However, we kindly ask you to provide additional details before we can approve your request. It would be helpful if you could provide us with more information. Remember – be kind. Be inclusive. Thank you. Best regards, Mabel Wainwright."

Oh dear, Mabel Wainwright and her bureaucratic approach to milk delivery is giving me flashbacks of dealing with the local council. I mean, what more do they need to know? Do I need to submit a full CV and cover letter to get my milk delivered?

But ever the people-pleaser, I take a deep breath and try to compose a post that will satisfy Mabel and her milkman approval committee but at the same time, not make me sound desperate.

"Attention all milkmen... or woman... or is it milkperson these days? Single lady, new to village, seeks early riser milk delivery to fuel her morning addiction. Must be punctual, reliable, and able to resist the temptation to take a sip from the bottle. Please slide into my DMs for more info."

And just like that, my post is approved and up on the community page. I get the feeling Mabel Wainwright was literally sitting, phone in hand, awaiting that text! I can practically feel the judgment from the other villagers as they read my sad plea for milk. But I don't care. A girl's gotta do what a girl's gotta do to get her dairy fix. Bring on the milkman…milkperson darn it!

Propped up in bed, surrounded by two pups and the cat with attitude, all staring up at me wondering why I was purposely starving them at midnight, I open "Slapface" and check my private messages. There are a few and scrolling through there are obviously some not meant for me. I stop on one from "The Milkman." Self-explanatory and to the point.

"Message me your address and I will deliver whatever you want in the morning. Welcome to the village." It reads.

"Hi. Hazel Cottage, on the triangle, opposite the walnut tree (the tree not the pub). I know it's short notice so will appreciate whatever you have. Any time before 6:30 would be good. I will probably be in the kitchen in my dressing gown, but the puppies will be out and about to greet you. Hope that's okay?"

"Perfect."

I can't help but feel a rush of excitement. Could it be that easy? Could I have finally found my milkman saviour?

I lay back against my pillows, my mind drifting off to visions of creamy milk in glass bottles, delivered fresh to my doorstep every morning. Maybe I could even start making my own butter or cheese with it. The possibilities are endless!

But then reality hits me. What if this milkman turns out to be unreliable, or worse, creepy? What if he starts leaving me notes or stalking me? I push the thoughts aside, reminding myself that this is a small village, and everyone knows everyone. Surely, it will be fine.

As I drift off to sleep, my mind still buzzing with thoughts of fresh milk, I can't help but feel a little giddy with excitement. Who knew finding a milkman could be so exhilarating?

And now back to today...

Having completely forgotten about the late-night text conversation, I haul myself out of bed half asleep, trip over a dog, three pillows off the bed and the silk pyjamas I attempt to sleep in each night (but always rapidly remove after they give me two static shocks, crutch burn and armpit strangulation), and head for the shower.

With trepidation, I enter said shower, which, like my mobile phone, is a work in progress. I prepare myself for the worst as I turn on the water,

11

recalling the three times I've been frozen and the two times I've been boiled since moving in. However, to my pleasant surprise, the water is at a comfortable temperature, and I get down to business.

I let the water run through my hair, over my face and body longer than required. It's my routine now to have a decent shower each morning rather than a quick session and out again, especially as I now have an airing cupboard full of toiletry gift boxes to work my way through.

Lathering up my hair, which now falls close to my waist, the smell of coconut fills the room. Can't stand to eat the stuff but quite like the smell. I continue the coconut themed experience as I sponge my body. Over the years I've become slightly "fleshier" and there seems to be additional curves, nooks, and crevices to wash; I have to lift my breasts now to clear the soap suds. For a moment, the thought of them becoming even larger crosses my mind. I imagine a scenario where they would be big enough to wear as a scarf or, in a more humorous twist, kick like footballs if gravity takes its toll.

Sometimes I wish Nate were still with me so he could wash my back. He'd sponge me over, lift my locks and kiss the nape of my neck. It was always such a sensual feeling. One I miss greatly, although it was about as close as we'd come to being intimate and partly the reason, he isn't here any longer... Instead, one performs increasingly varying awkward manoeuvres that once upon a time I did with ease.

I'm sure there is a spot right in the centre of my back, you know reader, where the bra strap goes across? I bet that gets completely missed each time.

And how exactly do you wash your lady bits with a fixed overhead shower? Do you swing your leg up against the wall and contort your body with the vague hope some water trickles between your thighs? Or do you reverse in and aim your backside upwards with your head towards your toes?

Ah, the joys of post-shower rituals! I step out of the steamy oasis and begin the awkward tip-toe dance towards the towel, which of course, is always on the other side of the room. After a quick rubdown that does nothing to alleviate the dampness, I launch into a frantic search for the last remnants of my stupidly long lasting and not much liked "Faint hint of autumn sun on a warm rain kind of day" moisturiser (the one your aunt gives you annually and you don't feel you can throw it away - but detest greatly.) Finally, I spot it lurking under the sink like a forgotten treasure and proceed to apply it liberally in long strokes up and down my body. The resulting scent is a confusing mix of pina colada and pine needles (or so I think) now its combined with the shampoo and body wash. But at least I can finally chuck the "autumn sun" into the bin where it belongs…until next Christmas again anyway.

With my unruly hair tossed up into a scruffy ponytail, I scuttle across the landing, praying to the gods of good timing that no one is up and about just yet across the way. The thought of Christa or her husband catching me in my post-shower state, or worse yet, one of the kids spying me through their bedroom window, can make me break out in a proverbial cold sweat. But alas for them, luck is on my side, and I make it across the landing unscathed. Another morning, another victory.

I check the time, and my heart sinks as I see that it's already just past six. The puppies are probably up and eager to wreak havoc in the garden.

With a resigned sigh, I throw on my trusty dressing gown and trudge downstairs, bracing myself for the inevitable onslaught of chaos and destruction.

The morning air is chilly and frosty, but I leave the stable door ajar so that I can keep an eye on the puppies while they do their business and explore the great outdoors. I watch as they scamper about, their, not so tiny, paws leaving little(ish) imprints in the grass, as they sniff and investigate all the new scents that have magically appeared since last night.

Once they're sufficiently settled, doing their thing, it's time for me to take a breather and enjoy a cuppa while I listen to some music. I yell across the kitchen to my temperamental device, which, as always, is perched precariously on top of the fridge to get the best signal.

"Margaret! Play some tunes!" I request, and joy of joys, OMD, one of Nate's favourite bands, starts playing "If You Leave." The irony of the situation is not lost on me - after all, he was the one who left. But I push the thought aside and allow myself to get lost in the music for a little while.

Leaning over the stable door with my hot drink in hand, I take a moment to appreciate Mother Nature's handiwork of the dark hours. The trees are frozen in time, adorned with large white crystals of ice on every skeletal branch and trunk. The grass glistens in the early morning sun, with just a hint of steam rising above, as a very cheerful Robin Redbreast sings from the top of the remaining fence between my property and Christa's.

As I watch the puppies chase the cat from next door, I feel a sense of belonging, as if I should have been here a long time ago.

It's been two years since Nate and I separated, and the first year was particularly challenging, as we didn't speak to each other. Over the past twelve months, we've made more of an effort, and have finally agreed to start couples counselling, but I must confess, I am now enjoying the single life. Looking back, I should have moved out of the marital home right at the beginning.

Do I really want to get back with him now? After what he said?

Hang on, what's that?

As I feel the pressure against me again and again, in perfect rhythm with The Lumineers' "Ophelia" playing in the background, I realise it's not the cat. With each touch, the pressure becomes stronger, and my body instinctively responds, moving in a way it hasn't in ages. The feeling of my dressing gown lifting up my back, tracing over my skin and giving me forgotten sensations, sends tingles down my spine, and I hear an appreciative murmur.

Suddenly, hands grab my hips and pull me away from the door, turning me towards the room.

The milkman has arrived.

Deeply brown with long, bovine lashes, his eyes have a mesmerizing effect on me. I feel like I would do anything he wanted, absolutely anything. Substantially taller than me he grins and presses himself hard against me pushing himself between my legs. It was an unusual way of introducing themselves but by jove I needed this.

His hands move from my hips to my chest. My gown, wanting to participate in the fun, falls wide open with a single pull of the cord revealing everything. I mean literally everything too – boobs heading southwards, stomach going left and right trying to hide around the back. Everything!

"Morning." he says, slightly breathlessly, as he lightly runs a finger down between my breasts. His voice is raspy and deep.

I about hold myself together with an "It is." response, feeling myself blush further than I am already.

His finger continues to trace the contours of my torso further down until it arrives between my legs. I let out a quiet moan as he touches gently, ever so gently, the skin.

I'm still standing facing him as his hand goes even further, and with the action of someone who knows what they are doing, quickly I feel his finger rub the top of my ...erm...lady parts... A shock wave runs through my body. Nobody has touched me like this. Ever.

I want more. He has two fingers inside me now. Slowly he pushes deeper. I close my eyes concentrating on the sensation and trying not to think how I look.

He murmurs again and leans in pressing his hand

against me, his fingers inside me and his lips near mine.

"You want more?"

Oh yes! I open my legs further, but he has me by my waist and takes me into the room.

My gown falls away to the floor and I am naked, complete with all my wobbly bits. He does not notice. I watch as he removes his white coat revealing a t-shirt pulled tight over his chest and biceps. Just as in the films he lifts his top over his head and begins to remove his jeans.

Is this really happening? Or have I unwittingly taken the catnip in my morning cuppa?

"Wait!" he says, as I move out of view of the stable door, feeling totally on show to the outside world. And let's be honest, there's a lot of me to see for any unfortunate person who happens to be looking!

Within seconds he too stands naked and pulls me against him. He smells really good. I mean really, really good. A cross between what everyone imagines George Clooney smells like and James Bond maybe. His...um... thing...rock hard and rubbing against me. Before I know it, he has lifted me onto the table.

"Lay back." he instructs. I do as I'm told.

"It's a bit hard."

"I know it is."

"No, not that. I meant the table. The table is hard."

"Oh. Hang on. Stand up." He picks my terry towelling gown off the floor and lays it on the table.

"Try again." He indicates for me to lay back down. I do.

I shiver. I don't know if it's the wintery weather and the door still open, the cold wood still touching areas of my body, or what I was anticipating coming. He lifts my arms above my head, holding then down with both hands, and begins to kiss my mouth. His lips move slowly towards my breasts. I can feel his breath on my body.

Then, he kisses and teases my nipple with his tongue before sucking it hard, I'm groaning. It's been so long.

Then he's working on the other before moving further down my body. His hands release my arms, but they seem to stay where they are. His head moves until his mouth is kissing the top of my legs, teasing me further.

I'm aching to feel him lick me, touch me with his

tongue. He hovers and sucks hard on me. No warning. My legs open wider as he licks and sucks me and then ...

Out of nowhere, my inner voice decides to make an appearance, and boy, as usual it's far too chatty for its own good. "Is it just me?" it asks. "Why didn't I buy the Veet?," "Be quite Diana. Concentrate!"

I can feel my belly jiggling with every movement, and I can't help but wish it were a little more toned. And to top it all off, I'm holding my breasts, trying my best to avoid looking like Christmas dinner prep time. Does he notice? I can't tell. But these thoughts are racing through my mind, and I can't seem to silence them. Oh, the joys of being a human with a constantly chattering inner voice? And then he sucks again, and he doesn't care. He really doesn't care!

And with that realisation I clutch his hair and push his head and, in turn, mouth harder on to me. I feel myself building up inside. His tongue is working, gently licking me then sucking me. His fingers are inside me again pushing slowly. Is it two? Maybe three? It feels so good. A pulse starts racing from my feet, up my legs and into me. I can't stop it. I tense my body, the pressure still building and he's still licking and sucking. I let out a loud, involuntary Meg Ryan impression "Yes! Yes! Yes!"

He looks up and smiles again. Those eyes ...

"Don't stop!" I blurt out. My body relaxes down, but I still need more.

He stands and pulls me towards him. My legs either side, I feel him enter me. Slowly. We're staring into each other as he withdraws, but not completely. He then flashes his perfect teeth and pushes right into me.

The music has changed and now just as the lyrics say, we start doing it like mammals. His rhythm and mine increasing. I feel him. He fills me. There's no waggling around. He's solid and it feels bloody fantastic! He turns me around and coaxes me to stand.

"Bend over." I do.

He pushes against me but this time there's no teasing, he penetrates. Grabbing my hips and ramming himself continuously until he releases inside of me. He pushes in hard and collapses onto my back and we stay that way for a moment.

I can feel his weight pressing down on me, and his muscled thigh is pinching my skin against the dense wood of the table. It's not exactly a romantic scene, but I'm too knackered to complain.

I also know I still need to make the walk of shame to the bathroom once he gets off me, so I'm just biding my time until then. It's definitely not the most glamorous moment, but hey, love-making is messy and sometimes involves being squished like a pancake!

And that, dear reader, is how I found myself upon the kitchen table. Rudely ended by the cat with attitude jumping at the leg of the milkman.

He must have smelt the milk!

2 Need A Hand

I'll be darned! The third week of February has just strolled in. A bit like the cat with attitude. The weather is as British as a cup of tea - frosty mornings, a bit of snow, and temperatures that never rise above lukewarm. And of course, let's not forget the rain - it's like someone's been turning on the shower every few hours just for the hell of it.

But fear not, for Dylan and I have a plan to combat the dreariness of the day - we're going to indulge in another cuppa and the cupcakes that were generously gifted to us by a vendor last night, whilst we trawl through the diary appointments. I mean, who needs sunshine when you have sugar, am I right dear reader?

Speaking of appointments, today's adventure takes me to visit Mr and Mrs Braye. They're part of the handful of folks who decided to ditch the hustle and bustle of the big city and move to the quaint Richdore instead. They used to run the local hardware store on the high street, but they are both in their eighties and Mr Braye had been diagnosed with dementia and now, just in recent months, Parkinson's.

They're hoping to sell their home and move closer to their son.

"Good morning Mrs Braye. It's Diana from Doors Estate Agency. Is it still convenient to call around this morning for our appointment?"

"Of course, darling. I'll put the kettle on."

Richdore, a rural town with a market where local farmers and small traders still sell their goods weekly, was named after a wealthy individual who resided at the top of a hill, in a manor with a gilded door.

In the thirteenth century, Richdore was recorded as a small hamlet that shared the church of St. Mary at Malthay with two other settlements. Over time, the town has grown into a reasonable size with many streets and lanes lined with ancient trees that once marked the horse tracks from surrounding farms, villages, and hamlets to the market square.

Most of these throughways are now named after local families, nearby landmarks, or random farm animals. One such lane, "Swinehogsow Lane," is a personal favourite of mine, and I often ponder whether the person who named it just stood there one day with the equivalent of today's clipboard and pen, went "Fuck It! If it's got to have the "pig" name why not have three?" and then walked off whistling, kicking their heels together and feeling proud of themselves for another day.

Doors Estate Agency is located in a position overlooking the square, providing me with a clear view from my desk of the old water pump and spring, the florists, and another agency called 'Buttards' (Whose name does unfortunately reflect their nature - if you understand what I am saying.) Additionally, I can also see the recycling bins that seem to be multiplying in nature over the years.

Meanwhile, Dylan's desk has a view of the public house, barbers, and the car park, provided he peeks around one of the ancient oaks that still stands. Overall, it is a pleasant view, particularly during the winter when we can spend a considerable amount of time doing the much under-rated hobby of people-watching.

At our agency, we handle a range of properties that cater to different preferences and locations. Some properties are situated in the heart of Richdore, while others are nestled in the glorious (in my eyes anyway), surrounding countryside.

Personally, I always find the latter to be particularly appealing, with properties like the Brayes' residence offering a peaceful and secluded lifestyle.

As you leave Richdore, the roads narrow and wind through the countryside, surrounded by fields and woodlands. However, it's worth noting that these roads are also used by agricultural vehicles, which can sometimes cause delays. It's a small price to pay for the tranquillity of living in such a beautiful and natural environment.

As someone who appreciates the charm of rural living, I always advise clients to factor in a few extra minutes for their journeys when exploring properties outside of the town.

As I make my way to the Brayes' residence, which is about five miles away, I am already regretting my decision to wear my full-length coat inside the beast. While the wool coat is incredibly toasty when I am outside, it becomes more like a toaster inside the vehicle, especially when I forget to turn off the heated seat in the four-by-four.

Despite being a bit battered, the vehicle gets me from A to B without any issues, and its large rear has come in handy on more occasions than I can count on both hands - mainly for when tenants purchase super king beds or corner sofas for small flats, having not listened to anyone pointing out the obvious flaw to their latest buy. It used to belong to Nate before he upgraded to one with a larger cargo bed, which he now affectionately calls "Enola Gay." I believe.

I park down the lane in a small lay-by. The Brayes say I can park on the drive but, as always, I am early. Plus, it usually gives me time to finish listening to whatever music is playing on the CD. I have music playing all the time and my taste varies considerably. Today happens to be a bit of northern soul. It helps me settle my thoughts and puts me in the right frame of mind for whatever the occasion may be.

And presently my rather vivid thoughts are recapturing the "milkman moment" as I have started to call it. Probably best not to dwell on it too much but rather learn from it and remember to make my adverts a tad clearer in the future. Don't get me wrong though… my body was absolutely craving for the attention, and I wouldn't mind a bit more of the "how's your father?" type of thing, but who in their right mind wants a potential divorcee, with baggage of an ex-husband as well as so obviously letting themselves go in the physical sense too?

Back to my music, I much prefer easy listening first thing when I get up, as my brain doesn't get frazzled from the boom, boom, boom of the latest stuff, whilst I have my cuppa. Whereas throughout the day anything goes I suppose. I blame my dad who loved a good sing song or "croon" as he would describe it when he listened to the radio at home or in his vehicle cab. In the bath it's got to be a bit classical. No candles or rose petals, they go everywhere and are a pain to clear up too. A bit of Pachelbel's Canon in D major will do nicely.

Deciding I need to add some exercise into my day, I leave the beast in the lay-by and walk the steep gradient up to the house, yanking my hat on as I go. There are only two properties in the lane, and each belongs to the Brayes. I'm already familiar with both.

The smaller one they privately rent out and the larger farmhouse they live in further along.

It is the farmhouse I am here to see today. I haven't been in the main family home really since childhood, where I spent every summer holiday in the orchards picking various fruits, and the autumn and winter breaks, stone picking with mum and Jack. Us and other mums and their kids would collect the largest flints, boulders, and rocks, piling them in small mounds at the edge of the field. It meant the machines at the time wouldn't hit them and get damaged (much). We'd use a large digging bar with a tapered end to stick into the ground and lever out the massive ones. I still have such a lever at the cottage that mum used.

Fond memories flood back as I look over towards the fields now. Still quite icy, I can feel my boots doing the odd slip and slide on the flint, which has long been used to top the track off, making it into the lane it is today. Thankfully, I arrive at the front door without falling on my backside first.

I look for the doorbell and my heart sinks to see it's one of those camera ones. I look awful in them –

today I'm a cloche hat wearing, blue eyed blob face with a massive mop of wavy hair. I take a deep breath, straighten my coat, press the button and instantly I hear a faint ringing sound from somewhere inside the house.

After a few moments, an older person's voice comes through the intercom.

"Hello?" It's Mrs. Braye, and I recognise her instantly.

"Hi. It's Diana Doors from Doors Estate Agency Mrs Braye" I shout at the doorbell.

As the door swings open, there stands Mrs Braye in her homemade apron, just as I had pictured her. In the shop, she was known for her skill in creating pinnies, which she wore while lifting heavy sacks of coal onto trucks or measuring nails and tacks for the local builders. The couple are greatly cherished within the town's community due to their long-standing help within the local people and charities.

"Hello, Mrs Braye."

"Now dear, please call me Veronica. You really ought to know better than to be so formal. I had the kettle waiting for you. It's just boiled."

We walk along the hallway; the musty smell takes me back to my preteen years visiting my grandparents here. The familiar little telephone table, still with the old GPO red dial telephone sat on it and the faded quilted seat where I sat as a young teenager, sobbing my heart out when Grandad died. Walls smattered with old black and white family photographs of the Brayes, mainly, clocks and even a newspaper cutting from when they retired. We head towards the back reception room and Mr Braye.

There are further photos of her husband in his demob suit holding a pint up in the air in what looks like an east end pub behind his chair. He was quite a handsome chap in his younger years.

"Reg, it's Diana. Diana Doors. I informed you earlier that she would be visiting today. Remember?" Veronica gesticulates towards me, and Reg fixes his stare upon me, tilting his head to one side.

"No, it's not!" he retorts with a touch of anger. "That person is not Diana!" ... deep breath, and here we go again ...

"Oh Reg, you old joker! You had us going there for a minute," I chuckle, trying to diffuse the tension.

"But I promise you, I am indeed Diana Doors. I'm the daughter of Thomas Doors, and the brains behind Doors Estate Agency." I try my best friendly smile.

Reg looks at me skeptically, but Veronica jumps in to back me up.

"That's right, Reg. Diana used to come in here all the time with her parents. And she's grown up to be quite the successful businesswoman!"

But Reg is not convinced. "Nonsense, Veronica! Diana died years ago! I remember it like it was yesterday. She was a real stunner, blonde hair, big boobs, died in 1984. "Oh, how I miss her" he trails off, realising he's probably said too much.

Veronica shakes her head in disbelief. "Oh, Reginald. You can remember the important things, can't you? But don't worry, Diana. It's just his memory playing tricks on him. He's been known to reminisce about singing in the pub in Benthal Green with 'that' Diana too!"

I can't help but shake my head, it sounds like he may have done a bit more than sing with her … I smile at the strange tangent our conversation has taken, however, it's not the first time.

My thoughts briefly turn to my dad's odd sense of humour and the naming conventions that have followed my brother and me throughout our lives.

It's not every day you meet someone named after a bombshell or a black-feathered corvid like the Jackdaw. And yet, here we are, two siblings with names that elicit either disappointment or bird noises from those we meet.

Growing up in this area, surrounded by nature and its various avian inhabitants, it was no surprise that the local kids had a whole repertoire of bird calls at their disposal. But oddly enough, the Jackdaw's distinctive "tchack" call was rarely used. I guess my poor brother was spared that particular indignity.

But despite the occasional awkward encounter, I wouldn't have it any other way. My dad's humour may have been an acquired taste, but it's also a daily reminder to not take life too seriously and to find joy in the unexpected. After all, who knows what kind of bizarre conversations and experiences await us in the future?

"Diana Doors and Jack Doors ... your father knew what he was doing. I bet he's smiling from above. How's Sauerkraut?" Reg asks.

I chuckle at Reg's comment about my dad's naming choices and nod in agreement. "I'm sure he is," I reply. "And Sauerkraut is doing just fine, thanks for asking. The cough seems to have cleared that has been hanging around all winter."

My mother, Rosa, locally known by her nickname purely due to her harsh German accent, was still alive and living in the adjoining farm my brother and I were born in, about two miles up from here.

As we continue to chat, I'm struck by how even in the midst of Reg's struggles with the dementia and

Parkinson's, he's still able to remember certain things and make connections to the past. It's a reminder that memory and identity are complex things, and that even as we age or face challenges, there are still parts of ourselves that remain constant.

"Before we start, how is your tenant getting on down the road? He's been there some time now."

"Daniel is lovely. So helpful. Does all sorts around here and at the cottage. Never see any visiting lady... or gentlemen guests, come to think of it. No bother at all."

Veronica takes me on a tour of the property, which feels more like a trip down memory lane than a new experience.

I will explore the grounds by myself later. Reg, who is unsteady on his feet and has visual tremors in his hands, chooses to remain seated by the television. His wife reliably informs me he will be asleep by the time I'm back indoors. She is correct of course. It's been a rapid process from first symptoms to where he is today.

As we make our way around the old house, it's like I'm stepping into a time machine. Memories from my own childhood rush back like a herd of wild horses, but instead of being greeted with hugs and ice cream, I'm here to sell it to potential buyers.

Veronica's doing her best to keep the place tidy and clean, but with fifteen rooms and two massive staircases, it's a bit like trying to herd cats. I can see the remnants of the grandkids' visits, with old-fashioned rocking horses, dolls houses, and an ancient tin train that belonged to Veronica and Reg's son. They're all grown up now and living their own lives, so the train doesn't get much, if any, use these days.

Like most houses, this one is full of happy and sad memories, but it's especially poignant for me because of my personal history with it. It'll be a real heart-wrencher when the time comes to shut the front door for the final time. But fear not, dear reader, for I will be here for them every step of the way, from start to finish. Because as I said before, that's the way I do things – I'm dedicated, determined, a glutton for punishment and maybe just a little bit sentimental!

The appointment is taking several hours, and I feel like I've been here for a lifetime (in a good way). Reg keeps waking up and asking which Diana I am and what I'm doing here, as if he's a secret agent trying to uncover my true identity. Veronica is doing her best to keep him on track, but the conversation still veers off in unexpected directions, from their days in London to their latest gardening woes. I'm starting to feel like I'm in the throes of a pleasant house arrest.

It's my half-day, and I have nothing better to do, I

might as well stick around and see if they have any more tales to tell. And by the time I finally extract myself from their chatty clutches, it's already mid-afternoon.

Hat and coat back on, I zip up my boots, say my goodbyes and head to the front door. I quickly send a text "On my way." and head out, back towards the beast.

The snow is falling heavily, coating everything in sight with a blanket of white. It's definitely cold enough for it to stick, but it's not a winter apocalypse or anything. Just a few inches of fluffy stuff. I was so engrossed in the warm and cosy conversation inside the house that I completely forgot to check the weather outside when I came back from the crew yard. But hey, who needs to worry about the cold when you're surrounded by good company and a roaring fire?

As I retrace my steps back down the 13° decline to the beast, it's like I'm on an ice rink, except instead of gliding gracefully like a figure skater, I'm stumbling around like a drunk penguin. Now, the smart thing to do would have been to grab onto the wrought iron fence or hedgerow for dear life, but of course, I didn't do that. Why, you ask? Well, it's because my brain took so long to process the danger that by the time, I started to think about grabbing onto something, my butt was already making contact with the ground.

Thankfully, I've been blessed with some extra cushioning in the derriere department (thank you, pizza, and ice cream), so my falls were cushioned... somewhat. I say somewhat because I proceeded to fall two more times before finally reaching the beast. It was like a game of whack-a-mole, but instead of moles, it was my own butt popping up and down on the ice.

As I made my way towards the vehicle, I must have looked like a flailing octopus, with one arm going in every direction while the other clung onto my precious folder for dear life. Eventually, I come to a stop, sprawled out on my back with my legs halfway under the beast.

All in all, it's safe to say that my graceful descent was a complete disaster. But hey, at least I got a good workout in and again, thankfully, nobody around to have watched.

"What a sight that was!" comes a voice. "I'm sorry. I shouldn't have laughed. Need a hand?"

"Bugger!" Apparently there was an audience after all.

"Interesting way to get back to your vehicle. What was that manoeuvre? Cats on ice?!"

"I agree. It wasn't the most dignified walk to a car I suppose. Ungainly, in fact." Trying to hold on to some semblance of self-respect and poise, I allow myself to be dragged out.

"Do you want to come in and warm up a bit? Unless you need to go somewhere else right now?"

"I wouldn't mind washing my hands if that's alright with you. I don't want to disrupt your day."

As I enter the snug little cottage behind Daniel, I can't help but appreciate the view from behind. He's definitely my type, and I can feel my heart racing with excitement. Of course, I'm just being professional - but a girl can dream? I'm sure he's noticed my blushes whenever we speak, but he probably just thinks I'm having hot flashes or something. Who am I kidding?

Anyway, back to reality - the cottage is tidy and well-maintained, with a row of wellies lined up in the porch and a warm fire crackling away in the front room. Bobby Darin's 'Heart of the City' plays from the kitchen. I love this song.

"Cuppa?" Daniel pulls out a couple of mugs from the cupboard. There's a familiarity about them. I've had them in the past.

"Yes please. I'd appreciate one."

"No problem. Take a seat and I'll bring it in. Feel free to kick your boots off and stay a while. Wait for the weather to settle and then I'll help you out the lane if you want. Saw your mum and brother the other day. Looking well. Don't get to see many peeps around here so that was nice. A quick chat and then they went back to the farm in the buggy. Think they had been to see next door."

Since I don't have any concrete plans for the afternoon, spending time with Daniel seems like a good way to pass the time. I've made up my mind. Besides, I really don't want to admit to feeling sore and bruised.

As I hesitantly try to take off my boot, trying not to show I'm feeling a tad tender, Daniel enters the room with two mugs of tea in hand.

"Are you alright?" he asks me with some concern.

"Let me help you."

With that, the mugs are swiftly placed on the solid wood mantle still dressed in fairy lights and tinsel, and he crouches down to unzip my boot.

"Bear with, haven't had much practice recently doing this. There is something about knee tall boots on a lady. Get the look right and it can be so feminine."

"Not sure I've got the look right! I don't think grass sods, mud and slush is a look to be honest."

"You always look lovely. The long-lined coat, hat, three quarter length skirt and then these boots. Black, leather boots with the sneaky laces up the back – it's the perfect combination." he reassures.

"I didn't realise men took that much notice about what women wear." I'm secretly quite impressed with his observation skills.

"You'll be surprised. Some of us do. Does that feel better?"

Without thinking Daniel begins to caringly rub my leg.

"Oh! I'm so sorry... again! Keep apologising today! I wasn't thinking."

"It's fine. Felt nice actually." Part of me didn't want him to stop. I've missed the affectionate touch of someone that you want to be near to.

He hands me the warm tea, and as his fingers graze mine, a slight tickle runs up my arm. Although I try to ignore it, I had often fantasized about being this close to "the" Daniel, never genuinely believing it could happen.

Let's be honest here reader, who wouldn't want a

Daniel in their lives? Even Dylan sighs when he sees him walk in. He's commented that there's no chance any average male could compete on looks in the same vicinity as the male currently here with me.

We sit in silence for a moment.

The song has moved on to Andy Williams singing "Walk Hand in Hand." I begin to sing along in my head.

"I love this song. It reminds me of my wife. We used to try and dance to it every time it played in the kitchen."

Daniel says, as he stands up from his chair, carefully avoiding the large dog bed on the floor next to it.

The way his jeans hug his figure, the way his broad shoulders move as he walks... he puts his arms around his imaginary dance partner and begins to waltz slowly across the room.

"Do you know this song?" he asks.

I hesitate, then hear myself say "Umm, no."

Why did I say that?! I know every word. Like, literally every word for Pete's sake! Shut up inner voice!

"Really?! That surprises me. Fair enough. Wanna

dance?"

In that moment, all I wanted was to dance with him. I yearned for his arms to envelop me tightly, to breathe in his scent, and to nuzzle into his neck while running my fingers through his hair.

However, I hesitate and say, "It's okay. I'm not a particularly good dancer."

In the middle of his twirl, Daniel halts and walks a few steps towards me before grasping my hand.

"Allow me to take charge," he effortlessly lifts me up while bringing me nearer to him.

We sway together slowly, moving around the room to the music. Another slow song follows, and we continue to dance, lost in the moment. The aches and pains from playing whack-a-mole, which had previously nagged me, seem to have settled, or perhaps I was just choosing to ignore them.

"I apologise for the playlist. I must have created it after a glass of wine or two, in a black cloud moment thinking about the ex."

BAM! Nate would also use that unusual term "black cloud moment."

As those words leave his lips, I am quickly transported to another time and place, surrounded by couples being swept around a large hall, all caught up in the throngs of dance lessons that had become popular thanks to a TV program. But like many things we tried to do together, that time didn't last, as he was always busy with work.

I feel Daniel's chest against my face, and suddenly I'm brought back to the present moment. The music stops, but he's still holding me close, and I can feel the heat from his body warming my cheek. As I look up, I notice that his mouth is right next to mine, and I feel conflicted.

I want it, but I know it's unprofessional. I pull away instantly, telling myself that I can't do this. Despite the attraction I feel towards him, I know he loves his blasted wife, even if she's not with him at the moment.

Oh, hang on. She's not here!

Sod it! I'm going in ...

Our lips touch and we share a brief but intense kiss. The warmth of his lips lingers on mine as we pull away, our eyes locked in a moment of understanding. The fire crackles in the background, casting a warm glow around us. It's a simple moment, but it feels like it has the potential to change everything.

And then it happens again. We are oblivious. Our world right here, right now is all about wanton passion. There's a connection! An attraction! And it's bloody mutual! This man wants me. Wants my body – there's not much natural daylight here and maybe he can't see very well. Oh, and I want him. All of him!

His lips caress my neck. His hands begin unbuttoning my blouse.

My mind is racing. Hello? Have you got decent lingerie on? What about those wobbly bits? Stretch marks?! What if he sees those?

His hands are now on my skin holding me tight against him. His fingers trace my nipples. They respond and through the lace they harden. He keeps teasing and they harden further. He kisses them gently in turn and returns his attention to my mouth.

"Touch me. I want you to touch me" He takes my hand and places it over the flies of his jeans.

My hand stays still. Just feeling the solid mass beneath the fabric makes me clench my legs together. I slowly begin to trace the contours. I feel Daniel twitch several times.

I'm tempted to undo the fly, but I hold back and instead, feeling brave and spontaneous, lower myself. His hands hold the sides of my head and gently guide me at his groin. I run my lips over him, and he twitches. I do it again and this time I stop over the head. I move my mouth onto the cloth and slowly breath warm air into the material. Again, there is involuntary movement as the shaft hardens even more.

I find his belt far too easy to unfasten and let it fall to either side. As I pull the zip, with my face still close, Daniel groans above me in anticipation. Lowering his jeans reveals tight, jersey boxers, everything neatly trapped within, with extraordinarily little room to enlarge. Sliding the boxers down, his penis lifts tall and lands perfectly at my wet lips, instantly entering my warm hungry mouth.

I encase the shaft, my tongue works around the tip, flicking, touching and down the length. Surprisingly, my gag reflex doesn't kick in, which is a stroke of luck. I'm known for gagging on the slightest thing from my electric toothbrush touching my rear teeth, to the smell of dry lavender on old ladies. Now is not the time for any of that!

I take him deeper into my throat. He's making all sorts of noises up there whilst pushing his body towards me.

My teeth gentle nibble causing moist droplets to fall. My tongue licks more. The taste of him. The smell of him. Oh my god. I tighten my lips' grasp and begin to suck. He lets out an even deeper moan and tries to push my head onto him more. I'm trying! I'm trying!

The more you do that matey the less likely this will end well!

I'm taking the whole length now with long, slow repetitive swallowing, teasing, licking, sucking. I can feel myself moistening down below. But this is about him right now and I want him to enjoy the moment. I start sucking with more pull. His legs are shaking. I slow down again. Getting a bit of jaw ache if I'm honest reader.

"Do you want me inside you?"

Well, that's a stupid question if ever there was one. However, this moment, right here, right now, is for him. A little tease of what he could expect to come (so to speak) if the clouds align our paths once more.

I hold him in my mouth and look up. I begin to tease with my tongue, and he gasps. Again, I deep throat his whole shaft and he hardens further. His legs, and lovely as they are, quiver more, and he holds my head tighter.

As I please him further, the quivering stops and an almighty rush of fluid fills my mouth. I have no choice but to swallow. It's new to me. The saltiness. It's not what I expected. Different salty to say, bacon. Bacon makes me happy. This also makes me happy.

The snow has stopped and is already beginning to rapidly thaw. I drive back to Malthay wondering if I've made a mistake and opened a proverbial can of worms, or have I just opened up my future life?

Back at the cottage I unlock the door and call out, "Margaret! Play my soundtrack."

The sound of Andy William's voice fills my kitchen once more ...

3 Dog Walker Required

Well, well, well, March has rolled around, and with it comes the day that sends shivers into my boots like no other.

It's been a year since my father passed away in my arms. The memory of that night still haunts me. It's like a wound that refuses to heal, reopening every time I think about it. I can still hear his cry out, the sound of his collapse echoing in my mind. For almost an hour, I tried to save him with CPR, but he was already gone. It was a cruel twist of fate that his pacemaker continued to jump start him, when we all knew he was gone. He was the one people called upon whenever there was a problem with their vehicle. He always had "all the gear," as he used to say.

That evening was supposed to be a joyous occasion, celebrating the safe arrival of all the new lambs on our farm. But instead, it turned into the worst night of our lives. Nothing could have prepared us for the sudden loss of dad, mum's husband, and life partner. There were no warning signs, no indication that anything was wrong.

In fact, he had been hauling bales around the barn earlier that day with far greater ease than my brother or me. And yet, in the blink of an eye, he was gone. It's hard to accept that he's not here anymore. Sometimes, I still feel his presence, as if he's watching over us. But the pain of his absence is all too real. I miss him more than words can express.

Waves of emotion have been coming and going for the past few days and I've had to control them, but today is officially a day off. I can be as emotional as I want to be.

An emotional wreck on the sea of tears.

I did pop in to work for a couple of hours earlier, whilst Dylan went to the dentist. He was thinking of getting veneers done "Like that Essex lot on telly." However, having found out the cost, he ceremoniously dumped the idea by eating a chunky chocolate bar instead.

Early morning has turned to late morning and I'm back on the community page, putting up another post, this time for a dog walker and pet sitter. I'm keeping my fingers and toes crossed that Mabel Wainwright and Co give the green light so I can finally arrange some cover for my furry little rascals and my cat with some serious 'tude.

But for now, I'm wiping away my tears with a holey, old handkerchief I found lying around, which probably belonged to Nate. Not hard to tell. He only ever had one colour.

I reckon it's time for the dogs to take me for a walk around the village and work off some of this emotional baggage.

Hat on. Coat on. I check my pocket for dog poo bags. Dogs? I look around and just see them disappearing out through the stable door. Where the hell do they think they're going?!

The Dick and the digging one shoot off into the garden.

They do have names but there seems to be no point. Even the three trainers I've had visit, have given up achieving anything with them, other than seeing it as a great way to make money out of me. £75.00 an hour one charged! I must have been desperate... I was desperate and it was probably written all over my face.

But now I just get on with it until the dog person can take over. I wouldn't mind, but these pups were Jack's gift to mum and dad days before dad passed. I took them home to mine to give mum a break; they never came back. Somehow, I think mum is happy the pups are still with us but not at the farm. They can truly be quite a handful, even a year on. (Understatement if ever there was one).

Stepping out into the brisk air, I take in the sight

of the garden. Fallen leaves still litter the ground, but new life is beginning to sprout from the plants and trees. Little buds, shoots, and blossoms are appearing everywhere.

I feel a sense of peace being out here. This place has become my sanctuary, my own little church, far from the worries of running my business, the stress of my failed marriage, and the everyday concerns of paying the bills.

But right now, I can't think about any of that. I'm too busy trying to wrangle The Dick (even the vet knows him by that name) out of Christa's hedging.

Meanwhile, the digging one is busy destroying her freshly dug flower bed. I can feel a sigh building up inside me, and before I know it, it escapes in a loud rush of air. It's moments like these that remind me that even in my sanctuary, I'm not immune to the chaos of everyday life.

"Hi," a young voice interrupts my frustration.

"I'll go and get the digging one out of mum's garden for you again."

I turn to see Trevor, grateful for his help.

"Thanks, Trevor."

"I'm Tony," he corrects me before stomping off to retrieve the pup. He promptly grabs the collar and brings a filthy, mud-covered canine back to me.

"Thank you. Come here, you stupid thing," I mutter, struggling to hold onto the wriggling pup.

Tony looks at me with a confused expression, and I quickly correct myself.

"Sorry, Tony. Not you. I meant this stupid thing right here. Tell mum I'll get the fence fixed when the weather warms up."

I take a deep breath, trying to regain my composure as Tony nods and walks off. Even in my few moments of frustration, I can't help but be grateful for the help of others, although I unwantedly pang for Nate to be that "other."

The haunting melody of Fleet Foxes' "Winter Hymnal" envelopes me as I set off at a very brisk pace with my pups towards the fields and woods. The woods hold a special place in my heart, reminding me of cherished memories with my father and dogs of my childhood. Jack, always up for a climb, would often fall from the trees and with a theatrical moan, he'd groan about imaginary injuries, while dad and I collected flowers for mum pretending to ignore him. Together, we'd craft makeshift bouquets with whatever woodland flowers were in season, if nothing available it would be what was to hand, maybe green leaves, and cow parsley, placing them in a washed-out jam jar on the kitchen table when we got home.

My father always carried an old pair of sheep clippers in his coat pocket, clearing away the overgrown briars and nettles that obstructed the animal tracks, which had over time become winding pathways beneath the tree canopies.

But now that he's gone, the access points are narrowing, if not disappearing altogether. I vow to bring my secateurs on my next visit.

As I take a moment to bask in the dappled shade and cool air, my peaceful reverie is shattered by The Dick's sudden yank on my arm as he chases after a squirrel, propelling us all forward at breakneck speed.

Out the far side of the woods and briefly blinded by the low sun, partly due to the speed we are travelling at, we head back towards the village along the edge of Barley Field, not that many people know, but the majority of farms have names for each field which are listed on the title deeds. It was a practical way of illiterate farmers to know which field to work in. Most names make sense, a few don't - but would have done many moons ago.

The open fields stretch out before me, bathed in the strong yellow and white from the rays of the sun. It's a beautiful sight, one that I just know dad would have appreciated.

I remember the days when we would walk this same path together, him telling me stories about the history of the land and the people who had worked it before us. He would point out the different crops, telling me which ones were ripe for harvesting and which ones needed a little more time. I miss those times, but I feel grateful for the memories. I can't help but feel a sense of loss of time gone by, as I walk the well-trodden animal track, and get that familiar lump in my throat back again as I hear dad's words repeat in my head.

The pups run ahead, chasing each other in the long grass. I watch them, feeling a sense of joy at their carefree playfulness. They remind me of Jack when he was younger, full of boundless energy and curiosity. I wonder if dad would have been proud of the pups if he could see them now.

As I make my way back home, I can't help but feel a sense of nostalgia wash over me as I pass by the old post office cum sweet shop once run by the Hoopers.

Memories flood my mind of Jack and me as kids, sneaking in to get our thruppence worth of sweets from the jars behind the counter. I can still taste the sweet and tangy flavour of the cola cubes, the strong and spicy kick of the aniseed balls, and the creamy and tart taste of the rhubarb and custard boiled sweets. Now, the shop is nothing but a private residence, and I can't help but feel a twinge of sadness that those childhood moments are gone forever.

As we continue walking, we come across "The Walnut Tree" pub, a once-thriving business that is now mostly frequented by non-locals. It's a reminder that the world is changing, and not always for the better.

Soon, St Mary's parish church looms ahead, and I can feel a sense of calm washing over me. It's a place that I know well, and I often find myself seeking solace within its walls, but never for long. The pups seem to sense the peacefulness of the surroundings are different today, and they slow their pace, no longer eager to cause chaos or destruction.

We wait at the entrance to the church in quiet patience.

We cannot cross. It would be rude to as the congregation make their way out of the stone building and past us.

It's at this moment I feel my phone begin to vibrate in my back pocket. No! No! No! Not here of all places!

I have that sinking feeling as my heart starts beating louder. The thing isn't on silent in case

Dylan needs to call. Oh shite! Why now? Why now?! I try to grab it but, being the size of a small encyclopedia, it's wedged in my rear jeans pocket. Putting all my effort into not being obvious, I'm twisting and contorting my arms, trying not to swear by putting my best smiley eyes and face forward.

The pups rise up and start to pull onwards thinking it's time to go on. I stop what I am doing for a second and they sit again. Ironically, standing outside this religious building, I begin to prey to the god of mobiles, and maybe to myself, these people won't hear the ringtone. Please, please don't hear the flipping ringtone!

A well-heeled gentleman appears, pushing an elderly lady in a wheelchair out from the service. As they stop in front of me, to let others go before them, I notice their similarities. Perhaps he is her son. Most definitely a relative - they have the same unique facial features (massive eyebrows and huge jaw).

"John, they said the bells don't work. Why are they playing that instead?"

"John" looks at me and smiles. "I don't know Auntie. Maybe Uncle secretly liked 'Don't fear the reaper.'"

Back at the house there's the missed call (Dylan) and a notification from the community page.

"Too many characters. I've helpfully removed them for you. Post now approved. Yours, Mabel Wainwright."

I open the "Slapface" app and there is my post, for all to see.

"My puppies need attention that I cannot give them in the day. My pussy too. PM me for details."

Like the previously mentioned dog trainers... I give up.

To my astonishment I trawl through quite a few messages and stumble on one from "@thedogwalker."

"Hi. If I understand correctly, you may need assistance with your dogs and cat?"

"Yes! Yes, I Do! Are you interested?

It's early Saturday evening, I've been on the phone to mum and didn't realise the time had flown by.

As mentioned before, she had a cough over the winter months and now she has been left with a dry tickle. It's been on her mind, and I've suggested she get it checked out to be on the safe side. She's not a fan of doctors or hospitals and I think I still have some convincing to go.

Funny how as we grow older our roles almost reverse when it comes to reminding our parents what they should do to look after themselves, whilst what do we get back? "You're old enough to look after yourselves now!"

I've just attempted to brush the pups to make them slightly more presentable. I glance down at my trousers and see that they still look like they've been attacked by a pack of wild animals. My attempts at tidying up the pups have clearly been in vain. I shake my head and mutter to myself, wondering why I even bother trying.

I've noticed I started doing that these days – talk to myself. Is it an age thing or because I'm on my own now and I'm just going bonkers?

I let out a huge sigh of frustration, feeling defeated by the never-ending battle against pet hair. Both pups look at me with their doleful eyes questioning what the noise was all about. The dog walker will surely see right through my feeble attempts and judge me for my lack of grooming skills. I can't help but feel a little self-conscious as I wait for their arrival, hoping they won't think I'm a terrible pet owner.

Ah, the symphony of the entitled feline - always a

joy to the ears! I hear the drama queen of a cat wailing at the stable door, as if he's been starved for days. You'd think he was auditioning for an opera with that kind of performance!

I mean, come on, it's been a whole ten minutes since his last meal. You'd think he was on the brink of fading away into nothingness. He could easily saunter in through the cat flap, but no, he prefers to summon his lowly human servant instead.

Cat fed (again) and pups settled just as the door knocker goes.

The dog walker has arrived.

I head towards the wellies and dog leads, kicking them to one side. Putting my secateurs back in my coat pocket, I then open the door.

All hell breaks loose.

I take a step back and watch as the over-enthusiastic hounds tackle the dog walker. It's like watching a group of toddlers greet their favourite uncle at a family reunion. The pups are all over him, tails wagging furiously and tongues lolling out in excitement. It's a wonder they don't knock him off his feet.

The dog walker looks equally happy to see them, although I suspect it's less about love and more about the wad of cash I'm about to hand over. But who am I to judge? Money talks, even to our furry friends.

Oops, spoke too soon...

"What a greeting! Hi, hi, hi, well hello, yes, I love you too!"

He continues chatting to the pups in a slightly awkward and high-pitched tone before gathering himself from the floor and standing again.

"Where were we?!"

With a brief chat and a greeting to the cat with attitude at the door, we venture out into the back garden with the four-legged furballs. The garden is massive, what drew me here in the first instance - it's like someone decided to throw a bunch of dirt and seeds around and let nature do its thing.

There's enough greenery to make a jungle jealous, and the flowers are so vibrant they practically jump out at you (allegedly). We follow the ancient brick path, which looks like it's seen better days, weaving around the flower beds - the sorrowful bench stranded in the middle of them, and the borders that look like they're trying to take over the world.

Meanwhile, the pups are having the time of their lives. They're bouncing around like they've had one too many cups of coffee, chasing each other and making it their life's mission to hunt down every bug in sight. And of course, they have to roll around in every mystery substance they come across.

After some time, we make our way back to the kitchen, with the pups looking like they've been in a mud wrestling match for at least three days.

"Nice table." He comments.

"Yes. The milkman liked it too."

As soon as the rather nice-looking dog walker leaves, I rush to Christa's house to give her the good news. I knock on her door so loudly, it's as if I'm trying to break it down.

"Hi Miss Diana"

"Hi Tony. Is your mum there?"

"I'm Terry. No, but she's in the bath."

"Oh, okay... can you pass a message to her Terry? Say I've sorted the dog walker out. Starts Monday"

"Yes. Will do." The door shuts.

"Hello neighbour!" A girl's voice comes from an open window next to me.

"Hi Daisy. Had a good day at school?"

"I'm Debbie. It's Saturday. Bye!" The window closes.

As I head back indoors, instantly I receive a text from Christa.

"What's happened? Is everything okay?"

"I've found a dog walker! He starts on Monday! What did you lad say I said?"

"Thank goodness! I was worried you were going to say one of the pups ate your sofa or something. He told me I needed to speak with you urgently. Something about you'd got your bus pass through."

"Piss off, did he! You're not that much younger than me missus!"

"Born in different decades... different decades, love."

"Alright. No need to rub it in."

I put my phone down somewhere safe (code for leave it where I can't find it again without a search party).

The pups are worn out, sleeping by the Aga. I put my wellies back on, head outside and light the fire pit. The night sky is clear of clouds, and I fancy a bit of star gazing and reading a book. One of the positives of being on my own is to have "me time" now and again without the guilt that comes when you live with someone.

Anyway, following on from my unscheduled visit to Daniel last month, I've concluded that perhaps I need to reign in the sexual siren within me for a bit. Having not heard from him, I can only presume he's not interested to take things any further. He's even made a point of only coming to the office when he knows it's my day off. Dylan says its coincidence, but then I didn't tell him fully what happened between us.

What's meant to be and all that … obviously for me that means life as a singleton.

It's time to crack open the vino and let loose.

As I fumble with the cork, I reminisce on the irony that the only bottle of wine I received as a housewarming present is from Nate.

He may not have been a great partner, but at least he knew my taste buds. The pantry is stocked with ancient, neglected bottles from the previous owner, but eventually they will see the light of day.

I'm not one for the booze. I know nothing about it

and most of the time I can't even pronounce the name on the label. Plus, it hits me like a ton of bricks, but hey, let's live a little tonight, right?

As I reach for the wine bottle, just about to pour a glass, the door knocker suddenly rumbles with a loud and insistent rat-a-tat-tat. I groan inwardly, wondering who could possibly be disturbing my peaceful evening. The pups stir from their slumber, casting curious glances in the direction of the door.

With a sigh, I reluctantly make my way towards the entrance, hoping it's not some unwelcome visitor trying to sell me double glazing or worse still, an urgent matter that needs attending to.

"Apologies. I think I lost something in the garden earlier. Do you mind if I have a look? I'm not disturbing you, am I?"

"Please, go on through. What is it you lost? I'll help you try and find it." Gosh, he seemed even more fanciable in the evening light.

As the dog walker speaks, I can sense whatever he is about to say is incredibly meaningful to him. I wonder if I see tears in his eyes. By the shaking in his voice, it is clear that whatever he is about to say is making him quite emotional. Great! I mean, I don't want to sound off, but all I need right now is a complete stranger off-loading his life's failures onto me when I have "me" things to do.

"It's difficult to explain, but there's this penny with a hole in it. To most people, it's just a penny, nothing special. But to me, it's everything."

Hold on, this could be interesting...

He takes a deep breath and continues, the words tumbling out of him in a rush.

"You see, someone I love dearly gave it to me years ago. We were walking on our favourite beach with our dogs, just the two of us. And she found it, this penny with a hole in it. It was lying there, waiting for us to discover it. And from that moment on, I knew it would be important to me."

He paused, his eyes flickering rapidly.

"I've been keeping it on my car keys, so I could see it every day and think of her. It just reminds me of that evening, with the sun low, the sea breeze blowing gently, causing strands of her hair to dance across her face, and the sound of the waves. I remember thinking it was just the two of us, lost in our own world, enjoying each other's company and the beauty of the moment, and then her seeing this random thing, this random coin half buried in the sand..."

The dog walker's voice trails off.

In that moment, I have a twinge of envy, wishing that someone spoke about me with such passion and intensity. I can't ever recall Nate speaking with such words. Listening to the dog walker I was transported to the beach with him. I could just imagine the scene - at the same time, I can't help but feel happy for this man, that he had experienced such a profound connection with another person and I kinda hope that will be me one day.

"I thought I must have dropped it in the van earlier, and I've been searching for it ever since. I've even taken out the footwells, but it's nowhere to be found. I'm hoping it will be here. I did try to call you but there wasn't an answer."

"Did you? (Make mental note to search for phone the size of a house later) We only followed the paths, so hopefully we'll see it. I need to get logs for the fire anyway. You should have brought your dogs with you tonight – they could have played with the pups for a bit."

His voice barely above a whisper. "The angels have sung to their beautiful hearts - I miss them every single waking hour."

Fuck! Didn't see that coming. Now what do I say?!

I wasn't sure what to make of his words, but there was a palpable sense of pain and longing in his voice. It was as if he were speaking of a deep loss, something he could never recover from. I do know it.

I've been there and worn the T-shirt, as all dog lovers have.

"Sorry. Didn't think."

I've lost many pups in my time. In fact, dad described the grief in his own unique way once and I have never forgotten it. "Nothing quite grabs you around the jugular more so than the pain left by the loss of your dog." How right he was. Every single one can still turn me into a teary-eyed trainwreck of a woman.

We venture into the depths of the garden, armed with nothing but a three cell torch with the illumination of four thousand candles, according to the box, and a sense of determination. The task at hand seems almost impossible, like finding a needle in a haystack.

Despite our efforts, we make little progress and conclude it's a job best done in daylight. Besides, I really feel the need for wine now.

Our next move is to head down to the wood store at the bottom of the garden. I had hoped to bring the logs I need closer to the cottage before now. However, I haven't had the chance to execute this plan yet, and it still sits on my "To Do" list duck taped on the inside of the pantry-cum-loo door.

"Load my arms up," he says, reaching out to me.

I can't help but notice how large and muscular he is and how capable he looks, his arms are strong, like, I mean really strong, his outfit exuding a sense of countryside charm that I find stupidly attractive. I begin to load up the cradle he has made with his forearms, conscious of the fact that his clothing is probably worth more than my entire wardrobe.

He sports a smart yet casual look, complete with a tweed waistcoat, gingham shirt, and deep navy jeans. I can't help but think he looks like one of those TV dog trainers, but it's a look that suits him well. In comparison, I feel scruffy and out of place, like I don't belong in his company. He does light work carrying the wood up to the fire pit.

"Do you want to stay for a glass or two of wine? My way of saying thank you. Was going to open it anyway."

Brilliant! Now dog walker man thinks I'm a lonely alcoholic!

"Go on then. It will take my mind off the penny. You pour and I'll stoke the fire and sort that out."

After two and a half bottles of wine and a ham sandwich, things were starting to get a bit spicy.

"Are you sure about this?" I ask, looking at my

companion with a mixture of excitement and trepidation.

"Yep! Never done it outside before. Time to start living, I say!" he replies, looking around the garden for a suitable location.

"Wood store or... um... grass thingy?" I suggest, my mind a bit fuzzy from the wine.

"Need a bit of light, my eyesight isn't that great these days. Grass."

And with that, we stumble towards the meadow, stripping off our clothes as we go. It is much colder away from the fire pit, and I regret, immediately, my decision to get naked. I scurry back to grab the blanket I'd brought out earlier to wrap myself in while reading my book. My wobbly bits are on full display yet again, but a combination of alcohol and excitement removes any inhibition I may have had.

Meanwhile, my companion is cackling and thrusting his hips. "I'm going to do you hard, missy! Come here, oh gorgeous one!" he exclaims, and I can't help but burst out laughing.

I guess this is what people mean by "living life to the fullest."

The meadow-turned-flower bed wasn't exactly what I would have in mind for outdoor fun, but the bench seems like a good option. I throw the blanket onto the seat and try to spread it out, but the chilly air makes me wrap it around me like a cocoon instead.

Meanwhile, the dog walker seems impervious to the cold. Maybe working outside in all weathers had toughened him up, or maybe he is just too excited to notice.

As I stand there shivering, the blanket barely covering anything, he comes up behind me and grabs my waist.

"You look good enough to eat," he whispers in my ear, making me quake for a different reason.

Before I know it, I am willingly bent over the bench, my backside in the air in a poor imitation of downward dog. His hands run over my exposed skin, sending love letters down my spine.

But then they stop.

Turning my head to look at him "What's wrong?"

"I think I just saw a spider, or it might not have been." His face contorted more in confusion than horror, although it could be hiccups.

I feel myself roll my eyes and pulling the blanket tighter around me blurt out "You're such a wuss. Call yourself a maaan?!"

With a loud snort in surprise, the dog walker scoffs back "You, you, you can't say that these days! You're bound to upset someone referring to me that way!"

"You are a maaan. A maaan. I can clearly see a pencil... I mean a pentacle... no, I... can...see a penis, that's it, a penis. There between your legs and that makes you a maaan! Well, in my eyes and learnings anyways ...is that a kitten down there or my foot?"

"Not from this position you can't. Anyway... where were we?" Still looking at my foot in a drunkenly distracted kind of way, I'm taken by surprise once more. Wetting his fingers with his mouth, the dog walker slowly traces my body until he reaches my bud. Brushing past and arriving between my legs.

"Very moist. Very moist indeed" he purrs. Then, he moves his fingers, and starts to touch me - where nobody has gone before.

"Oi! Wrong hole!" I shout rather too loudly. The instant thought the neighbours may hear passes quickly, when I remember they're out for the evening visiting family.

I can't believe this is happening! I'm bent over a bench in the middle of the flowerbed, in the freezing cold, now with a man's tongue exploring places I never thought possible. I should be outraged, but I'm just too damn turned on to care. His fingers are doing magical things inside me, and I can feel myself getting wetter by the second.

A cold flurry of air abruptly arrives over me, and I realise that the damn blanket has fallen away. I'm completely exposed to the chilly night, and my nipples are as hard as diamonds. It's like having ice cubes rubbed all over my breasts – or so I imagine. It's both painful and rather exhilarating at the same time.

As I catch my breath, my garden companion leans in close to me, a wicked smile playing on his lips.

"You're insatiable." I can feel his hot breath on my neck.

He's right. I am insatiable. I want more, and I want it now.

Without another word, he positions himself behind me, and I arch my back, offering myself to him. I can feel his hardness against my skin, and I quiver once more, this time with anticipation.

With his hand around his erect penis slowly pleasuring himself to be as hard as he can be, he places his shaft ready to penetrate. Helped by my natural juices he slides in easily. He enters me slowly, and I moan with pleasure as he fills me up completely. He starts to move, thrusting in and out of me with a steady rhythm. Each time he enters me, I feel like I'm on the brink of exploding like a ball from a cannon, and I cling on to the bench for dear life.

The pleasure is almost too much to bear. But just as I'm about to reach my peak, he pulls out of me, leaving me feeling empty and unsatisfied.

"What are you doing?" I gasp, but before I can say anything else, he takes me again, and this time it's even better than before. I know I'm close to coming.

I begin to pulse my inner muscles, clenching him each time he thrusts. Thrust after thrust. He grabs my hair and yanks it to him pulling my head up towards the night sky. With a mighty shove of the hips, into me he releases.

Well, I did want to do a bit of star gazing tonight I suppose but I'll get neck ache if he doesn't let go soon ...

4 To Buy Or Not To Buy

It's April, and another day in the thrilling world of estate agency. Dylan's taking a day off, leaving me to handle the excitement solo. Unusual for me, with a cup of caffeine in hand, I glance at the diary and see that we've got a slew of viewings booked for the Braye's farmhouse. It hit the market over the weekend and after separating the looky-loos from the serious buyers, we set up a block of appointments for yesterday and today.

Just as I'm about to close up shop and head out, the phone rings. I answer with my best professional tone.

"Doors Estate Agency. Diana speaking. How may I help you?"

I'm greeted by a voice that seems to have been chugging gravel for breakfast.

"Hey, do you have that farmhouse on Whites Lane up for grabs? I've got a bucket of cash and I'm looking to swing by this morning to take a gander if that works for you."

Suppressing a chuckle, I can't help but find the guy's attempt at sounding sophisticated rather amusing. I mean, "swing by"? Is he trying to impress me with his '60s slang? It's not exactly the most eloquent way to express interest in a property. However, I manage to keep my composure and respond politely.

"Yes, sir. We do have it. Do we already have your details, or do you need to register with us?"

"You do. The name's Lawrence Barker," he replies.

I pencil in a time slot for Mr. Barker at the end of the existing bookings, throw up the 'Back Soon!' sign in the window, lock up, and make my way to my trusty old beast. It's been very loyal to me but is starting to show its age. A bit like me, really - got that well-loved look, and the engine's been acting up a bit lately. I'll have to schedule an appointment with Robert or one of his mechanics to give the engine a once-over on Friday.

The beast comes to life on the third try and we hit the road, winding our way down the narrow country lanes. Spring has fully sprung. I'm greeted by a breathtaking sight, what with the fields stretching out before me, a patchwork quilt of emerald, green grass, and brown earth. My windows wound down, I can hear the adorable lambs, with their white and black woolly coats and wobbly legs, frolicking and bleating in the sunshine.

The fields themselves are separated by stone walls that have stood for centuries. Some are made from large boulders, while others are built from neatly stacked rocks. If not a stone wall, native hedgerows have grown, which are bursting with life. They're a riot of colour, with hawthorn and black elder trees covered in delicate white flowers. Dog roses, with their pretty pink petals attempting to bloom, wind their way around the branches, while hazel and other shrubs are beginning to tease the creatures that live in this magnificent rural wonderland, with their bounty yet to come.

As I continue my journey, I'm serenaded by the sound of birds flitting in and out of the foliage. The air is alive with their melodies, each one a unique tune that blends together to create a symphony of sound. I hear the chirping of robins, the trilling of larks, and the sweet warbling of blackbirds. It's a sound that fills me with joy and reminds me of the beauty of nature. It's never appropriate to race through these lanes, who would, when you can miss all this life around you?

I park in the same lay-by as before and take a quick peek over at Daniel's cottage. Haven't seen him around much lately. Last I heard, he's been keeping busy in the West End working at a couple of theatres. He runs his own business, "Marlowe Makeovers," which not only builds stage sets but also provides props and costumes for each production. Maybe it's for the best that I haven't bumped into him recently, not after what happened last time!

Veronica and Reg are both staying put at the farmhouse, while I go about my business of conducting the viewings. I will have to manoeuvre around them, as they will be occupying the front room during my visits. It's a shame to see Reg's condition has worsened since my last visit, currently rendering him unable to leave the house.

The first two viewings were as exciting as watching a kettle boil. Neither of them thought the property or the grounds were suitable for their plans.

The third person was a complete joke. They didn't even know how big an acre was, which didn't help. I mean, seriously? You come to a viewing with the intent to buy a farm with mass acreage and you don't know how big an acre is?! I can't help but wonder how they managed to get dressed in the morning without assistance.

But that's not even the best part. When asked why they were interested in the property, they replied with, "Just thought it sounded good to say got fifteen hundred acres and a ride on lawn mower." Wow. Just wow. Yet another appointment being a complete waste of time.

Now, I'm waiting for Lawrence Barker. I try not to

make assumptions about people, but this guy is a special case. I see his car coming up the lane, music blaring from his S-Class Merc. He probably had it imported from a country where they don't have noise pollution laws. As he gets closer, I notice that he's driving a long wheelbase model with extra legroom. Of course, because why wouldn't he?

The car screeches to a stop, and "Common People" by Pulp blasts from the driver's window. The door opens, and a pair of exceptionally long legs unravel onto the flint lane.

And there he is, the immaculately dressed Lawrence Barker, head-to-toe in a navy suit, probably from Savile Row or equivalent. His highly polished brown brogues and matching paisley tie finish off the look. He scrubs up well, as my mum would say.

The look does nothing for me Yes, he's a good looking chap of a certain age – But I much prefer the overall appearance of the dog walker last month with his jeans and waistcoat. Shame he did a disappearing act on me. Seems to be the way of things around here. Or is it just me? Am I putting men off by being so willing? If it were the other way around, I don't think I'd be offended. Probably flattered if anything! Sorry, distracted with my thoughts once more. Back to Mr Barker and the Braye's place.

Let's be real here. What would a guy like Lawrence Barker want with Veronica and Reg's lovely home in the middle of nowhere? It's far too earthy and homely for this man. I've seen it all before. He's probably just all mouth and no trousers, as my grandma would say. This viewing is going to be a complete waste of time, but at least I'll have some entertainment watching him get those expensive shoes filthed up.

The husky voice kicks in again "Good afternoon Ms Doors. Lawrence Barker."

He holds his hand out to shake mine, or so I thought.

Instead, he pushes a strand of hair from my face stroking my cheek at the same time. Looks like Mr Barker tries to be a smooth talker on the phone (unsuccessfully), but also a bit of a touchy-feely one in person. Someone forgot to tell him that it's not appropriate to invade someone's personal space, especially when you're meeting them for the first time. Maybe he should have taken a class on social skills instead of spending all that money on a fancy suit.

But let's give him the benefit of the doubt. Maybe he's just trying to charm his way into getting a good deal on the farmhouse. After all, he did say he's a cash buyer, and we all know money talks? But then again, maybe he's just looking for some peace and quiet in the middle of nowhere, and

Veronica and Reg's home seems like the perfect place to hide away from the world.

Either way, I'm not too keen on this Lawrence Barker character. He may be dressed to impress, but his actions are not exactly winning him any points in my book. Let's just hope he keeps his hands to himself during the viewing and doesn't try any cheekier moves.

We head indoors past the wellies, coats, and log stack. I quickly update the Brayes that the last viewing had arrived, reminding them it would take a while again due to the amount to see.

"I thought we would start in the kitchen first if that's okay with you. Most like to start their tour in the kitchen."

"Lead the way Ms Doors. I'm more interested in the upstairs personally, but still need a kitchen. Must have room for a large table to munch on when starving."

"As you can see, the Brayes have quite a dining set-up in here along with an American fridge/freezer, neither of which dominate the room at all." I try to concentrate on the job in hand, but the distraction of this irritatingly attractive man running his hands slowly along the wood grain of the table doesn't help.

"Is that one of those that makes ice? I do like to

use decent size cubes, don't you Ms Doors?"
Barker stifles a cough.

Maybe he's getting over a cold.

My nipples react instantly. Jeeze, my hormones
are playing up as much as the car is today.

"Yes, I believe where it says "Ice" might be a clue.
Perhaps you would like a glass of iced water for
your voice – sounds a bit hoarse?"

I walk through the rest of the downstairs trying to
refocus on the task.

"Time for the main bedroom."

"Thought you wouldn't ask."

"Sorry, what did you say?"

"I apologise. Bad joke. You probably get it all the
time."

"As it happens, not really. Apology accepted.
We'll take the far staircase and work our way back
to this one."

"After you." Lawrence indicates me to go first.

Immediately after placing my heel on the first step,
I can't help but feel a wave of regret wash over me.
Why did I have to choose this particular staircase?

Of course, it's the most decorative one, with intricate carvings and elaborate handrails, but it also happens to be the longest one.

And now, I am stuck in front of Lawrence Barker, with my backside practically in his face the whole way up.

To make matters worse, I can feel his eyes burning a hole in me. It's making me feel incredibly self-conscious. I'm wearing a floaty, 360-degree summer skirt, which can be quite revealing at the wrong angle or in a gust of wind - think Marilyn Monroe in "The Seven Year Itch."

It seemed like a promising idea this morning when the sun was shining brightly, and I wanted to wear something light and breezy. I paired the skirt with a cute blouse and a vintage-inspired cardi, which added a touch of retro glamour to the outfit.

However, now that I am standing in close proximity to Mr Barker, I can't help but think about how much cleavage I am inadvertently displaying. I never intended for so much to be on show but it's quite difficult sometimes to gather enough material together in an outfit to disguise these assets! But there's nothing I can do about it now. I'll just have to soldier on and hope that he doesn't notice.

"Nice posterior by the way. The sort you could nibble or lick constantly."

I choose to ignore and head quickly towards the last door. As we step into huge main bedroom, I can feel the tension rising. Barker's eyes roam around the room, taking in the wooden bed frame and the exposed beams.

"The beams," he muses. "Are they original? And have they ever been treated?"

I nod, trying to maintain a professional demeanour. "Yes, they're original. I'll double check about treatment. But the vendors have assured us that there's no woodworm or anything of the sort. They even said that you could swing off them, they're that strong."

Barker raises an eyebrow, a smirk playing at the corners of his lips. "Really now? Swing off them, you say? A swing seat or maybe a person?"

I can feel the blush creeping up my cheeks. "I don't think that's what they had in mind, Mr. Barker. They're in their eighties. Shall we go on to the next room now?"

I'm concluding this man must have a secret hobby. The questions keep on coming and I answer them all as well as a professional agent would do. However, I am beginning to wonder if he is trying to fluster me on purpose.

It's beginning to work.

The en-suite to bedroom two as been refurbished to a really high standard – Veronica requested one room for herself where she could relax away from farm life. It is a luxurious oasis, with its large, free-standing copper bath and spacious shower. The room is decorated in shades of cream and gold, with plush towels and fluffy bathrobes hanging from a heated rail next to the sink.

I walk over to the copper bath and without thinking, run my hand over its smooth surface, marvelling at its beauty. It's big enough for two people, maybe even three, and I can already imagine sinking into its depths and letting my troubles disappear.

Then my mind is drawn to the shower. It's a walk-in, with a large rain showerhead that looks like it could accommodate at least two people at once. The thought of sharing the shower with someone sends yet another shiver down my spine, and I feel a flush of excitement course through me.

"You could have sex in that bath or shower quite easily" Barker states. "Is that something you do Ms Doors? Do you like to fuck in the bath?"

Experiencing a sudden, intense warmth spreading across my face, I avert my gaze elsewhere. Was he just thinking the same as me or could he tell what was going on in my head?

"That will be a yes then."

"Bedroom three next. That's across the hallway and down the two steps... and mind what you're saying."

I'm no stranger to house viewings, but this one is a real doozy. Lawrence Barker, the potential buyer, has got under my skin with his sheer cheek and confidence – or is it just arrogance?

As we move on to the outbuildings, yards, and fields, I mind is still pondering as to what Lawrence Barker would be doing with somewhere like this. This is the countryside after all, and things can get a bit muddy, and he doesn't look like he "does" mud.

"Have you got any wellies with you Mr Barker? You'll need some around here if you purchase this property. Talking of which, have you had any thoughts on that yet?"

The response I get is typical Barker. "No, and no wellies. I'll have staff do the hard work. I'll do all my 'dirty' stuff indoors." Barker gives me a sly grin and a wink. "And who knows? Maybe I'll have some dirty work for you to do indoors too."

My mind goes into overdrive at those comments. What on earth does he mean by "dirty stuff indoors"?

I try not to let any of my imagination run too wild, but I am beginning to feel a little hot under the collar.

As we walk, Barker continues to talk about all the things he'll have his staff do. He'll have them tend to the gardens, mow the lawn, and even clean the stables. He'll just be the one enjoying the fruits of their labour.

I'm unable to prevent my eyes from rolling at his entitled attitude. But at the same time, I'm kind of impressed. The man has some serious confidence, even if it borders on an air of self-importance.

We pass through the yards to the field track at the rear.

The Brayes have put hardcore down and it's a relatively dry, if not long, walk to the old red brick barn. Handy, these shoes and mud don't mix.

As we walk, I can't help but notice Lawrence Barker staring at me. It's not the first time he's done it, but this time it feels different. I get a tingling sensation when he licks his lips, which he does several times before finally starting to speak.

"You know, Diana, I can't help but think about all the 'dirty' work we could do indoors," he says, his voice dripping with innuendo.

Yet again, I roll my eyes and try to brush off his

suggestive comment.

"Mr. Barker, I'm just here to show you the property. Let's keep things professional, shall we?"

But he doesn't seem to be deterred. "Oh, come on now, Diana. Don't be such a prude. You can't deny the chemistry between us."

Chemistry? What chemistry? The only chemistry I feel is the urge to throw up in my mouth. Or so I tell myself.

But before I can say anything else, Barker's attention is drawn to the old red brick barn beginning to appear around the bend in the track.

"Now this is more like it. I can just picture my vintage car collection in here," he says, changing the subject.

I'm grateful for the distraction, but as we make our way into the barn, Barker's gaze never leaves me. It's like he's undressing me with his eyes, and I can't help but feel uncomfortable.

"Ms Doors, you have an exquisite taste in fashion. That skirt suits you perfectly," he says with a suggestive tone.

I feel my cheeks redden as I reply. "Thank you, Mr Barker. It's just a simple skirt I picked up from a vintage store."

"I beg to differ. It's not just the skirt, it's the way it hugs your curves and flows as you walk. You have a way of turning heads, Ms Doors," he says with a smirk.

"I find you incredibly attractive Ms Doors. Extremely sexy and really want to fuck you hard!"

That word again. "Oh! Um... I'm, err, flattered. I think."

"Do you think the same of me?"

"I find you rude, slightly arrogant even! That you feel you can say that to me, having never met me before or know me, is completely bang out of order! Besides, I'm married."

"Lucky man."

"Tell him that."

As we stand in the old, well used, barn, I take a deep breath and inhale the earthy scent of hay. The smell takes me back to my childhood, growing up on our own farm. I remember playing in the fields, running through the tall grass, and jumping in the hay bales. It's a comforting smell, one that always puts me at ease.

Looking around the barn, I see the remnants of this past year's bales scattered in one corner. Most of it has been used to overwinter the cattle of the tenant farmer, a widespread practice in these parts. The Brayes are good landlords, always willing to help out their tenants when needed.

As I take in the surroundings, I notice Lawrence Barker staring at me with an intensity that makes me feel uneasy. His eyes seem to be searching for something – he's looking all around us. Suddenly he grabs me and throws me against the door. I feel weak at my knees. His hands work swiftly lifting the hem of my dress.

"You've not got on any underwear you dirty whore!"

He cups me between my legs, and I gasp. The tension building up over the past hour or so has made me quite wet. His other hand is firmly massaging my breast. He puts his lips on mine and pushes his tongue in deep.

With one hand he partially unbuttons my blouse and swiftly moves into my bra. My nipple is swollen and firm. His fingers pull and lengthen it and pull again in a repeat motion. He rolls it between index and forefinger.

Somehow this is painfully pleasurable. I'm wincing but groaning at the same time.

Barker looks around, ensuring that we are alone in the barn. Then, he starts to undo his belt. It's not just any old belt in his hands.

I know, I know, I shouldn't be admiring a belt when I have bigger things to worry about, but I can't help it. Lawrence Barker's belt is simply stunning. I mean, it's not every day you see a belt with a clasp like that.

It's clear that this belt was not cheap, very likely worth more than my monthly mortgage payment. The craftsmanship is exquisite, with swirls of crystals and gems interwoven between the gold. It matches perfectly with his paisley tie, and I can't help but wonder if he has a whole collection of accessories like this.

"Is something catching your eye, Diana?" Barker asks, noticing my focus being on his waist.

"Oh, no, it's nothing. Just admiring your belt," I say, trying to play it cool.

He chuckles. "Ah, yes. It's one of my favourites. The clasp is actually one-of-a-kind. I had it custom-made for me. For moments like these…"

Of course, he did. I wouldn't expect anything less from a man like Lawrence Barker.

"It's truly stunning," I say, unable to take my eyes off it.

"It's nice to know that someone appreciates the finer things in life." He smiles. "Give me your hands."

Before I could think what was happening, his belt is entwined around my wrists and he's using the clasp to fix them high above my head on the metal meat hook there; I'm stretched as far as my body will allow.

He takes my heels leaving me standing on tiptoe, then tears the rest of the buttons from my blouse and lifts my bra above my breasts, allowing them to fall onto my chest, nipples hard, pointing forward. I don't think I could be more vulnerable than I am right now.

He teases. Pulling, tugging, and then sucking hard on my chest. Sucking really hard. So hard that I can feel the tug under my arms. I've never been treated so roughly. He's like an animal going at my breasts. He seems starved of sex. Starved of a woman's body.

Lawrence Barker removes his jacket and shirt, revealing a well-toned torso that almost shines with layers of his perspiration. I can't help but stare as my eyes trace over his bare chest, taking in his defined pecs and abdominal muscles. He looks like he spends hours in the gym every day – bet he has his own in his current palatial pad!

But then, something catches my eye. Just off to the

side, there's a thin scar - an appendix scar. Nate had that too.

I try to push the thought out of my mind. It's just a coincidence. Lots of people have appendix scars. It doesn't mean anything.

Barker doesn't seem to notice my distraction as he starts to set to work. Swiftly he relieves me of my skirt, pulling it down over my thighs, puddling it at my feet. His face level with the top of my legs, he pulls me wide open and sucks firmly. He nips. I moan loudly. I can feel I'm getting wetter as his mouth works. My wrists being tied high restricts my movement. Barker holds my waist and turns me.

I'm now facing the door looking up at my hands with my breasts rubbing against the wood causing friction on the sensitive skin. I pull away as far as I can and allow them to hang free. He grabs and massages with his able hands but it's hard and almost aggressive in nature.

My face is now to one side. My breathing is heavy. This man is manipulating me, exactly where he wants me to be. I have no control. He expertly works me down below, my lips there are swollen and sodden. His thumb continues to circle, stop, press, repeat. Circle, stop, press, repeat. Two fingers are just inside me holding me in place. Each time he stops I feel my body tense.

Barker speaks straight into my ear "Don't you dare! You're mine and I will tell you when you can release!"

"I want to. I want to now" I whimper.

"Don't answer me back or I'll punish you!"

Barker is moving quicker with his motions. My body is writhing, and my arms are aching.

He stops.

I can just about see him out the corner of my eye lowering his trousers and pants, revealing his magnificent erection. He comes towards me and touches me again. I moan loudly.

"Hush!" Another warning. "Do that again and I will punish you. No joke."

Coming up behind me he touches again, this time his fingers work deep and fast against his thumb. I'm biting my lip. I can't shout out. What does he mean by punishing me? Oh God! I cry out. Loudly. I can't help myself.

A sharp sting flies across my butt cheeks. He's slapped me. I don't like it. He does it again. There's a warmth after the sting. Then his hand is back in me. No. Not his hand. He has penetrated me with full force. If it's possible he's getting bigger still. He withdraws. Turns me back around. What now?

He lifts me off the ground with ease, sitting my legs around his waist, and thrusts into me. We're looking at each other. He thrusts, I moan, he thrusts again. My breasts are moving in tandem with my body. He thrusts in repeatedly. My wrists are killing me, but I don't want this to stop.

His eyes are really looking deep into mine. After all the noise and frenzy, he climaxes quietly and pushes into me one more time. He pulls away but he's not finished with me yet.

Lowering my legs, he leaves me tied, then, crouching down, Barker opens me up and begins to lick. Once again, my body betrays me, and I begin to push towards him. Suck it! Suck it! Oh, please suck it! He seems to know what I yearn for and begins to pull me inside his mouth and suck. Hard and long. He doesn't tease with his tongue. He just sucks, the pressure building each time. Suddenly I ejaculate my juices whilst my muscles spasm and clench. I feel the orgasm right into my backside. It's deep. It's long and it's bloody amazing.

But he carries on going. Wait! I can't! Oh, sweet Mary, not again!

My muscles are clenching. My legs quivering, my eyes are tight shut. I'm concentrating so hard on this feeling. It's strong. Stronger than the last. It's internal. He sucks and sucks until I come again. My legs give way, but I'm held fast by his belt. My chest heaving, and glistening beads of sweat are running down my front into my naval.

After all this, I hope Lawrence Barker buys this place...

5 The Post Men

Nothing worse than an itchy bum."

Dylan doesn't seem to have a care in the world as he disappears into the depths of the back rooms, leaving his statement hanging in the air. It's not clear if he's talking to someone in particular or just making a general observation, but the way he said it with such glorious nonchalance and enthusiasm is hard to ignore.

"As I was saying Mr Hardcastle, the property has only been on for a fortnight, but you've had a good amount of viewings and an offer already, at a realistic figure nye on the same as I valued it at. I don't think the extra fifty thousand you want is going to happen. I also believe the feedback confirms that. Not everyone wants a new build, four bed house without parking or any gardens."

"I think it's worth the extra. Bob's down the road sold for more."

"It has two acres and a double garage. It's not

comparable."

"I think we wait. If they want the place they will offer more."

"They've already said first and final offer. I'm happy to go back to them and ask again, however, that could send them elsewhere."

"Do that. If they want it, they will offer what I'm saying it's worth."

Dylan strolls back into the office, a wide tooth filled smile plastered across his face.

"Still here, Mr. Hardcastle?" he quips, taking note of the older gentleman's prolonged stay. One could hardly blame him for wondering if the man had taken up permanent residence at the office.

"Sorted your arse out lad? I'll be getting back to the yard now."

Well, here we are in May, the fifth month of the year, and the fifth month of this couples counselling torture with Nate. Yesterday's session was a no-go yet again. I swear, he's always too busy working or coming up with some lame excuse to skip out on our sessions.

The only progress we've made is agreeing that we both need to try new things and step out of our comfort zones. Big whoop. And to add insult to injury, Melanie just talks to him and then repeats everything to me, like I'm some kind of idiot who can't understand even the most basic of communication. I'm starting to question this counsellor, but of course, Nate insists on sticking with her because "the family" recommended her. Ugh.

"Right-o, I'm outta here like a cat from a bathtub. See you later, alligator! Oh, and I have complete faith in you but don't hesitate to give me a holler if you need anything… but try not to!"

Shrugging on my jacket, snatching my floppy hat, and tugging it onto my head, trying to contain my unruly waves and, after making sure my fringe is sat flat, I turn to playfully strut out the door. That's the fun of being the boss of one, we can have a laugh and not take life too seriously with each other.

Dad used to say it was the people you work with rather than the job itself that helped to get you up in the morns. He was correct in his musings.

I make my grand exit from the office and head over to the family farm. My dear mum is currently struggling with that pesky pleasure known as hay fever, or as the Germans like to call it, "heuschnupfen." Ever since dad passed, my brother Jack and I have been stepping up to help her out with farm chores.

Today, I received a call alerting me that some of our fluffy friends have gone rogue and made their way into the neighbouring Brayes' fields. So, I grabbed some clothes and boots and prepared to get down and dirty fixing fences and chasing sheep. Oh, the joys of wrangling sheep... not!

Ah, sheep. The silly, woolly creatures that seem to exist just to make our lives more difficult. They don't listen to a single command, and they'll play dead at the drop of a hat. Don't even get me started on their birthing habits! Give birth in a nice, safe barn? Nah, let's just pop it out in a muddy ditch and walk away. And again, don't waste brain power even thinking about leaving them near mud - they'll sink up to their necks and just look at you like it's a normal Tuesday.

And have you ever seen a sheep stuck on its back, legs flailing helplessly like a turtle stranded on its shell? That's when you have to stop whatever you're doing, climb a wall or fence, and heave the darn thing back onto its feet. And let's not forget the cost - it costs more to keep them than what you actually get back for them.

Honestly, who needs sheep? Well, apparently my mum does, but that's just because she hasn't been stuck in the mud – well, since we were old enough to do that job for her.

As I drive my faithful beast past the Braye's farmhouse, Lawrence Barker's cringeworthy image appears forefront in my mind, complete with his appendix scar and flashy belt (it was a nice belt). I can't help but wince at the memory of my poor judgement. What was I thinking?! I mean, I know I'm supposed to be open-minded and all because of what was agreed with the counsellor, but Lawrence Barker?

That was a mistake I'm pretty sure I won't be repeating. Lesson learned: never walk up the stairs in front of a guy who's more interested in shagging than buying a barn. On the bright side, I discovered that I don't mind doing the deed outdoors every now and then, what with the dog walker and now Barker. Who knew?

"Only me. Your favourite daughter!" I shout towards the kitchen. "I'm just going upstairs, get myself sorted and all that."

After a few minutes, I emerge from the bedroom wearing jeans that looked like they had been vacuum-sealed onto me thanks to being tumbled, and one of my mum's knitted jumpers. I did bring all my clothes with me - except a top, so I had to improvise.

Unfortunately, my mum is petite and flat, and her top hugs every curve and bulge on my body. I look like a balloon in a straitjacket.

"Thought Nigella had walked in then."

"You're so funny Jack."

"Nice haircut. Good luck with the fence. Bloody sheep."

Jack and I may be a few years apart in age, but we share a mutual distaste for the cows and sheep that roam the fields around our childhood home. It's a bond that has only grown stronger over time. We've both tried to avoid getting involved in the family farm, opting instead to pursue our own passions – partly by choice but partly because both mum and dad wanted us to live our own lives; lives we have chosen for ourselves.

For Jack, this meant starting his own plant hire business, which has proven to be a remarkable success. He works with farmers all around Richdore and beyond, using some of our dad's old machines and some he has acquired on his own. It's been great to watch him carve out a successful career for himself, even if it means he has to deal with the very animals we both can't stand.

Mum and I hastily throw together some sandwiches, snacks, and drinks, whilst enjoying a cuppa. I then take the beast through the yards and out to Foxhole Field to sort the fence. The guys should already be working with the fence driver and stakes down there. Even though it's unseasonably warm we shouldn't need more than the handheld one. Not like we're on clay which goes waterlogged in the winter and solid as rock in the drier months.

I can see the two of them near the wood line and pull up next to Reggie's quad. Future head's "Hounds of Love" playing extremely loudly, they are oblivious to my arrival.

It was then I realised it wasn't Pete with Reggie.

"Where's Pete?"

"What's wrong with me instead?!"

Oh, my dizzy aunt … There he is, my secret childhood crush - Reggie, my brother's best mate from school, and the ex-professional rugby player.

And wait for it...

Standing next to him is Daniel with his shirt already off! I couldn't believe my eyes. I mean, seeing the two of them together like that made me feel a little light-headed and giddy. It's like a dream come true, or at least a very vivid fantasy! I have to pinch myself to make sure I wasn't hallucinating! Thought I'd only witness these two together in the same place at the charity bike ride coming up.

"I've brought food and drink as promised. Won't be anything like your mum's cooking Reggie. How is she?"

"Gone home to Jamaica. Sis is having another sprog there. Any grub will be good. Got pies? Do you want to set up whilst we finish this section?"

Earlier I searched high and low for the family picnic blanket, not able to find it, and now as I set the spread of food and drink out in front of me, my mum's voice echoing in my mind, her insistence that I bring the double quilt from the spare room. According to her, it would be much more comfortable to sit on than any old picnic blanket anyway.

I doubted the guys would even notice at the time, so I, now somewhat regrettably, grabbed Jack's old "Frankie says Relax" bedding, hoping it could maybe pass for a picnic blanket - if you closed your eyes and pretended hard enough.

"Couldn't find the picnic blanket eh Di? Last time I saw that old thing there I was probably seventeen!"

"Mum's idea Reggie. Not mine."

I can feel Daniel's focus, appearing stuck towards my direction; was he thinking the same as me I wonder. If it were just him and me here, would we be making use of the quilt? Would he be tracing every contour of me with his tongue, his fingers stroking my body...

"Di, bring over another stake." Perhaps not then.

Between us we did another three more sections before stopping for a late lunch.

Picture this: the scorching sun blazing down on us as if it had a personal vendetta against our skin. The guys are here, blessed to be able to bare their naked chests, and already basking in the heat like lizards on a rock, while I'm sweating bullets in my mum's now itchy and damp jumper that fits me like a sausage casing, working like a thermal layer.

As I stand there, feeling as out of place as a nun at a strip club, I can't help but stare in admiration at the two of them. It was like they had no idea of the magnetic effect they had on everyone around them. Were they completely clueless to their charisma or was it all part of their master plan to make me feel like a soggy sock (in more ways than just the heat issue)?

"Take your jumper off Di, you're sweltering. Got a 'T' underneath? We're all mates here don't forget."

Typical Reggie. I suddenly feel quite bashful.

"It's ok. May go back and get a t-shirt as no, haven't one underneath. I stupidly went and forgot to pack one first thing when I made all the calls."

To top it off, I woke up this morning to a 'fat' day. I'm just not feeling the body positive vibe right now, if you know what I mean reader?

"We'll be in the shade for the last few sections, I'll be fine."

"Go on Di. You'll make yourself ill. It's only like you'd be wearing a bikini." Daniel piped up.

I peer down my top to double check which bra I have on. Fairly sure it's a bit more revealing than the average bikini top...yep. As I thought, I'm wearing my going out on special occasions "show off" bra. Nipples on full blown display through the sheer fabric inserts. Soft now but I could almost guarantee I'd be poking someone's eyes out with them as soon as they see daylight.

In a rush this morning, I threw my everyday undies down for the wash and just put on what was on top in my lingerie drawer. Obviously, I wasn't thinking I'd get the call from mum nor end up here in a 1970's porn scene with two gorgeous (in my eyes), and topless hunks. I've got fencing to do. We've got fencing to do...

On the plus side, I stand by a bit of advice my grandma gave me years back "Always match upstairs with downstairs in case of an accident. You don't want the doctors to think you can't afford matching underwear my child." The other clothing quote from her being "Never wear white – in case you shit yourself." A lady of wise words.

"Come on guys. Need to get this fencing done."

"Spoil sport!" One of them says aloud.

"Agree." Says the other.

We reluctantly pack up the remnants of our picnic, tucking everything back into the cardboard box it came from. Reggie suggests we leave the bedding out in case we want to take another breather later.

As I turn to respond, I catch Reggie giving Daniel a sneaky wink.

Suspicious, I demand "What's with the wink? What are you two planning?"

Next thing I know, the scoundrels have grabbed the waistband of my jumper, yanking it inside out and over my head!

"Hey, not fair play!" I protest through my laughter, but it's too late. My arms are now suspended (yet again) in mid-air, trapped by the tight confines of my mum's impeccable choice of cable-knit. The woollen masterpiece made for excellent blinders, blocking my vision completely.

The infectious well-known beat of "Pump up the

Jam" by Technotronic blares out, flooding the air with its energy.

As I bob my head to the rhythm, I can't help but feel a rush of nostalgia wash over me. The memory of carefree summer days spent messing around with friends in the fields and woods comes flooding back, accompanied by the soundtrack of a battered 90's ghetto blaster blasting out some classic tunes in the background.

Despite being momentarily trapped in my dear mum's skin-tight jumper, I feel a sense of joy and freedom. The music has a way of transporting me to a time when the worries of the world were far from my mind. It's as if the beat has the power to unlock a hidden part of my soul, reminding me of the simple pleasures in life.

With a thud I come back to the moment as I suddenly feel arms around my torso, and my ankles taken hold of too. Swiftly I find myself laying on my back. One of the lads helps remove my jumper completely.

"There you go. Bet you're feeling cooler now?!" Reggie teases.

"Actually, I feel a bit hotter now the sun is on me."

What was that about agreeing to try new things and moving out my comfort zone again? Well here goes...

"I don't know about you guys, but I think it's time for some sunbathing action!" I declare, already peeling off my boots and struggling to free myself from the vice-like grip of my jeans. It's not a pretty sight, but my two friends seem to be transfixed - either with awe or horror. I finally manage to wriggle out of my denim prison and plop down on the ground, basking in the warm glow of the sun like a contented hippo in the Serengeti grasslands.

"Join me, boys! We can forget about the fencing for now. After all, we don't have any sunscreen, and we wouldn't want to end up looking like lobsters. At least if we get too warm here we can move elsewhere."

Daniel and Reggie exchange a quick flick of the eyes before sheepishly shaking their heads.

"No way, mate. I don't want to risk becoming a human barbecue," Reggie quips, eliciting a chuckle from both of us.

I close my eyes and let out a sigh of contentment, soaking up the rays and letting my mind drift. Ah, this is the life. I feel like a celebrity sunbathing on a yacht in the Riviera. We may not have a yacht, but we've got the next best thing - a cooler-box picnic and a quilt. It's all about perspective... all about perspective.

There's silence for a few moments before Daniel speaks.

"The glitter in the nail varnish matches the silver of your toe ring. I like it."

He begins to suck the toe with the ring on it. I jump, not realising he was anywhere near my feet. Oh, my, God! How can such a small action send such a big wave right to my lady parts! He continues. Is this the same feeling as me sucking his solid cock? Behave Diana!

"Come on Reggie. You gonna join in?" Daniel doesn't wait for an answer before carrying on.

"Na mate. I'm a free spirit and all that, but toe sucking ain't my thing! I prefer other stuff."

"Like what? This is actually quite nice." Even I'm curious now. Eyes still closed and enjoying the warmth of Daniel's mouth sending mini shock waves into me.

"I'm a boob man. Love boobs! Just love, love, love boobs!"

"I love mine being played with..." Shit! Did I say that out loud?!

"Don't be the spare. Join in!" Daniel hints to his friend.

I hear a belt being unbuckled and fly pulling down.

Turning, I see Reggie removing his trousers

revealing crisp, white and very new looking boxers. Kneeling, he's unsure what to do next - he always was well mannered. I find myself guiding his hands to my breasts and showing him how I want them to be played with.

At first, he flicks my nipples through the bra. They need no prompting or assistance. Standing like soldiers on parade he begins to tease them further. He leans over to the cool box, lifts the lid, and grabs an ice cube. He likes ice play! Yes! This is going to be good! I can feel Daniel pulling at my briefs. They're sliding down over my thighs, creating goosebumps on my skin. He parts my legs and moves between.

The ice cube is melting along my collarbone, the freezing chilly water trickling down towards my back. Then I feel the cold move to my décolletage, between my breasts. Reggie slides his hand under my back and with a singular move, unclips my bra; my breasts now totally uncovered.

He begins to circle my nipple with ice. A shooting pain, or is it pleasure, races around my chest. He does it again. I feel the water running down my sides. He leans in for more ice and just as he circles my other nipple Daniel places the tip of his tongue on to me and digs down in between my wet, swollen lips.

He's hungry. He's licking and sucking, and it feels so good. I spread my legs wider. His hands are exploring. Reggie has the ice in between his teeth taking turns with each nipple before dropping the cube to my navel. He fills his mouth with as much of one breast as he can and sucks firmly. His groans are long and deep.

Pulling his cock from his pants he starts to pleasure himself whilst sucking me hard. I've never seen anything quite so big. It must be big. Reggie doesn't exactly have small hands!

Meanwhile, Daniel is sliding his fingers into me.

Pumping me slowly. There's a new move happening. I've not felt it before. He has fingers inside me, but another is sliding back and forth across my…um…rear entrance? Not inside. Just outside.

The nerve endings there make me clench tight. It's a good feeling. I'm being played with, top and bottom, so to speak, and these men are completely in control and by the sound of it, enjoying themselves greatly.

Reggie straddles me, pinning my arms with his legs. His cock is there waiting to enter my mouth. I want to taste it. Shall I taste it?

I can't believe I now use the word 'cock.' Never in my wildest dreams did I think I'd end up in a threesome, let alone it be Daniel and Reggie with me. My mid-life sexual liberation has truly begun!

Reggie's muscular thighs continue to hold me down. His large black cock enters my mouth. I need to relax. I need to relax my mouth. I can do this. I want to do this. Daniel is working me down below. I can feel I'm very wet, almost too wet. He's lapping and sucking my bud. Oh, it's so good. He's really so good at that! I'm trying not to bite down on Reggie. How do they do this in the films?! It's downright impossible! I can feel myself ready to climax already. Don't do it Di, concentrate!

"Ahhh... Leg cramp! Leg cramp!" I yell, my leg twisting in agony, almost hitting poor Daniel in the face.

Reggie jumps back, and then immediately snaps into action, assuming the role of a seasoned sports trainer. He kneels down beside me, furiously rubbing my calf with his strong hands.

"Is it getting any better?" he asks, concern etched on his face.

I try to catch my breath and suppress the urge to scream. Instead, I manage to choke out between gritted teeth.

"Noooo! And now your backside is in my face too!"

The absurdity of the situation is not lost on me, and despite the pain, I can't help but laugh at the absolute ridiculousness of it all.

Daniel grabs the cooler box and throws the ice over my leg, and most of Reggie.

"Christ! Why the hell did you do that?" We both say together.

"I panicked? Was funny though."

And then I laugh again. The spasm is easing. "That wasn't the sort of ice play I had in my head for this kind of scenario!"

The sun beats down on us mercilessly, the heat still intense even as the cramp in my leg begins to subside. We scramble to move the quilt to a shadier spot, finally settling under the cool shelter of an ancient weeping willow after a round of rock, paper, scissors – Daniel won. These trees are scattered all around the farm, their graceful branches reaching out like welcoming arms.

As we lie there, enjoying the relative coolness of our new spot, I can't help but admire the lush foliage that surrounds us.

The boundary between us and the Brayes is marked by a deep drainage ditch, which seems to have become a haven for these majestic trees, along with many other varieties that have taken root in the rich soil.

It's a peaceful and idyllic scene in anyone's eyes. Other than the fact we're all starkers or semi-naked and should be fencing right now.

Reggie is in his full glory to one side of me, Daniel to the other, still in his jeans.

"Take your jeans off Daniel. You shy or something?!" I jest.

It didn't take another request. His jeans fly off like clays from a pigeon trap. He retakes his position on the word "Relax."

"Right boys, not done this before so bear with..." I slide down until I can reach both their cocks, Daniel's is already rock solid, Reggie's needs a helping hand... or mouth.

Positioning myself, purposely showing Daniel my "everything", I place Reggie's soft cock into my mouth. It stirs slightly, he murmurs. I sense it growing, as I continue to flick with my tongue, nibble and take as much as I can without choking. He involuntarily moans and twitches. My head moving as I deep throat him, sucking hard as I pull back up. I don't want him to come yet. I lift away and straddle him, sitting on his thighs.

Leaning over I place his cock between my breasts and rub him up and down slowly. Very, slowly. His moans are louder. I rub him harder. With each motion I place his cock in my mouth on the downward stroke. He feels the wet warmth inside. I repeat the action increasing the rhythm until ...

"Fuck! That's good!" Reggie cries out as he ejaculates over me. I wait for him to relax, then turn my attention to Daniel.

If it were possible, he is stiffer now than before. I want him inside me. I need him there. I'm so ready and have that aching yearn for cock. Thick, large, cock. Holding on to the branch above me I reverse cowboy him and lower myself down. His cock pushes my swollen lips apart and fills me completely. I don't move, savouring the feeling.

Daniel holds my hips, pushing me harder on to him, he thrusts upwards. My muscles pull tight around him. Again, I close my eyes and instantly I feel something else. Reggie. I feel Reggie near me. I can feel his breathing and then I feel his mouth on my bare breasts again. His tongue is tracing me until he reaches between my legs.

Already parted with Daniel's cock there, Reggie begins to nuzzle in. He sucks hard. I'm being fucked and sucked at the same time. The cock inside me is pushing into me hard but slow. My bud is engorging as the sucking carries on.

I'm using language my mother would be so proud of... not! With her strong German accent, she'd likely tell me a few, choice words, clip my ear and wash my mouth out with soap! Luckily, she cannot see me hanging on to a branch being hard screwed by Daniel, and Reggie face first in my lady bits sucking me like a popsicle!

Daniel quickens his pace. Reggie instantly increases the pressure on me, I'm clamping around Daniel as I feel myself getting more excited. My legs are shaking, and I hold the branch with all my strength as my body gets wound into a muscular frenzy of fighting the climax.

The tightening from my feet, into my calves, through my thighs going right up into me as the release of all the pressure exploding is too much and I shout out loud some sort of primal scream.

As my orgasm pulsates my inner muscles against Daniel's hardened cock, he throws a final thrust and comes deep between my legs.

Five thrusts later he releases his grip from my hips and collapses backwards on to the quilt.

Reggie, ever the gentleman, hands me his handkerchief...

"You may need that."

6 There's Always Two Sides

June 21st. As I stand here in my ridiculous cycling shorts, I can't help but think how funny it is that all of these people are voluntarily subjecting themselves to a gruelling bike ride on a beautiful Saturday morning. And for what? To raise money for some charity or another. I mean, don't get me wrong, it's a great cause and all, but there are much easier ways to donate money, like just writing a cheque, some would say.

But I guess there's some kind of draw about the physical challenge that brings people together, even if it means squeezing into spandex and sweating like a pig. I spot a few familiar faces from the town, including Mr. Wilson, retired primary school headteacher, who looks like he's about to keel over before we even start. I guess I'm not the only one who's been roped into this thing against my will.

I check my phone again, still no word from Diana. It's not like her bailing on a commitment, even if it is just to cheer me on from the sidelines. Maybe she really is tied up with family stuff, or maybe she's avoiding me and Reggie like the plague after the field incident.

I can't say I blame her; it was pretty embarrassing afterwards, but at least we continued with getting the fence repaired before driving off with our heads bowed in shame! Maybe she's being a bit dramatic about the whole thing.

It's taking ages for the ride to start and I'm beginning to feel a bit self-conscious standing here in my skin-tight pants. Let's do a few laps around the field to warm up.

As I turn the corner, I pass by a group of teenage boys who are eyeing my bike like it's a Ferrari.

"Nice ride, mate!" one of them calls out. I hear another of the boys rather loudly whisper to his friend, "I bet he's got a mansion and a personal butler too."

I almost laugh out loud. If only they knew that I had to save up for months just to buy this thing, and my idea of a butler is a microwave that can reheat last night's leftovers.

I give them a friendly wave and keep pedalling, feeling a bit happy about my fancy carbon fibre frame and high-tech gears. It's not like I need all this fancy gear to ride a bike, but it sure does make it more enjoyable. And let's be honest, it's nice to show off a bit. I've worked hard since leaving education and don't treat myself very often.

In fact, the only reason I have this fancy thing between my legs is because my old Raleigh, Daphne, finally gave up on that last fell ride.

RIP Daphne. Thank you for all those fantastic rides uphill and down dale, as they say.

I push myself a little harder on the next lap, feeling the burn in my legs. Suddenly, a girl on a bright pink bike whizzes by me with a huge grin on her face. I can't help but chuckle at the sight of her helmet covered in fake flowers. Maybe I should have gone for something more outrageous than my plain black one, but it was on sale, and it fits my head and mass of curls. Crikey, I'm feeling old seeing the fading pink blur now in the distance!

As I finish my warm-up laps and head over to the starting line, I can't help but feel a little nervous. I've done this ride so many times before, but it still feels like a huge challenge every year. And this year, without my trusted other half in tow, it feels even more daunting. But I take a deep breath and remind myself that I'm doing this for a good cause, and that's all that matters.

As I make my way back to the starting line, I spot Jack and Reggie in the crowd. They're both decked out in matching cycling jerseys and helmets, looking like they're about to tackle the Tour de France. I can't help but let out a childish snigger at the sight of them. They're both so competitive, it's like they're trying to outdo each other with their cycling gear. Typical old school mates. Do everything together when they can. They were known as the terrible twins in their teens.

"Hey, old man!" Jack's calling out, waving me over. "Ready to crush this ride?"

I can't help myself from chuckling, knowing full well that Jack's idea of "crushing" a bike ride is probably very different from mine.

"I'm just here to survive it, mate," I reply. "You know me, only here to do my annual bit for the wonderful Marlowe Foundation."

Reggie nudges him with his elbow. "Don't listen to him, he's just being modest. I've seen him tear up some pretty gnarly trails in his day."

I roll my eyes, but secretly appreciate the compliment. It's nice to know that my skills on a bike are still appreciated, even if I'm not quite the daredevil I used to be.

We line up, surrounded by hundreds of other riders from around the county, all revving their engines (or at least, their pedals). I take a deep breath and remind myself why I'm doing this. It's not just about the charity, it's about pushing myself to do something that's difficult and uncomfortable.

It's about proving to myself that I'm still capable of doing hard things, even when I don't feel like it, and at my age, I am beginning to feel everything, from my knees creaking to my neck clicking in time to the beat of a good banging dance track whilst driving my trusty steed. And maybe, just maybe, it's about showing Diana that I'm capable of being a mature, responsible adult who can handle himself whilst out in public and can refrain from having my pants down all the time she's anywhere near me!

Trying to focus on the twenty-one miles ahead of me, secretly cursing to myself asking why I've agreed to do the long route up to Dalebank and back again, I can hear Reggie and Jack behind me. I'm wondering if they may have had "one for the road" before getting here. Seem far too happy to me. I regularly forget they are a good few years younger than me and have yet to join the clickety-clack, groaning back club.

"You seen the padding on those shorts of his Reggie?!"

"Well, you know he needs it after his beloved Daphne lost her saddle that time!"

"Rest in peace dearest Daphne. Hope you're having a lovely time on the scrapheap in the sky!"

"Leave it out lads and concentrate! There's Dave, the butcher, with the klaxon out front there!"

And with that, we're off.

We shall be embarking on a leisurely ascent, which can only be described as a snail's pace, out of Richdore. Our path shall be tracing the steps of the old railway, and it shall lead us straight to the esteemed Dalebank station - now a café that caters to bikers, and much to our delight by the time we eventually get there, we shall be blessed with the pleasure of icy beverages and scrumptious sandwiches before we turn back around.

Now, let me tell you, the true adventure begins at this point. The track we shall be traversing is so narrow that it can only accommodate two or three cycles side-by-side. And of course, I shall be the straggler grunting and sighing on the way up, while the likes of Reggie and Jack zoom past me with such ease on their descent.

I'm fifteen minutes in and getting seriously distracted by some heavy huffing and puffing... hang on, is that me?! Well, that's embarrassing! There's me thinking I'm as fit as a fiddle. Time to hit the gym again me thinks!

The incline is seriously deceiving. I'm hoping to literally ride out the ache in my thighs that's building up. Let's hope I don't do a Diana and get leg cramp … that was quite amusing though. I really didn't think twice about sloshing the two of them with the ice water. Thought I was helping at the time.

Jack is sailing ahead of me, just disappearing over the brow. He's making this look too easy, but he's built like Thomas, and, like father and son, the lithe body frame no doubt helps with this cycling lark.

Unlike me, built like a lot of the family; must be the Dutch gene pool at this bloody height. Heard it all, you know "Is it warm up there near the sun?" or "Can you change the lightbulb whilst you're there?" or the classic "Wow! You're tall."

No idea where Di gets her rather lovely curves from. The first time I saw her I knew I'd like to get to know her better. Seeing her with her floaty dresses, masses of wavy hair and those doll-like blue eyes peering out from the agency window... makes my heart skip a beat every time I go in there. Cocked that one up now though, haven't I?!

Pulling over to one side for a glug of water and another check of the mobile, I see Reggie coming up behind me with a massive grin on his face. Those rugby player thighs pounding down on the pedals.

"What's kept you?"

"Went back for my pods mate! Had to start again."
He points to an ear, wobbling hard for a moment
on his wheels. "I'll see you at the top!" he calls out
as he speeds off into the distance, leaving me in
the dust.

Ah, here comes Mr. Wilson, the man whose face
matches his bright red football shirt. He manages
to muster a nod my way as he trudges onward,
sweat pouring down his face like a waterfall
thanks to the late morning sun beating down on
him.

"Need some water Mr Wilson?" I hold my spare
bottle out to him. He carries on. "That'll be a 'No'
then?"

Well, time to carry on with this bike ride. At least
it's not a timed event, so I can take as many breaks
as I need to catch my breath. I haul my leg back
over the saddle and am immediately grateful for
the extra-padded bike pants I'm sporting, even
though the lads were mercilessly teasing me
earlier. My saddle may as well be made of solid
rock, it's so hard and unforgiving.

But I don't let that stop me. I shift my weight
forward and stand up on the pedals, determined to
keep moving onwards. It's a bit of a struggle at
first, my legs feel like lead weights, but soon I find
my rhythm and start to make some progress. But
just as I start to get comfortable, I feel my backside
start to ache from the hard saddle once again. I

shift my weight back down onto the seat, hoping the padding will provide some relief. It does... for a few seconds, at least.

But soon enough, I'm standing up on those pedals again, trying to find a balance between comfort and progress. All in all, it's a struggle, but I know it'll be worth it once I reach the top of this hill. Or at least, that's what I keep telling myself as I keep pedalling forward.

I reckon I'm about halfway up this hill now. Most of the local kids have whizzed past me, including that little girl with the pink cycle helmet. I swear, she couldn't have been more than six years old, and yet she's already got more biking stamina than I do! It's times like these that I realise just how unathletic I am.

In school, my specialties were the long jump and high jump - short bursts of activity that I could handle. But why they thought I'd be any good at rowing or hammer throwing is beyond me. Every year it was the same thing "You! you're on the hammer, rowing, and cricket teams this term."

Now, cricket was alright. I loved the sound of the ball smacking against the willow bat. In fact, it was my love of cricket that got me interested in crafting my own bats from the willow trees that surrounded our town. And that's actually how I started my business, believe it or not.

But biking up this hill? That's a whole other story. My thirty-five-inch legs might be good for short bursts, but they're definitely not built for this kind of endurance. I can feel the burn in my thighs and the ache in my lungs, and I'm starting to wonder if I should have stuck to crafting bats instead of trying to bike up this damn hill! But hey, at least I'm giving it a shot. And who knows, maybe all this pedalling will give me some killer quads or something. A man can dream.

Finally, the top is in sight! Yay and all that jazz...

A last push, literally, wheels all a wobbling left and right like a crazy toddler when it first learns to ride a trike, and I reach Reggie and Jack.

"Why do you look as if you haven't done a thing yet?!"

"Been here half hour already mate. My sister will be deeply disappointed in you!"

"Thanks for that bud. Just what I need to hear!"

"Nah, she'll be alright." Reggie winks at me

"You'll be seeing those jiggling babies soon enough again I reckon!"

I raise a disapproving eyebrow and quickly try to

change the subject.

"Think you are getting me muddled up mate with someone else?" I continue frowning at him.

"Don't know what you mean mate! Can hardly get you muddled up when I was there!"

What is he not getting? I try indicating with my head towards Jack in a "not now" kind of way.

"What do you mean Reggie? What do you mean? He ain't been shagging Di?"

"We both have mate! Together! Same time, same place, and everything. She's a bit of a goer is your Diana."

"Woah! This isn't the time nor the place. There are kids here around us. Enough Reggie."

I wave my arms in various directions trying to justify my point. The kids in question are not taking a blind bit of notice – bit like Reggie right now.

There's an awkward silence in the air. It's obvious Jack is visibly upset and quite rightly so. He shouldn't have found out like this. I've got a sick feeling in my stomach as I see his face. Please do not say anything further Reggie. Please don't.

Jack looks around for his helmet, straps it hard to

his head and, flinging his legs over his frame, flies off down the hill, narrowly missing Mr Wilson who has just arrived.

"Wait Jack! I can explain!"

I kick myself as he vanishes out of view. I'm not one for reacting. I hardly have a temper, but right now I can feel what I can only describe as boiling blood growing inside me.

"Why the fuck did you tell him Reggie? Of all people you are the one who knows not to push his buttons!"

"It's no big deal, man. He'll be alright once he cools down a bit. Bet he's jealous and wishes something like that happens to him one day. About time he got his leg over again with someone."

"I doubt that very much Reggie! Doubt he'll cool down at all! You're talking about his sister!"

Right at this second I don't want to hold any further conversation and walk off to top up my bottles at the grotty looking water fountain next to the dog bowls. Some fun day this has turned out to be!

Reggie has found someone else to talk to when I return to my bike, but his attention is back to me as I saddle up.

"Calmed down yet mate?"

"Leave it Reggie. I'm off to find Jack."

My legs are still feeling a bit like jelly as I make my way down the decline, trying my best to avoid the slower cyclists. It's like a scene from The Walking Dead, only with bikes instead of zombies.

The sun is beating down on me, and I swear I can feel my skin sizzling like a strip of bacon on a hot griddle. As if that wasn't bad enough, the trees that line the trackside seem to disappear just when I need them the most, leaving me to face the full force of the sun's wrath.

I feel like I'm in a never-ending game of laser-quest, only the rays of blue light are in fact rays of sun, and they're not exactly friendly either. To make matters worse, the sweat pouring down my face like a salty facewash, makes my eyes sting like a swarm of angry bees biting at my skin. I must look like a beetroot on wheels, a tomato on a bike, a fiery hot chilli pepper pedalling down the track. The embarrassment is cooking me faster than a roast chicken at Gas mark 8. I'm pretty sure my face is redder than Mr. Wilson's when he caught up with me earlier. And let me tell you, that guy was looking pretty darn red in the face himself.

Maybe he's related to the tomato I've become?! But hey, at least I'm still moving? Slow and steady wins the race, or so they say. Although at this rate, I'm pretty sure I'm going to be the last one to cross the finish line. Oh well, at least I'll have a good story to tell.

Assuming I survive Jack, that is.

I'm still seething and feeling I've really let Jack down. Diana too. I'm sure she wouldn't have wanted her own brother to know what went on that day. But why should we be ashamed of it? We were all consenting adults, and what we did was natural. Sure, it's not something that is commonly accepted in this conservative town, but that doesn't mean we have to feel ashamed of our desires. We weren't hurting anyone - until now that is.

I think my guilt is causing me more pain than this gruelling bike ride. I've got to find Jack.

Oh, great! Just what I needed, a surprise dismount from my trusty steed. I don't know who's responsible for this act of treachery, but they better have a good excuse. My foot, the size of a small car, slips off the pedal like a greased watermelon, and my chain follows suit. Next thing I know, I'm on the ground, my knees and elbow becoming intimate with the rough and tumble of the gravel.

Meanwhile, my bike, eager to continue the adventure, decides to take a solo trip through the briars - blackberry ones if I'm not mistaken. Looks like we're both having a rough day!

Who did that? Who clipped my rear wheel? Was it one of those pesky local kids with nothing better to do than cause trouble?

As I peel myself off the ground, I can't help but feel like a baby giraffe taking its first wobbly steps. My spandex has now seen better days, but at least it's not ripped open like a bag of chips as far as I can tell. But just when I'm about to regain my composure, I see Reggie, and the tension in my body starts to build again. I swear, if he's responsible for this, I'm going to give him a wedgie he won't forget.

"What the actual fuck are you doing? Twat!"

"Didn't mean to mate. Pulled up a bit late and caught your wheel."

"Well, you can help by putting the chain back on whilst I sort out what's left of my knee."

"Bit of an over exaggeration, but okay."

I sit back down on the grass verge and examine the wound. It really isn't much to be honest, could have been a lot worse. I'm a tough guy me (grunting in pain). A little bit of pressure with a handkerchief should patch me up in no time. Ain't no big deal, just another day in the life of a clumsy guy like me.

In no time, Reggie fixes my bike like a pro and plops it next to me on the ground. He then joins me for a sit-down - probably to rest his ego.

"I don't get what was wrong with what I said earlier mate. Not like you haven't done it with her before is it?"

"Jack obviously didn't know we'd caught up. You could see that from his reaction. I thought, what with your job, you'd be able to read people!"

"What do you mean, in my job?"

Oh dear, I may have hit a nerve.

"My job is bloody serious mate. I may be life and soul of the party, but I take my fucking job as serious as I take my mother's wisdom. I cocked up earlier with Jack. That's all. I thought we were having a laugh."

"Alright pal. Don't over-react. We just need to find Jack and explain."

"Yeah, you're right. He probably didn't need to hear his sister is the local bike …"

Whack! I miss my mark and land on top of Reggie

instead. I don't know what I am thinking; I've never been much of a fighter. Maybe I was trying to re-enact some epic movie scene or something.

Turns out Reggie is no fighter either, but his rugby skills come in handy. He tackles me like a pro and sends me flying to the side. As I struggle to get back on my feet, I watch in disbelief as Reggie swings past me, flying straight into the hedgerow like a rogue bird.

I wait as several cyclists fly past at warp speed, nodding and smiling at them as they go, before reaching into the hawthorn and grabbing Reggie's arm. He instantly grips my wrist with both hands and pulls me down with him. I'm face to face with him and don't know what to do now … so I peck him on the forehead (I know, you're asking why? Well, I wasn't thinking … again!).

Apparently shocked, this action seems to anger him for some reason, and he shoves me off with full force into the path of Mr Wilson who stops abruptly and falls to one side. Both of us spring to our feet and help Mr Wilson back onto his bike.

"Sorry Mr Wilson" I hear myself saying as I pick up his reflector off the ground. "I won't do it again Mr Wilson."

"Yes, Sorry Mr Wilson. It was him." Reggie adds, slapping me in the back.

"Ow! Ow! Ow!"

"Had enough?"

As Mr Wilson rides off, I turn to Reggie with a very mischievous grin on my face.

"You ready for round two?" I ask, preparing to lunge at him.

Without hesitation, I grab Reggie's shoulders and attempt to take him down with a swift kick to the legs. But he's too quick for me, and he grabs onto my waist, causing us to stumble around like two drunk penguins on an ice rink – reminds me of Di sliding down the road by my place that time.

We continue to miss each other with our clumsy moves, spinning and swaying along the path like a scene from a slapstick comedy. The looks we're getting from other cyclists range from amusement to confusion to utter disbelief. We continue with our comical tussle, constantly missing each other with our attempts to trip the other up. We're like a couple of clowns waltzing along the track, our bikes forgotten as we prance around.

Suddenly, I can't help but laugh at the ridiculousness of the situation. I turn to Reggie and give him a childish glint in my eye.

"You ready to dance, partner?"

Reggie gets the memo and nods back at me. "You lead mate!" and offers his arms to me.

Oh, what a sight to behold! Two grown men in spandex, waltzing their way back towards their bicycles like Andy Pandy and Loopy Loo. If only we had some music playing in the background, it could have been a scene straight out of Bridget Jones or other!

Bike bells a ringing; I hear a loud cheer from a group of cyclists passing by. "Bravo, bravo!" one of them shouts, clapping their hands. I turn to them with a theatrical bow, before continuing the dance with Reggie. We finally collapse onto the grass, exhausted from our impromptu performance.

"We should take this on the road," I say, panting for breath. Reggie just chuckles and shakes his head.

But as we sit there, catching our breath and wiping away tears of laughter, I conclude that this silly little moment has been the highlight of my day. Sometimes it's the unplanned and ridiculous moments that make life worth living…that's not to say I still need to get to the end of the pesky bike ride and sort things out with Jack.

Back on our trusty steeds, Reggie and I pedal away down the old track, the tension between us having dissipated like a fart in the wind.

As we approach Whites Lane, my heart skips a beat at the sight of The Brayes' farmhouse looming in the distance to our right. And lo and behold, there's Di's really filthy, and I mean really filthy, 4x4 parked outside my humble abode. About time she cleaned that.

"Speak of the devil, Di's in the field over there!"

Reggie exclaims, waving frantically at her like a lovesick puppy on steroids. He's so distracted that he almost crashes into my rear wheel, again, But I forgive him because I'm just as smitten with Di as he is.

Could she be visiting my landlords? Or did she actually lie about helping out at her mum's place? The suspense is killing me, but I try to play it cool as we pedal towards her, my heart racing faster than a pro-cyclist drinking Red Bull.

Is this the epiphany that I've been waiting for? Have I been blind to the true meaning of love all this time and taken everything in my life for granted? What about my wife and our marriage? Have I failed to appreciate all that has passed between us? As I see Diana, I can't help but wonder if the same feeling should still be there for my wife even after all these years.

And then, the track turns away as it winds its way back towards Richdore and the moment has passed.

We finally spot Jack, hunched over on the old railway embankment, surrounded by a sea of people. None of them seem to notice him, though. They're too busy basking in their own sense of accomplishment, proudly displaying their phony gold medals.

"Hey there, mate. We've been looking for you everywhere."

I call out to him as we make our way over. I dismount my bike and begin to push it over to Jack, feeling a pang of guilt as I take in his defeated expression. I know that Reggie and I are the reason for his misery. But Jack doesn't seem to want to see us.

"Go away, both of you. Just leave me alone," he mutters, barely lifting his head to acknowledge our presence.

Reggie, however, refuses to back down. He crouches in front of Jack, casting a looming shadow over him.

"No, mate. We're not going anywhere until we've made things right with you." he declares.

"I shouldn't have said what I did. It was wrong," he continues, looking genuinely contrite. "And that big lug over there already gave me a good seeing to about it," he adds, nodding in my direction.

Not the first time I've been referred to as that. I'm glad to see him taking responsibility for his actions.

But then, out of nowhere, we are pounced upon by the town mayor and some "paparazzi" from the local newspaper, chasing us down and demanding we pose for a photo with our "golds" (aka medals).

So, there we are, in our skin-tight spandex, looking like three wise monkeys who had just stumbled into oncoming traffic.

And then, to make matters worse, the photographer yells "cheese" and blinds us with his camera flash.

I mean, talk about a surreal experience! It was like we were in some kind of bizarre sitcom, but with way less laughter and way more lycra.

As Jack turns to me, his face twisted with deep disappointment, I can feel the weight of his accusations bearing down on me.

"What do you have to say for yourself?" he

demands, his voice full of hurt. "I put my faith in you, mate. You promised to keep me in the loop about my sister, and you let me down!"

I can't help but feel like I'm in the spotlight, caught in the midst of a dramatic scene. I glance around, half expecting a stagehand to appear and turn off the bright lights shining down on me. But of course, there's no such luck. This is real life, and I'm going to have to face the music.

"I know, Jack." I reply, hoping my tone is sincere as the sincerity in my words.

Jack continues to scowl.

"It wasn't planned. Pete couldn't help with the fencing, so Reggie called me up to be his second pair of hands. Your mum was in a bit of a pickle, and she needed it sorted before the sheep got back out again. Di arrived, and maybe the heat got to us all. But I swear, it was a one-off. We're not trying to keep anything from you or your family." I explain, scratching my head sheepishly.

I can feel the weight of Jack's disappointment lifting slightly, but there's still a lingering sense of hurt in his eyes. It's going to take more than just words to make things right between us.

Meanwhile, Mr Wilson has wheeled up to us on his bike, looking non-plussed about the medal that's just been handed to him.

"Gentlemen, have we resolved our stupid conflicts, or are we going to have to call in your mothers to straighten you out?" he admonishes us in his best headmaster voice, before casually stowing his trophy into his cycle bag and riding off towards the stand offering refreshments.

I wouldn't be surprised if he secretly had a stash of rulers in that bag, ready to whack us with if we didn't behave. That man means business.

"Alright, alright. It was a one-time thing. Didn't even get to stick it in her..." Reggie starts to chuckle. I quickly cut him off with a sharp jab to his side.

"Did a few other things though..."

"Reggie! You never know when to quit!" I exclaim. Earning him another elbow jab in the ribs.

"You're missing the point, mate! It's not about whether you three have been sneaking around behind my back and my mum's back or not. It's about the fact that you can't even confess without acting all smug and proud." Jack pipes back up. "It's not on, just not on."

Well, well, well. Looks like we've got a bit of tension in the air. But hey, we're all friends here? Let's inject some humour into this conversation and lighten the mood.

"Reggie, my man, you seem to have a talent for putting your foot in it. But what other talents do you have hidden up your sleeve? Maybe something that doesn't involve getting yourself into trouble with the ladies?"

Reggie responds with a sly grin, "Oh, I've got plenty of talents, but I'll stick with having fun with the ladies. It's just way more enjoyable if you catch my drift."

"Woah, hold on there, Reggie! Seriously, I was trying to change the subject!"

Jack chimes in with a chuckle, "You know what, mate? You're way too laid back for your own good. It's hard to stay mad at you for long. Even when you're being a twat, like you were back up the track just now."

"Funnily enough, that's just what I called him before he rugby tackled me!" I snigger, then snort, like a small kid.

And so, we all burst out laughing, the tension rapidly dissipating like a cloud on a sunny day. It's moments like these that make us really appreciate the true value of friendship. Ah, there's nothing like a good laugh to diffuse a tense situation! The power of humour is truly amazing.

We agree to put today's argument behind us, at least for the time being, and make our way towards

Bobcats and Boots for a well-deserved pint or two.

After all, what better way to mend fences than over a cold one with your best mates?

7 The Birthday Present

Can you believe it? We're already halfway through the year, and before we know it, summer will be in full swing. As for me, work is busier than ever, but I'm feeling pretty good about where things stand.

And yes, I'm still standing despite my unexpected, but rather enthralling threesome in the field! Not sure I'd do it again, but at my age I'm very unlikely for it happen more than once anyway, and when would I be likely to end up in that position again, my childhood crush and the extremely lovely Daniel … Sorry reader, the memories are quite distracting don't you know!

Back to June …

The sales are flowing like a river, and we're close to completing a few deals that are sure to knock it out of the park. But let's not get ahead of ourselves, because we all know what's coming in just a few short weeks - the dreaded school summer holidays.

When July hits, it's like the housing market suddenly slams on the brakes. Everyone's too busy soaking up the sun or packing their bags for a well-deserved vacation to think about moving house. I mean, who wants to deal with that when there are beaches to be lounged on and cocktails to be sipped?

As the clock strikes four, I realise it's time to lock up the office until Monday. I take notice of the other local businesses across the way, such as Buttards, who still follow the traditional market hours of only being open for half a day on Wednesdays and Saturdays. However, when I first started my business, I made a deliberate decision to remain open during times that were more convenient for working locals who may not have been able to visit us during regular business hours.

This strategy has proven to be successful, as we continue to gain returning clients who appreciate the flexibility we offer to accommodate for their constant ever-changing circumstances in life.

I'm feeling fabulous today (not), thanks to a mishap this morning. Having the sheer audacity to pack up and go bang mid-cycle, the washing machine has left me with a severe lack of respectable things to wear, and so today I resorted to an all-in-one bright red jumpsuit - something slightly regrettable as really not designed for quick access on toilet breaks - neck scarf to hide some cleavage, sandals and now, sunglasses, aviator shades to be precise.

I've had three comments about working for the Red Arrows and one about having a nice bum.

Plugging my headphones in, I attempt to access my playlist on the phone, unintentionally deafening myself with the previous half-played "Sunday Girl" by Blondie. Endeavouring to decrease Debbie Harry's mellifluous tones by continuously pressing the volume button (and basically half the screen too), I manage to delete a new notification from Alex, Nate's cousin. However, I did catch "laters x" and assume I'll get another call or text towards the end of the day, as per usual.

With the pleasant weather, it's an ideal opportunity to do my Thelma and Louise impression - minus the open top car, baseball caps and police car chase - I have the windows open full, sunglasses on and, with my hair smacking me full on in the face as I drive, I take the scenic route home in the beast.

Me time, enjoying the afternoon peace and quiet on the roads here, other than my "Now That's What I Call the Nineties" CD playing loudly. It's just so green around the curving lanes, past various farms, mills, and workers cottages. The journey lifts the spirits, on what would be a pretty dull birthday otherwise.

"Hi Sid! How's your mum and dad?"

"I'm Sam. They're doing ok. Saying us kids doin' their heads in. Happy birthday. Mum said you're 63 today."

"Your mum's taking the pi.... I mean..... say 'hi' to the rest of the family from me and the furry things!"

Talking of which, The Dick and the digging one greet me with a good old jumping up session whilst the cat with attitude sticks an imaginary finger in the air and stares me out at his bowl. After placing a parcel on the table, left helpfully under the door mat so that I could trip over it, I let the pups out, feed the attitude and I pour myself a much-needed glass of wine. Ahh, that's more like it. This wine drinking malarky seems to be catching on in my house. Is this what grown-ups do?

I'm not entirely sure whether it was the sound of the wine pouring into the glass or the sight of the liquid flowing from the bottle that triggered it, but suddenly, without warning, I feel an intense and urgent need to relieve myself.

Despite having put off this task for most of the day because of the hassle of getting out of my jumpsuit, I quickly make my way to the outdoor toilet, which, these days, is cleverly disguised as a pretend pantry in the corner of the kitchen, all the while struggling to unravel myself from the all-in-one combo.

However, as I strive to remove the jumpsuit, I find myself cursing like a sailor, struggling to release my left arm from the wrap-around frontage and then, stumbling across those mandatory tie things that seemed to be of no use that have decided to knot themselves (despite the fact I didn't even do them up in the first place).

As I try to do the same with my right arm, the jumpsuit seems to have a mind of its own and exposes an additional triangular panel that I am almost certain wasn't there earlier. I am exasperated - this is an emergency pee situation for crying out loud!

As I sit there, catching my breath, weeing for England, and wondering if I'll ever be able to stand upright again, my phone starts buzzing like a swarm of angry hornets. I grit my teeth and ignore it - I've got bigger problems to deal with at the moment. But the buzzing just won't stop, like a persistent mosquito in the middle of the night. I shake my head and try to focus on more important matters, like the fact that I need to stock up on the recently discovered coconut scented toilet paper after this epic pee session.

Finally, I emerge to check the phone, only to find a blank screen staring back at me. Was it a ghost call? A poltergeist trying to mess with my already fragile state of mind? Or is it just some dodgy telemarketer trying to sell me a timeshare in Skegness?

The phone has been fine all day. As proven with all the birthday messages from people I haven't spoken to in fifteen years or more. Do they really think a generic "HBD" on "Slapface" counts as a heartfelt greeting?

Oh, and then there was the one from Malthay village community page. Not that I've used it since the dog walking debacle (the ad, not the shag.) but less said about that the better me thinks.

With a glass in hand and the dogs safely back inside and taken care of, we - me and the animals, all settle in front of the television, although it isn't actually turned on.

Margaret, still perched on top of the fridge, is blasting one of Nate's playlists, which consists mainly of 80s synth with the occasional surprise thrown in.

Seizing the opportunity to finally read the latest issue of Farmers Weekly, which has been sitting around for the past couple of weeks, I plop down in my favourite wingback chair by the fireplace, overlooking the garden outside through the window.

As I curl up and start to read, I come across a section on seasonal workers that I think might be of interest to my mother. She used to be one herself, when her and dad first came back from Germany, and now hires and accommodates "her helpers" every year to assist with the potato crops we plant.

It's pleasant to feel the warmth of the summer sun through the glass pane, even at this time of day, but it doesn't last for long.

The glass of wine has appeared to have emptied itself.

Wandering back into the kitchen, I hear the mobile again. Looking at the screen once more I can clearly see it's not doing anything. Not even lit up. The buzzing is coming from elsewhere.

My phone pings and a new notification flashes up.

"Sorry I can't be there but hope Alex makes up for it. N"

'N' being Nate of course. He agreed to celebrate with me as part of our "couples counselling" plan, but it seemed like he was flaking out on his end of the deal. Luckily, he has had the foresight to organise Alex to keep me company instead and they happen to be great fun to be around. If I'm being honest, quite easy on the eyes too - although I wouldn't dare tell Nate that!

"Pour one for me too. Been a long day and my hands are killing me. Banging tune by the way!"

"Rhythm is a Dancer" Snap! verberates off the

kitchen units just as Alex makes an entrance through the back door.

I'm greeted with a double cheek kiss and a smacker on the lips. Soft lips still, just as I recall.

"Oh! You got the parcel! How exciting! Happy birthday by the way! Fuck him for not coming. His loss. Love him really. He's just a fucker. He's forgotten he ever married, the way he treats you. Just fucks off and leaves you. You're the forgotten wife you are. That's exactly what you are. The fucking, forgotten wife!"

Alex tends to talk a lot, generally without engaging brain first, and normally effing and blinding away.

"What have you been up to?"

"Fuck knows. Been ages. You look great. Nice outfit. Shows off the curves and those fuck off massive tits of yours."

We head into the front room. The pups have stolen the two armchairs for themselves. With limited seating options, we are left to decide between the worn-out dog sofa or the rug as our next best alternative.

Alex chooses the dog sofa (The dog sofa - It's seen more tails than a dog park, and more fur than a sheep shearing festival sees wool. It's been chewed on, drooled on, and scratched up to the point where it looks like it's been through a tornado. But despite its tattered and, worn appearance and now, severe lack of springs, and foam, is still remarkably comfortable…IF YOU'RE A DOG!).

Dumping a large, half empty, holdall down on the floor, which appears to have seen better days, Alex crashes out like a sofa sloth alongside the cat with attitude, who looks less pleased than an albino black widow. I place the wine bottle on the side table next to my magazine - immediately giving cause for Alex to start ribbing me being a farmer's daughter shagging on haystacks or behind tractors.

I'm used to it though. Known Alex as long as I have Nate. With my legs twisted underneath me, I make myself comfortable and prepare for a much-needed gossip session over drinks.

The self-emptying glasses continue to be refilled for several rounds.

Although it's June, the room is beginning to get chilly. Alex decides to light the fire already prepped in the hearth. The room immediately fills with smoke.

"Open the flue up Alex! We'll be smoked out at this rate!"

"Oops. Fuck! Sorry Fuck! Shit! Bloody smoke!"

The smoke persists, making the room increasingly

uncomfortable to be in. I suspect it's one of the old cherry logs that's been lying around since I moved to the cottage.

Even with the windows open, the room remains hazy, and the chimney doesn't seem to be drawing any air. I go to the kitchen and grab a tea towel, soaking it under the cold tap. It's a good thing it isn't an actual fire, as I have to stand there like a muppet for several minutes due to the very low water pressure.

It takes several verses of "Nellie the Elephant" before I re-emerge from the kitchen and, after ruining said tea towel, I finally manage to put out the fire.

"Well, that was a pointless exercise, wasn't it?!" Alex grins with a wonky toothed smile.

"And now I stink of bonfire!"

"Not the only one! Are you staying over?"

"Obviously didn't read my text, did you?! I'm here for an all-nighter with you courtesy of my cockwomble of a cousin!"

"Really? Good o'. Is this where I admit I accidentally deleted your message when it came through?! Blondie was too loud and wouldn't quieten. I also managed to call the GP at the same time. Amazingly got straight through to the dreaded receptionist, which is bloody typical, being that I didn't need them this time!"

"Yeah. Typical!"

"Want food? Think I may have some bits here we can make into a meal."

"Thought you wouldn't ask! Starving and been thinking all day about this evening. Didn't want to ruin my appetite."

Not sure what that means. We're only sitting, drinking, reminiscing and soon to be, munching. Yazoo's "Only You" is now playing.

"You be Vince and I'll be Alison!"

Alex starts to sing (badly) from the other room whilst I plate up a load of out-of-date Christmas snacks that still smell okay. I join in, equally out of tune. Must be the wine... I promise readers, I really do sound perfect in the shower.

Swaying and clinging to each other, glass in hands, crooning away, we make our way through Nate's eighties playlist until we reach Human League's "Electric Dreams," which Alex puts on repeat.

The residual smoke still hangs from the ceiling. Even though there are just the two of us, this isn't my front room now, this is the infamous Stacey's Eighties night, circa 1995 and the nostalgic feelings of our days of youth are back; that time in my life when Nate and Alex walked into it and never really left. Until Nate uttered those bloody awful words one evening.

The pups continue to snooze on the chairs. The cat with attitude just stares at the imaginary spider running across the carpet, following 'it' along the skirting board and up the wall.

A serious amount of wine later, the evening is now early morning. Alex and I are quite jolly.

"Oh shit! I forgot all about the package Di! Was supposed to open it earlier."

"It'll wait until the morning Alex."

"Best not. Anyways, technically it is morning."

"Good point." I look at my watch to confirm. "I'm going to go make your bed up. Let the pups out and lock the backdoor after."

"Will do. I'll bring the package with me."

The cottage has two bedrooms. Only one has a bed in it. The other is the "don't know where else to put it room."

I stand in the doorway for a good few minutes observing the mess in front of me.

"Fuck it. We'll share mine." I walk back out, shutting the door behind me.

"Alex! You're in with me." I shout down the stairs and go to my room.

Alex is already there at home under the quilt.

"Got to clean my teeth." I step into the adjoining bathroom to do my usual. My choice of clothing, once again, strikes back.

"I can't get out this stupid jumpsuit! It's fighting with me again!"

Alex leaps out of bed stark naked. Wasn't expecting that. Perfect in every way, perfect smile, perfect hair, and now perfect body.

"Let me help you."

Gently unravelling me from my clothing with all my wobbly bits on display I feel totally inadequate in the looks department.

Without questioning it, my bra and panties are removed. I just stand there dumbfounded at the vision of perfection in front of me.

Then, without warning, Alex leans in, kissing me softly on my lips. I melt. My legs turn to jelly. I almost pee myself.

Another kiss, again soft. A pulse races through my body. My hand is held, and I'm pulled onto my bed, together we lay down, bodies touching. This is new to me.

I think it's my turn to instigate the kiss. I want to. That attraction for my husband's cousin has always been there.

Our lips meet. The kiss is firmer. Our tongues entwine. It feels different. (Anyone else think kissing with tongues is like clothes on a washing machine cycle? No? Just me again.) This is gentle. This is intimate. This is something else!

I lift away, gazing down at Alex. I move forward and kiss along the collar bone, then the little dip in the neck, working my way down. I cup her breast with my hand. It feels firm, unlike mine. I place my mouth around her nipple. Holding it there for a moment whilst I take in what's happening. I begin to tease her with my tongue and feel it swell and engorge. This isn't the same as taking cock in my mouth. It's smaller, feminine of course, the skin feels soft, and she smells sublime.

I kiss between her breasts now before taking the other into my mouth. My tongue plays before I suck gently. I can sense the skin tightening around the budlike bullet in my mouth. I have an ache between my legs growing. No. Not an ache. A throb.

I put my body over hers, sitting astride, and lift her arms above her head. I know I like the position. It stretches me out and every sense is heightened. She seems to like it also as she arches her back. My ample breasts hang down towards her mouth. She sucks hard. I hold her arms still as she moves her head and mouth between each nipple.

I'm savouring the feeling. Sliding down I release her arms and kiss her on the lips once more. It's firm. It's extremely passionate. Our hips meet. Our breasts touch. A spark of electricity flashes through me.

Suddenly she wraps her arms and legs around me and flips me over with some ease - thanks to her school wrestling days no doubt. Now she is the one on top. Our bodies are tight together. Our hands grabbing each other where we can in the moment, as the gentleness goes and adrenaline kicks in. That urge between my legs ... I really want Alex to go down on me and explore me as only another woman would know. I go to speak...

Alex suddenly sits up. "The package!"

She grabs the box from the side and shoves it at me. "Open it! Open it!"

Hold up, hold up, hold up! Do I really have to do this right now? I'm not ready to give up my precious time for this. But nope, Alex just won't quit, and now I'm staring at a not very exciting cardboard box on my lap. I reluctantly tear off the tape and expose the contents within.

Lo and behold, a shiny gold bullet vibrator winks back at me, along with a bunch of other mysterious tools that I either have no clue about or only heard of in shady corners of the internet. It's like a kinky treasure trove in there!

"Game on!" Alex exclaims as she snatches up the vibrator. "And would you look at that, batteries included! Talk about convenient!"

Oh no, oh no, oh no. This is not good. I've never dabbled in the world of sex toys before, and my social circle is all about treating them like they're on par with soliciting on the street corner. I'm in uncharted, potentially scandalous territory here.

"Lay down Di, there's a look of horror on your face!" Alex laughs. "Believe me. You don't know what you've been missing! You're not ready yet though ..."

She puts the vibrator back down (to my relief) and swings her leg back over me. Her breasts, pert and small, jiggle with the movement. I watch my hands as they begin to move towards her chest. I stroke her skin and see goosebumps appear. Her nipples double in size before my eyes. I've never been this close to another female.

Her body is stunning. I slide my hands down to her

waist. She's sat astride me. I trace my finger from her hip, along an imaginary line until I reach her pubic mound. I hover by the natural split and brush gently, caressing the blond, downy baby hairs there. I look up at Alex's face, almost asking for permission to explore further, she nods and lifts herself off my chest. She moves upwards, straddling my face, above my mouth. High enough for me to see and lust for, low enough for me to smell her womanly scent.

Her legs spread slightly, my mouth waters as I tentatively part her lips with my fingertips to reveal her glistening pierced jewel. I touch her with my index finger and a small droplet appears. She almost purrs. I touch her again then gently circle her; more juice appears. I press, circle, repeat. Press, circle, repeat. She's pushing towards me with her hips. I want to taste but I hold back.

Why am I hesitating? What if I do it wrong? I'm a virgin to all this.

"Just go for it Di! I want you to taste me. I want you to lick me. I want you to suck me. I want your tongue to long for everything about me Di!"

The mustiness mixed with floral tones of her body wash is mild but totally intoxicating. I hold her soft buttocks. My mouth salivates, my taste buds erupt as I slowly envelope her. I take as much as I can, parting her with my tongue.

Searching for her bud, I relish the affect I am having on her whole body. I hear the noises coming from her mouth as I lick and suck her, alternating from soft and gentle to hard and long. I move my tongue further down into her. I trace her inner lips, running the tip of my tongue, edging her, before returning to her piercing.

"More Di! More!"

I can feel her thighs tensing as I suckle her.

"Keep going! Don't stop!"

I do keep going. I suck and release and suck and release, then I am sucking harder still until I feel the pulsations of her in my mouth. I can taste Alex's womanly juices as she quietly climaxes. Quite exquisite. I keep sucking, harder and harder. I now know, as a woman, if this momentum is kept up, she will come so hard, so much more than just then. The secondary climax has to be brought from the depths within but when it blows, it blows!

Alex is holding my head to her. She's fighting the feelings, but she knows. She knows to hang in there and concentrate on the feelings happening. I suckle her hard. This is not the time for licking. Suck Diana! Suck! I want her to come. I want her to spurt her juices.

She's groaning. Her body is writhing, she's so close. Pushing her hips and holding my head, it's almost stifling me and then she releases all that tension, thrusting her hips high into my face. Clear juices are pouring from her in short, sharp spurts. Female ejaculation close up looks amazing.

How many years have us girls thought we are wetting ourselves in orgasm rather than this? This is so fucking cool!

And then it's my turn. Alex carefully moves back, kissing my forehead, my mouth, my neck, my breasts in turn, she traces her tongue over my navel and down between my legs. It doesn't feel like a man. The touch is tender. She knows where to place her tongue to send tingles up my spine.

She takes her time, working me with her fingers. I'm too wet, too moist, but she keeps pumping me with her slight hand. My bladder full, again heightening the sensation. Pumping and sucking me until I finally climax, my muscles clamping and throbbing around her fist.

She hasn't finished. I feel her fumble over the bed looking for the toys. Her face still low to me. Her breath warms my skin, her tongue touches my bud once more. I jump with the sensation then push my body towards her face. I want more.

And then I feel it. She slides the toy within me and gentle pulls it in a back-and-forth motion. It's not cock. But it fills me. Rhythmically the full-length slides in and out of me to the sound of "Wicked

Game" Chris Isaak. Margaret is still playing loudly in the kitchen below.

"Do you like?"

"I do. I do like it."

Alex turns the end, and my body is a mass of buzzing, cheek wobbling, delight! The vibrations pulse right throughout my lady parts and into my rear. The back and forth of the long shaft slipping into me sends shudders from my toes to my head. Why have I not explored this before?!

Moving from inside me, Alex follows my inner lips slowly towards my bud. Oh, sweet Mary! I'm ultra-sensitive from the orgasm. I feel like I'm going to wet myself as the vibrations reach me. Concentrate Di!

Alex moves alongside me while her hand masterfully works the vibrator between my legs.

She suckles my breast coordinating the suck with the vibrator reaching my tip each time. Fuck me, my body can't take much more of this. I feel my toes clenching, the muscles tighten in my legs, my body fighting fire burning within. I climax again, stronger, and harder, with such force that I involuntarily pull my legs to my chest and push straight out again trying to control it.

Alex flips me over. I'm face down. She pulls my

hips up and rams her face between my legs. Sucking and licking me, moving her tongue around like a pro, she pushes the vibrator expertly into my now tight inners. Turns the end to full speed and I literally explode...

The following morning, I wake with a slightly sore head. Alex is sat up next to me all bright and cheerful.

"Morning! Made you a cuppa. It's on the side."

"Thanks. I need it. You hit parts of my body last night I didn't know I had! I've got a right ache now in my lower back!"

"Roll over, and I'll give it a rub."

Why do I suddenly feel like a bumbling, awkward mess? Maybe it's because Alex is a pro at this stuff and I'm just an amateur in the game of bodies.

I reluctantly comply with her request to roll over, my mind racing with thoughts of my imperfections. It's daytime, I'm sober, and there's no special occasion to excuse my behaviour, unlike last night. Nope, that was just a one-time thing. Just a random, isolated event that definitely won't turn into a regular occurrence. Definitely not... maybe.

Suddenly, Alex whips out a bottle of massage oil from her trusty bag. "I was thinking we might have used this last night, but no worries, it'll definitely come in handy now," she says with a naughty grin.

Straddling me once more, she pumps a generous amount of the slippery substance onto her palms and gets to work.

Starting at my back, she glides her hands in long, sweeping strokes, up over my shoulders, down my arms, and back up along my sides. I can feel the tension in my muscles melting away as she works her magic. Up and down, back, and forth, her hands firmly knead and stroke, sending me into a state of pure bliss. It's like my body is a piece of dough and Alex is a master baker, moulding and shaping me into something new and delightful.

"Alright, just scooting down a bit here." Alex announces as she manoeuvres a pillow under my hips and "bits."

I feel her settle between my legs. "There we go, that's much better. Now I can work on your lower back area properly." She says with a sense of purpose.

As she applies more oil, I sink deeper into the mattress, my face and shoulders softening while my derriere basks in the spotlight. With her skilled hands, she rubs and presses her thumbs into my lumbar region, working out all the kinks and knots.

I have to admit, it feels pretty damn amazing.

How have I never had a massage before? Maybe I should indulge in this kind of pampering more often. I mean, I do have a holiday coming up next month...

Alex's hands continue to move lower, now gliding over my bottom in swift, brush-like strokes, the oil making everything slick and smooth. But do you know what? I don't even care anymore about feeling self-conscious. Alex saw it all last night, and this is just a massage after all.

With her expert touch, she works her magic on my flesh, manipulating it with precision and skill. She rubs and pinches, even giving a little slap here and there, sending warmth radiating across my skin. Suddenly, my mind drifts back to that rather wild session at the barn with Lawrence Barker. But no, no, no, this is just a massage. Nothing more, nothing less.

Did she just touch me?!

There it is again. Alex pours more oil into her hands. Is that oil dripping between me, between my cheeks and legs? She's rubbing me again, parting my cheeks, touching me, releasing me then repeating her moves - parting, touching, releasing, parting, touching, releasing ...

Wrong hole Alex! Wrong hole!

She isn't hearing the words rushing through my mind right now. She touches me again and oh God, I like it. The oil makes her movements light and teasing. Her fingers slide in between my lips and right into me. She begins to finger fuck me.

"You really like this don't you?"

I nod.

"What about this?"

Her hand moves back between my cheeks, a finger pressed firmly, not entering. I pucker. That, dear lady, that area is forbidden. Do you not agree reader?

Alex starts to pour more oil and repeats parting my cheeks, touching, and now teasing my very tight hole with her fingertip. I want her to stop but I don't want her to stop.

Alex moves back, resting on her heels, and I hear the familiar sound of the lid of the oil bottle flipping open.

My heart sinks – please, no more oil. I mean, don't get me wrong, the massage feels amazing, but the last thing I want is to ruin the sheets with an oil slick.

She parts me and starts to tease again. It doesn't feel like before. Something is entering me, not by much but it's there. Is it a finger? Nope. That's definitely not a finger! It feels different, almost blunt. She's pushing me harder, adding yet more oil...

"Want me to carry on?"

"I don't know what you're doing Alex?!" (I think I like it though.)

"Butt plug, dear. Butt plug. It was in the package."

"Was that not a dog toy for the pups?!"

She slaps me. Her hand being so much smaller than Lawrence Barker's but still leaving a sting.

She continues...the plug pushes against my hole repeatedly. Each time it moves further in until I feel myself open enough to take the silicon covered toy inside of me. This feels weird. Am I supposed to feel dirty or ashamed or am I supposed to feel enlightened to a new experience that feels bloody wonderful?

At this point, I'm not entirely sure if I'm fully enjoying this part of the "massage" yet. It's like my grandma always used to say, "Try it once, otherwise how do you know you don't like it?"

And boy, have I been taking that advice to heart this year? But despite my initial apprehension, I'm determined to give this "massage" a fair shot. Who knows, maybe it will end up being the best massage of my life!

Alex pulls at the plug, pulling it in and out of me. Oh my, this is strangely nice. She pushes it back in, places her thumb inside of my lips, her fingers onto my wet bud and begins to rub slowly.

Oh, fuck me that's good! Is that the 'G' spots her thumb has found?

Don't stop Alex! Don't stop! My butt is clenching hard around the plug; my teeth are biting into the mattress. Fuck! Fuck! Fuck! What the hell is she doing to me?!

"Come Di! I can see you want it!" Alex expertly keeps the momentum, pressing on the plug with her other hand at the same time as my bud with her fingers – until I absolutely erupt. The pulsations inside of me – the plug blocking me from pouting my tight hole further. It's a restrictive feeling but something quite glorious that I've never felt before.

"Bloody hell Alex! Where did you learn that manoeuvre?!" I splutter, after I regain consciousness that is.

"You're forgetting I'm a professional Di. Plus, it's in the genes."

Did Nate know Alex would make this birthday one

to remember? Is that why he asked her to see me?
I don't know. But I'm glad she came...

8 Sand Between Their Toes

As I hop up and down on my bed like a kangaroo, sitting on... I mean, packing... my bags with all my favourite clothes, "toys" (and snacks), I feel like a kid again! I'm so excited to go on an adventure for a whole week that I can hardly contain myself. The thought of all the fun and mischief I can get up to in seven days on my own had me giggling, or rather, gaggling like a silly goose!

If I compare myself now, to say, even six months ago, I feel like a completely different Diana. I've lost weight, gained confidence (mainly needed in the sex department – box half ticked.) had various new hairstyles to go with newfound single life and clothes now resembling more my namesakes – rather than Mother Teresa. All, I feel, heading in the right direction; that marriage counsellor will be pleased.

Before I set off on my main journey, however, I want to make sure that mum is all sorted over at the farm. So, I plan to make a quickish stop with her to drop off the replacement brake discs for grandad's tractor.

The little International B275 has been in our family since it was brand new in 1958, and it holds a special place in our hearts. With an extra 5 horsepower compared to the B250, it is a little bigger and more powerful. Despite its age, it has remained an eminent sight around the villages, often pulling a carnival float filled with small children from the local primary schools in the summer months. Unfortunately, it is currently off the road, awaiting repairs from our trusted mechanic, aka, Jack. He is busy helping the Brayes with their silage collection and baling at the moment, and next month he'll be moving on to the barley and maize harvests.

As we find ourselves in the middle of the year, the scorching heat of July has taken hold, leaving many of us feeling like we can't bear to wear anything too restrictive or heavy. I, too, am beginning to reach the point where I care less about what I wear and more about staying cool and comfortable. In fact, I even decided to brave wearing shorts on my daily walk with the pups yesterday, which is unheard of for me.

Despite my desire to stay cool, I try to maintain a formal appearance for work, aside from my beloved floppy summer hats. As someone with stupidly pale skin and blue eyes, I know all too well the dangers of overexposure to the sun's harmful rays, and the unpleasantness of sunburn, thanks to growing up in the decades of no sun cream… just add butter… (Thanks for that mum).

Back to packing …

Various fitted, yet daringly sexy, floaty, dresses, cropped trousers, jeans, jumpers, and smaller, much, much, smaller, every day undies are already 'neatly' shoved in the red one. Blue is for all the toiletries, footwear and all those bits and pieces such as chargers, toothbrushes, and stuff. If I work it out well, I can bag up the dog bowls, leads etc. and food at the other end saving on taking another bag.

Or maybe not. The pups are sat next to me along with a year's worth of dog towels, a couple of doughnut beds, several bowls and who knows what else. Christa will take care of the cat with attitude as he can't be trusted elsewhere without taking somebody's throat with him.

The beast loaded, brake discs on the spare seat, I'm heading off for hopefully a relaxing week away from work – left in the capable hands of Dylan of course.

"Drive By" by Train playing loudly as I pull out on to the lane, reminds me of Nate. It's his CD, found in the footwell when he bought the vehicle and been wedged in the player, well, until I took over ownership and pressed the "release CD" button.

I'm feeling a growing sense of grown-upness, as I prepare to head out on my latest adventure. The last time I went away was with my now half in half out husband, and it was a complete disaster. He chose that moment to drop the bombshell that he didn't want to continue our marriage as it was, and we spent the whole trip as emotional wrecks, crying and pouring out our hearts to each other. It was a real mess!

But this time, it's just me, The Dick, and the digging one. I have a feeling this trip is going to be one for the books!

Oh boy, mum's at it again! She's up to her elbows in the flower bed – her favourite place when not with her beloved sheep. I'm not about to pull a Jack and honk the horn just to make her jump – I'm not that brave (or stupid)! Even when I was a teenager and just called for a ride from the bus stop, I'd sweat bullets waiting for mum to pick up the phone. Her sharp "Ja?" and eerie silence made me feel like I was in trouble before I even said a word.

That's why Jack and I came up with the genius plan of calling and hanging up after three rings. It's the international symbol for "come and get us mum!" without the heart attack-inducing greeting.

"Here already? All packed?"

"All sorted. Do you need a hand with anything

before I go? I'll stick the brake discs in the barn in a moment."

"Might as well have a cuppa, love. It's a bloomin' trek to get there, all the way down to the edge of the country."

My mum and dad really, other than his National Service, were always a bit of a homebody, and never left the farm unless it was absolutely necessary. But my trip is only a couple hundred miles – nothing compared to her dramatics! Once I hit the main road, it'll be a piece of cake.

And it's not like I'm going to the underworld or anything – it's just a straight shot across the country. Mum always makes it sound like I'm embarking on some epic quest to the end of the world!

"Mum, are you trying to fatten me up before my big journey? A cuppa and some biscuits won't hurt, I suppose." I say, eyeing the plate of sugary treats she'd laid out for me.

"I'll put the pups in the crew yard for a few minutes."

I am feeling a weight on my mind as I prepare to leave my mum behind for a week. I have asked Jack to try and do everything he can to help her while I am away, but he seems to think that I am worrying too much. However, I can't shake the feeling that something isn't quite right. Even though my mum isn't saying anything, I can see that the constant upkeep of the farm is taking its toll on her. She's getting older, and I can't help but wonder if there's something else going on with her. Perhaps she's missing my dad, who she used to work very closely with during the summer months.

Whatever it is, I just want to make sure that she's okay and that she has the support she needs while I'm away.

I've moved on from the Train CD and am now listening to Fix Radio (it's a real thing) where the host is talking mental health in the trades industries with various experts.

I do wish the farming/agricultural industry were mentioned too or had a similar station to listen to. So many workers have their radio on in their cabs and would realise they weren't the only ones feeling the way they do. Did you know reader that farming has the second highest suicide rate behind trades in the UK (last time I checked anyway).

The amount of 'tradies' calling in talking about their own personal experience is quite impressive. A good few years ago Jack went through a horrendous time when one of his best mates from secondary died in a farming accident. Jack was there at the time and couldn't help; he has suffered ever since with PTSD, although recently he has got involved with several charities promoting farm safety and positive mental health which in turn is helping him.

We'll be on to "carpentry hour" soon but I should, in my theory anyway, be arriving at the holiday let in twenty minutes or so.

An hour later, through the large metal gate, the beast is taking me down a long, narrow, and winding private track with a marram grass/sand combination down the middle of it. The property should be at the end. The Dick and the digging one play Russian roulette with the hedgerow plants coming through the window. The air conditioning has been fighting the whole journey to keep us cool and now to have the windows open and a slight sea breeze, along with the hawthorn and hazel coming in, is quite a relief.

Oh my gosh, there it is - the Glass House. This property is so stunning it makes my eyes water with joy! From its perch high above a private cove, it's much, much, more impressive than the online pictures suggested. And let me tell you, I value my privacy on holiday, so this is the perfect choice for me - even if it did cost an absolute packet.

I punch in the pin code and the grand double oak

doors swing open to reveal the open-plan living quarters. This place is clearly not designed for families or many, as the sleeping quarters and bathroom are separated from the living and kitchen areas by a mere concrete half wall.

But who needs privacy when you have three floor-to-ceiling glass walls that offer unobstructed views of the water? That's what I call a room with a view!

The fourth wall features a far too "arty" painting of the immediate area, which is a bit too fancy for my taste, but who cares when you've got a swing seat hanging from a queen post truss in the corner that looks like it was made for lazy afternoons gazing at the sea.

And let's not forget the pièce de résistance - the largest leather sofa I have ever seen! It takes up most of the space in the middle of the room and looks like the perfect spot to sink into and let the holiday vibes wash over me.

As the sun starts to make its descent, I decide to go on a little adventure and explore the rest of the gardens and property.

While walking around the perimeter earlier, to find the main entrance, I saw a small wooden gate that leads to a path winding up the hill behind the house. My curiosity gets the better of me, and I eagerly follow the path. It's a steep climb, but boy, is it worth it! The view from the top is simply breathtaking.

I can see for miles around, with rolling hills and lush green fields stretching as far as the eye can see. Far in the distance, there's a quaint little village, and beyond that, the glimmering lights of a town. It's so peaceful up here, with nothing but the sounds of nature to keep me company.

But as the sky starts to darken and evening approaches, I reluctantly make my way back down to the house.

After snatching a quick shower, I slip into my pyjamas, enjoying the refreshing coolness of the air conditioning.

The glass walls are now reflecting the last rays of the setting sun, casting an ethereal glow over the room. It's like I'm in my own little magical bubble, and, right now, I never want to leave!

Feeling a bit peckish, I decide to put my cooking skills to the test in the impressively well-equipped kitchen. But as I rummage through the cupboards lacking the whatever it is I seem to be craving, I find myself drawn to the fridge, where I spot a promising looking bottle of wine. Before I know it, my planned cuppa has turned into a large glass of vino, and I'm feeling very content with my decision.

As I sit down to enjoy my meal, I notice a small

note attached to the bottle. It reads, "I hope you all have a pleasurable time! Look out for the sand between their toes moment."

Hmm, pretty standard note, I guess. But I can't help but wonder what they meant by the sand between their toes moment. Maybe I'll find out soon enough!

Now that the night sky has settled in, I can hear the soft, gentle lapping of the waves against the shore. It's so peaceful and tranquil here, a world away from the chaos of everyday life. The pups are curled up on their doggy doughnut beds, completely exhausted from their earlier adventures. It's just the three of us, and it feels like we're in our own little paradise.

After dinner, I settle down on the giant sofa with a book, but I find myself getting lost in the view instead. The stars are starting to twinkle in the sky, and the moon is reflecting on the water casting a golden glow across it. I can see why this place is called the Glass House – it's like living in a giant terrarium with the most magnificent view.

As I drift off to sleep in the comfortable bed, with the sound of the waves lulling me into a peaceful slumber, I think to myself that this is the perfect place to disconnect and recharge. Tomorrow, I'll wake up to another day in this beautiful paradise, with the sound of the waves and the salty sea air filling my senses. I know I keep using that word

"Paradise" reader, but I just cannot think of any better one to describe what I have been truly blessed with this week. Who knew there was anything like this on our own little island?!

On the third day, I'm still struggling with the bathroom situation. It's basically an outdoor toilet with a view. I mean, I don't mind nature, but I don't need it to be up close and personal when I'm doing my business. It's like a public toilet, except instead of strangers, it's the seagulls and the crabs that get a peek at my private parts. (Not those sort of crabs... naughty!) And let's face it, seagulls are not exactly known for their discretion.

But then I remember my sexual exploits and think, "Come on, Diana, you've had more eyes on you than a YouTube video." I mean, I've done it with the dog walker, the milkman, and even Alex, who's Nate's cousin. Not all at once, of course. That would be a logistical nightmare. But still, I've got nothing to be ashamed of.

I take a deep breath and remind myself that I'm not the same Diana who used to be afraid of undressing in front of her own husband. I'm a confident, free-spirited, and slightly chubby goddess who's living her best life. If the seagulls want to watch, let them watch. I'm sure they've seen worse.

I shake my head and push those thoughts aside, again reminding myself that I am on a fabulous holiday and it's time to embrace the new me. As I saunter into the kitchen, feeling free and confident, I can't help but notice the strange looks on the faces of the pups. Perhaps they're not used to seeing me in my natural state either. I pour myself a cup of coffee, or rather a glass of wine, and head back to the glass-walled living area to enjoy the beautiful view.

As the day progresses, I find myself feeling increasingly comfortable with my new-found confidence. I even venture outside to the deck to soak up some sun, clad only in my t-shirt and knickers, much to the surprise of the seagulls flying overhead. I'm sure they're thinking "what is she wearing?!" but I couldn't care less.

Later on, as I'm cooking dinner in the nude, I catch a glimpse of myself in the reflection of the glass walls. "Wow!" I think to myself, "I'm a goddess!" The pups seem to be impressed as well, wagging their tails with over-the-top enthusiasm.

As I sit down to eat, I realise that this holiday has given me the chance to rediscover myself, to let go of my inhibitions and embrace my true self. Who knows what adventures tomorrow will bring? Perhaps a little skinny-dipping session in the cove or a spontaneous dance party with the pups. The possibilities are endless when you're a midlife crisis having, slightly curvier than average, gorgeous singleton!

Ah, nothing like a relaxing day at the cove? Well, at least that's what I think until I realise, I have left my precious blankets and towels back at the house. Talk about a beach bummer!

So, I put on my thinking cap and head underneath the raised decked area. Maybe there's a surprise waiting for me there? Spoiler alert: there isn't. Instead, I find a trunk full of useless straps, rags, and steel rings. I mean, unless I plan on tying myself up like a Christmas ham, they are completely useless.

But desperate times call for desperate measures? So, I lay my sorry self on the sand and hope for the best. I mean, who needs a plush towel anyway? If the sand gets too much, I can always wash it off in the sea. Easy-peasy-lemon-squeezy!

Well, well, well, looks like someone's feeling bold today! That's right, it's me, the queen of the private cove, and today is a special day because I'm having a 'thin' day! Cue the trumpets! I mean, let's be honest, getting all these curves into a good fitting bikini seems like a truly major impossibility most days, but not today, my friends. Nope, today I'm embracing the summer weather and whipping off my top like I'm auditioning for Baywatch.

Look out, Pamela Anderson! It's just me, in all my glory, basking in the sun like the sun goddess I am.

And let me tell you reader, it feels quite liberating to be topless. It's like I'm breaking all the rules and living life on the edge. Who needs a top when you've got a personal beach all to yourself, am I right? And let's not forget, this is a very adult decision. I feel like a responsible, grown-up human being who can make her own choices. Take that, mum!

Alright, folks, it's time to get that SPF game on point! I start slathering myself in sun lotion like there's no tomorrow. Sure, I probably should have done it inside, but hey, I got distracted! Better late than never? Now, usually, my sun lotion routine involves a certain someone named Nate who would do my back and I'd do his in return.

But today, I'm flying solo, baby! I just aim the spray nozzle and hope for the best. Front, arms, and legs done; I take a quick glance at my knicker area. And that's when it hits me: what's the point of even having them on, Di? I mean, they're just going to come off eventually. Might as well get a head start on that all-over tan!

And so, with a devil-may-care attitude, I strip down and let it all hang out. Who needs knickers anyway? It's all about freedom! (I think the sun's getting to me already!).

Okay reader, it's time for a quick check-in. I'm still lying here in the sand, and let me tell you, the struggle is real. The only positive thing is that, while lying on my front, I can dig a well for my heaving breasts to reside in. But the negatives? Oh, boy. I'm breathing in sand granules despite lying on my old t-shirt. It's like I'm trying to give myself a lungful of the beach. Maybe a trip for a blanket or towel wouldn't be such a bad idea after all. But before I make my move, I need to check on my pups, who seem to be crashed out next to the trunk. They're living their best lives while I'm here suffocating on sand.

Massive sigh. Time to go back up to the accommodation. I put on my sandals, left at the bottom of the steps, and stride up the stairway like a boss. That's when I get the sense of being watched. Uh-oh. I look back, but there's nothing there. I'm being paranoid!

To be safe, I grab the nearest thing, which happens to be a large throw on the sofa, and head back outside to my dent in the sand. I place the throw on the ground and settle in for some serious tanning. Face down, legs and arms out, starfish style. It's like I'm becoming one with the sand. I wake up to the sound of the pups excitedly barking.

"Hi! Hi! How are you?!" I hear someone say.

Wait, what? Who the hell is that?!

"Don't mind me over there. Seen it all before," a cheerful, yet mysterious, voice continues.

My mind is racing. What the fuck is going on? Forgetting my lack of attire for a moment, I'm more concerned that someone has invaded my own little private cove without an invitation. I roll over and sit up, and that's when it happens. My breasts strike each other with a loud clap. It's like they're applauding the stranger's arrival. Great. Just great. At that point, I go into full-on panic mode and have a mad search for my t-shirt. I hurriedly yank it over my head and pull my legs up, trying to hide my lady bits. And then, I put on my best angry face, ready to confront the intruder.

This is not how I envisioned my day at the beach. Not at all.

"This is private land. You are not welcome!"

"Sorry! I haven't introduced myself. I'm Bearsted Faversham Montgomery, or "Bear" as I prefer to call myself. Your host. This is one of my family's homes that we let out. Diana, I assume?"

"Whoa, hold up! Bearsted Faversham Montgomery? That's a name that could break a jaw! Did your parents have something against you or what? Oh no, shit! Did I just say that out loud?"

"Don't worry. It's a family name passed down through generations, meaning mound or hill or something. I just happened to be the lucky one to inherit it. My brother got stuck with 'Montague Capulet,' so I'd say I came out on top!"

"Well, when you put it that way, I guess you did dodge a bullet there. Your parents, fans of Shakespeare's "Romeo and Juliet" by chance? Lovely home by the way. Really glad I booked it."

"Where are the others? Always have group bookings for this place."

"How? There's only one bed and a sofa. And no, no others. Just me and the pups over there."

"What site did you go through? Just out of curiosity."

"Now you got me... hang on, I saw it on several." I go to check my phone but remember that's up in the kitchen. "Think it was one of the more obscure ones. Anyway. I'm glad I found it. Love the privacy. You didn't answer how group parties fit in up there."

"Tend to hire out for film shoots and private videos. That kind of thing. Don't normally stay here, leave their stuff overnight and go into the nearest town to sleep."

"Why wouldn't you sleep here?! It's stunning."

"Perhaps I should elaborate more? Because of the privacy. They tend to use this place for ...um... adult... um ... X-rated stuff. Do you get my drift? I spend a fortune getting the place cleaned after each time. Having said that. I've been able to join in now and again so must not complain! Dare not tell ma and pa." He starts to chuckle.

"Wait, what?! So, this place is basically a kinky paradise?!" I exclaim, trying to hide my shock and amusement.

Bear nods. "Yep."

"No wonder the cleaning bill is so high and added to the end tab! And here I thought I was just getting a nice little beach getaway!" I chuckle, imagining all the wild and crazy things that must have gone down in this house.

Then the brain kicks in "I mean, I'm not judging or anything. To each their own?" I add with a wink. "But I gotta say, I'm pretty relieved I brought my own whips and handcuffs just in case." I burst out laughing, unable to contain my sense of humour in what seems such a ludicrous situation.

Silence... this chap seems to have a puzzled look on his face, or is it he's just computing my last sentence?

"Joke... Who knew a beach house could double as a sex dungeon? This is like something out of that film, Fifty Sheds or whatever it was! You've got your very own playroom – just with more daylight."

"Could say that. Just don't have anyone to 'play' in

it with me!"

Bear steps to the side, finally letting the sunshine through. I have to lift my arm to shield my eyes from the sudden glare and I can't help but take a closer look at him. He's definitely a beefcake - I bet he works out under that polo shirt. Those massive biceps straining against the sleeves look like they could crush walnuts. I mean, he could probably bench press me without breaking a sweat!

Without thought, I drop my knees to either side. Feet together still of course.

Bear's gaze head straight between my legs. "Nice. Very nice. Want to play?"

Have I just subconsciously invited myself to something?

"I'd like to see the toys first before I say yes."

I hold my hand out ...

"There are so many!" Bear seems to be very pleased for a new playmate and I have to say, this impromptu play session is already beginning to make me moist.

As Bear pulls me up the steps, I'm grateful that he's walking in front of me. If he were behind, he would notice my favourite butt plug, which I had slipped in after my shower this morning. It's a beautiful piece of jewellery with added benefits. Made of glass with a diamond rose, it's still quite small.

After my birthday with Alex, I discovered that I enjoyed the sensation of being "plugged" from time to time. I tried out some of the toys in the package, but not all of them, and bought some more. I brought them all with me on vacation, thinking this would be the perfect opportunity to try out the others, as I am alone.

Little did I know I would meet Bear!

"Stay right here." Bear's voice commands me.

I obediently stand in the doorway and watch as this hulking great figure saunters over to the sofa. With one powerful arm, he lifts the cushion, revealing something hidden beneath it.

From my vantage point, I can't quite make it out. As he returns to me, I notice he's carrying a blindfold and some other items in his hand. What could he be up to? My mind races with every possibility under the sun.

"Take your top off."

I can only imagine the thoughts running through your mind right now reader, but don't worry, I'll keep it semi-PG!

As I stand there, Bear walks up behind me and ties a blindfold over my eyes. I can't see a thing, but I feel the soft cuffs on my wrists and ankles, and a cold shiver runs down my spine. Is this some sort of kinky game he wants to play?

Suddenly, his hands caress my body, stopping at the plug. He can't help but let out a little "Mmmm." Taking it all in I can only assume.

He then takes me by the hand and leads me to the centre of the room.

I feel like a mix between a damsel in distress and a wild animal being led to its cage. But hey, in for a penny, in for a pound?

"Do you like soft or hard play Diana?"

"To be honest this is all new to me. I'll let you take the lead."

"Wait there."

I'm listening to Bear as he swiftly moves about me. He's gathering things, I think. There's opening and closing of doors. Placing items by my feet and now he's gone outside.

There is excitement within me but also a huge thought of what danger I may have put myself in, yet I don't try to remove the blindfold. I just stand there and wait...

He's back. What is he doing? There's a grunt and the sound of something being thrown. He grabs my cuffed wrists and clips them to whatever is in his hands. My arms are being pulled above my head. Its rope he has attached. Working quickly, he forces my ankles apart, fixing them in place somehow; I can no longer bring them together.

Then, silence.

He's walking around me. I don't know how many times. Just walking. There's been no touch. I can feel him. He's just there. His breath is on my neck, but he hasn't touched. Why hasn't he touched?

I don't know if I should be turned on or scared out of my mind right now. All I know is that Bear better have a safe word because I have a feeling, I may need it soon. I can hear him breathing heavily, like he's excited about something. Suddenly, I feel a sharp sting on my thigh.

"Ouch! What was that?" I exclaim.

Bear just laughs, "Don't worry, it's just a little love tap. You'll thank me for it later."

I'm not so sure about that, but I trust him... I think. The silence is deafening, broken only by the sound of my own breathing and the occasional rustle of something nearby. I can't help but wonder what he's going to do next. Is he going to tickle me? Spank me? Feed me grapes?

Gone now. Where is he? I look around but obviously cannot see a thing; the blindfold does its job well. I don't know what to expect.

Why isn't he saying anything?

He's gone to the kitchen. What for? The fridge door is opening or is that the freezer. I'm all alert for the next noise or feeling.

He's pouring...

A wine glass is placed against my lips. I feel Bear lean in towards my ear. "Drink. Take a mouthful but don't swallow. If you spill, I will whip your heavenly arse to hell and back."

Oh, sweet Mary! Bear begins his assault of my senses immediately I take the wine into my mouth. With what feels like a feather or small brush he strokes up the back of my legs, following over my butt cheeks and up my spine, making me arch as he travels with the lightest of touches.

Grasping my hair unexpectedly he bears down biting into my neck, sending signals to my brain to pull my legs together (or try to) before sucking hard.

He trails what I've come to believe is a make-up brush over my shoulder and begins to move down the front of my body, stopping to tickle and tease my achingly solid nipples on the way.

I feel the brush touch me - down there.

My body's immediate reaction is a want to close my legs again, but they stay solidly apart. It must be a spreader bar he's used upon me. Must be. The brush is slowly tracing my outer lips. The sensations are tingling through my whole area there like nothing before. He repeats the move several times before working towards my sodden bud. It's got to be so swollen right now.

The brush runs over the bud and a pulse shoots right to my rear as well as my head. Picking up moisture as Bear moves the head in large circular manoeuvres, each time, getting wetter and wetter and each time getting deeper and deeper as it reaches further in me. I can feel the excitement building through my stretched-out body. It's coursing its way in clenches and jerks...

I forget the instruction. Wine spills from my mouth down my face, down my body. Bear notices and ceases his actions bluntly.

"If you can't keep your mouth shut for me, you can keep it wide open!"

He's moved and stands behind me. I can smell sweet leather.

His hands come around by my face "Open" he firmly instructs.

My mouth opens as he pushes the ball gag into place. I cough. I didn't expect that. Relax Di, breathe slowly, I tell myself. Try and work out what he's doing next. His hands are fastening the strap around the back of my head. He lays something cold onto my shoulders and walks back over to the sofa.

Oh boy, here we go! Blindfolded, bound, and feeling more excited than a squirrel on a sugar rush, I'm eagerly awaiting whatever this Bear person has in store for me.

The suspense is killing me - is he going to tickle me with a feather? Give me a surprise makeover? Or maybe he's just making himself a sandwich and forgot about me?

I'm trying to keep calm and remind myself that I asked for this. But let's be real, who in their right mind would willingly subject themselves to this kind of torture? Oh right, that would be me. I guess I'm a glutton for punishment – nice punishment of course.

I can hear Bear moving around me, and I can't help but wonder what he's up to. Is he setting up a surprise belated party for my birthday? Or is he plotting to take over the world?

Either way, I'm in no position to stop him. All I can do is wait and hope that whatever he has planned isn't too embarrassing or painful.

So here I am, blindfolded, bound, and with a racing heart full of anticipation and a dash of fear. It's like waiting for Christmas morning, except instead of presents, I might get a mild case of thrush. Yay for me!

Suddenly, there it is again, yet another sharp sting on my thigh, I gasp in surprise. Another one follows, then another, each one slightly harder than the last. I realise that Bear is using a flogger on me, and my body starts to respond to the sensation. I feel a warmth spreading through me, and I can't help but moan softly. Bear continues to flog me, varying the intensity and the location of the strikes. I'm lost in the sensation, my body responding to his touch in ways I never imagined. As the flogging continues, I feel my arousal building, and I realise that I want more.

Finally, Bear stops, and I stand there, panting and trembling, waiting for what comes next. I can hear him moving around me again, and I wonder what he has in store for me next.

Then I hear a familiar noise.

Fuck! Straight between my legs! I convulse with the vibrations of the wand in his hand. Never have I felt anything so powerful down there. My legs held apart by the bar and my arms up high, I am completely at the mercy of this man. He holds the tool static. The vibrations work through to the butt plug, making all the muscles contract and tighten further around it.

Everything going on is a ginormous sensory overload. My body contorts against the pulses running through it. I can feel myself drooling around the gag; unable to see or speak. Bear is in charge and that only makes me want more.

And then he stops again. On purpose. He can tell I'm right at the tip, ready to explode. I want to scream! I feel his hand take hold of whatever it was he laid on my shoulder. His other hand is now on my breast pinching the nipple firmly. Is he going to place it in his mouth? Oh, please do...

Ouch! What the?! What was that?! The pain quickly subsides as Bear pincers the nipple with the clip. I turn my head to wear he now stands pulling the chain, from the clip to the gag, enough to send an instant reminder it is there. He manipulates the other nipple and clamps it. If I move my head now, I'll bloody know it.

The whirring and buzzing sound of the vibrator starts up again. This time he comes up from below hitting everything at once, throwing my head upwards I yank at the chains. My nipples burn, my bud wants to erupt, and my legs are shuddering. He continues holding it there for what seems minutes and minutes, each time I let more juices flow from within me and each time I reach "that" point, he moves the wand head away. This is sexual torture!

I don't know if Bear is in front of me or behind me. As I get to the point of no return he grabs my hips, not before launching the wand across the room. He pushes me forward and rams into me with his enormously engorged cock. Thrust after thrust he solidly pounds me.

My breasts hanging low, the clips giving me that painful pleasurable I'm far too familiar with these days, as they move to the beat of cock hitting my inner walls. This must be the most degrading position I have ever put myself in, but it doesn't feel that way. Although, saying that, being hung from a meat hook in the barn probably takes some beating.

To let someone else take over and control my body and mind like this. I must do more!

Bear's stamina knows no bounds, he thrusts and pounds into me. Holding my waist as his cock rubs internally against the plug, his balls hitting my lips, I hear his breath getting heavier and heavier as he closes in on climaxing. With a final swelling and a massive push of his hips he comes. A further few mini thrusts and silence.

My blindfold and gag are removed. With Bear's face rosy with a gorgeous, post sex glow, or could just be the perspiration on his tanned forehead in front of me, my arms still held high, he leans in and kisses me softly on the lips.

Crouching down, his eyes level with the top of my legs, he reaches down and removes the spreader from my ankles. Parting my legs again he performs the same soft kiss on me "there." No hard suck, no lapping, just soft and gentle kisses. His hands on my butt cheeks he kisses along the groin line. Little shockwaves run into me once more.

Back on my bud he tips it with his tongue, humming pleasurably at the taste, sending me into uncontrolled bliss. Pouting and pulsing, my orgasm resonates through my legs, into my back and chest over and over again. He now sucks, firmer, harder, and even harder still until the already tensed muscles release with such force I shove him off me with my hips; I just can't take any more.

He leaves me strung up whilst he tidies away.

"Want a cuppa? By the way, I noticed you have sand between your toes..."

9 There's Something About A Uniform

The month of August has been horrendous, especially for the farming industry throughout the country. We've been experiencing an intense and scorching summer, which has caused widespread damage and destruction everywhere. And now, having seen it on television, heard our colleagues speaking on the radio and read about it in the national press, we, on our little farm just outside Richdore, are right in the thick of it.

Very rarely will mum be quiet. Last time was the moment she knew dad had gone.

The three of us stand silently, taking in the devastation in front us. The once lush barley crop in Sycamore Field has been completely destroyed, leaving behind only charred earth and stubble.

Annoyingly, we were a week behind on the harvesting of it, due to Jack finishing up at the Brayes. Luckily, it was the last to be done, if you can call any of this occurrence "lucky."

The drainage ditch prevented further spread elsewhere – no water or rain meant no weeds or roughage, to alight, had survived living on the banks of the cutting.

It was a kick in the teeth but nothing we hadn't dealt with before. We've lost several crops of rapeseed due to flea beetle in the past, alongside other losses. Frustrating as it is, you must just accept and move forward. This did seem different though, more ominous, almost as if it were a sign of things to come - if the summers continue getting hotter and drier each year.

Sycamore Field was the first locally to light. Although it's almost ninety-nine percent of the summer heat that caused it, we await a visit from the crew manager at the local fire station at some point soon to confirm no foul play was involved. We've already had the incident team visit.

As we gather around the kitchen table at the farmhouse, the topic of conversation inevitably shifts back to Nate and me. My poor mum, trying to mediate between us, looks like she's about to throw in the towel and run away to join the circus. Can't say I blame her.

I fill her in on the latest of many, non-developments in our relationship. Nate says he wants to give it another go, but then conveniently forgets to show up for our online counselling sessions. I mean, seriously, he doesn't even have to leave the comfort of his own couch to attend! It's like he's trying to break some kind of world record for being the most flaky and unreliable partner in history.

At this point in our twelve-month counselling session, I'm almost tempted to hire a private investigator to track the bloke (commonly known as Nate) and make sure he's not living a double life as a secret agent or something. But then again, knowing my luck, he's probably binge-watching films and eating breakfast cereals straight from the box.

So, here we are again, discussing the same old thing. It's like Groundhog Day, but instead of Bill Murray, we have Nate - the king of empty promises and missed opportunities. Maybe one day he'll surprise us all and actually follow through on something, but I'm not holding my breath.

"He's throwing all those years down the drain sis. And look at you! You look bloody amazing compared to this time last year. You've even sorted out that horse's mane of a hair style and got clothes that fit you now rather than hiding the inner 'Nigella'."

He's called me that ever since I wore mum's knitted jumper back in May. I'll take it as a huge compliment - especially coming from a guy who looks like he got mauled by a bear on his way over.

Bear. That word. That name. That time.

"What are you going to do with yourself and no Nate, darling?"

"As I keep saying, it's been two years mum. I'm fine. Honestly. Business is doing well; I had an amazing holiday last month – in fact, it was so incredibly enlightening in many ways...got a bit tied up with a few things while I was there. Nothing I couldn't handle."

"She got a shag mum! Sis got a shag! Nigella got her knickers down! Naughty Nigella!"

"Jack! Say sorry to your sister! You may be a grown man, but I do question it sometimes."

"Sorry mum." Jack looks at me "Sorry Nigella. But I bet you grandad's tractor you did get your knickers down!"

Back at work, Dylan has taken a call from Veronica Braye asking to take the farm off the market. Reg had taken a real turn for the worse and she needed to concentrate on him for the time being.

Disappointing but totally understandable. I would have done the same. I arrange to collect the board on the way back through to mum rather than wait for the board man to visit Richdore on his rounds next week.

Well, it looks like things are about to get interesting on the farm.

My mum just called to tell me that the Crew Manager is coming over on Friday. Apparently, he's a new guy at the station but already knows the ropes. Let's hope he's not all hat and no cattle. With any luck, this visit will be the end of all the drama, and we can finally start focusing on next year's crops. We've got ploughing and cultivating to do, and it needs to happen ASAP if we want to get a good yield. It's like a race against time, but instead of a finish line, we have rows of dirt waiting to be tended to.

I just pray this "lovely young fellow" knows what he is doing and doesn't turn out to be a city slicker who's never seen a cow before. We've got a lot riding on this, and the last thing we need is someone who's all talk and no action.

But hey, at least we'll have something to look forward to - besides the usual excitement of watching paint dry. Fingers crossed that the Crew Manager is the real deal and not just another smooth-talking salesperson.

The combine has packed up! Jack is very much

feeling the pressure from the other farmers that hire his services. If he doesn't get the parts and back up and running, he loses the business to others. He simply cannot afford it. Those "others" undercut his prices and he's almost on bare minimum already.

I can tell by his voice he is struggling. I can't tell mum he is in a state and give her something else to be concerned about but have told her the machine needs attention. Dad brought both Jack and I up to fix the equipment as much as we can rather than pay someone else to do it.

Dylan is holding fort again (I really don't know what I'd do without him.) and I'm on way to my brother rather than the farm to meet the Crew Manager with mum.

Jack is at the Brayes' Orchard Field – long gone the orchard after it was moved closer to the barns – works out about four miles from mum. I may be able to catch up with her later.

As I arrive, I see Jack pacing back and forth while talking on the phone. His face is smeared with oil, and his work clothes are covered in dirt, making him look just like our dad. At first, I even did a double take because of the resemblance. It's both obvious and scary how much we can become our parents as we grow older.

As Jack notices my arrival, he raises his oiled hand to acknowledge me before delivering a powerful kick to the combine's tyre as he ends his phone call.

"Fuck this for a living. Over four grand without VAT included. I've just about got that in the account. Has to be an easier way of life. Fuck! Fuck! Fuck!"

"Let me cover the cost, Jack. Do you reckon you can fix it?"

"Yeah, I can fix it but four grand Di. Four fucking grand!"

The combine is probably the most expensive piece of kit on the farm and can run into hundreds of thousands to purchase new. Jack bought second-hand from a local farm sale.

We know the farmer and Jack knew the machine. Unfortunately, it being an older model, things break on it. It's not been anything major, until now.

"I'll cover it through the books somehow. It'll be all right."

Admittedly I have a feeling it may be coming out my savings, but I'm not prepared to see Jack getting to the point we were at with him after the farm accident. He doesn't need to know. Not now.

"Go ahead and place the order. If you want me to, I'll go in the beast and get it, after I finish with mum."

Fifteen minutes later I arrive at the farm. There's a fire service incident van parked next to mum's reliable old truck.

Walking into the kitchen I hear an awfully familiar voice.

"Reggie!"

"Nigella!"

"Don't you bloody start!" I put my arms around his massive shoulders and give him a big hug.

"Why didn't you say it was you coming?! Jack's having a meltdown over at Orchard Field. He'll be so pleased to see you."

It hadn't even crossed my mind it could have been him today.

Reggie's been in the fire service for donkeys' years. Soon after he gave up professional rugby, he went into full time firefighter mode. His mum said he needed to get a "sensible" career.

"I thought you were based in Dalebank?"

"Came back this way last week. The opening came

up and I got the chance to apply. I'll be taking over from Jim eventually."

I don't know who Jim is but nodded anyway.

"Mum, why didn't you say anything?"

"I didn't recognise the voice. He sounds so grown up now."

"Mum! It's been years since we were all spotty teenagers! Reggie's voice broke before Jacks! His name's a bit of a giveaway surely?!" I laugh and look at Reggie, getting a wink in return, unexpectedly making my heart jump slightly.

"Shall we go down to the field? I arrived a bit later than expected and your mum and I have just been nattering and playing catch up."

As we all pile out of the beast in the middle of Sycamore Field, I become fully aware how different Reggie looks in his uniform. It's a strange sight to see him in something other than his usual T-shirt and jeans, but I have to admit, it suits him. I mean, standing in the middle of a field in a neatly pressed uniform isn't normal but then, of course, I'm not exactly dressed for the occasion either. I'm sporting a lovely, fitted dress I picked up from Marks, which probably makes me look equally out of place as Reggie. The only thing that's remotely appropriate are my trusty wellies.

As I glance over at my mother, I notice that she's sporting her typical bib and braces, but they seem to be hanging off her small frame more than usual. It's clear that she's not feeling her best, and it's understandable given everything that's been going on lately. I can't help but feel concerned for her well-being as she appears quite fragile at the moment.

Having said that, I stifle a childlike snigger at the juxtaposition of the scene - a group of mismatched individuals standing in the middle of a field, trying to make sense of the chaos around them.

Who knows, we're probably even getting a few odd looks from the cows grazing in the field over the way there. But hey, as long as we can find a solution to this mess, I'm willing to wear a tutu and dance the macarena if it helps. Okay, maybe not the tutu...but you get the idea.

Reggie is speaking with authority and confidence as he breaks down the findings and conclusions of the fire investigation. "The fire started over there, slightly out from the corner. The team found broken glass, which potentially was thrown over the hedge from the road..."

As I listen to Reggie speak, I find myself briefly drifting off into a daydream, remembering the silly antics he and Jack used to get up to on the school bus. But the sight of him now, standing there in his uniform, speaking with such expertise and confidence, is hugely impressive. And that smile of his... I could stare at it all day long. It lights up his entire face and is truly infectious.

We walk over to the area in question. I make a mental note to let Jack know to grow the hedge higher. And, hopefully, it would eventually prevent this scenario from happening again in the future.

Back at the house Reggie and I leave mum to sort the sheep and head back to our vehicles.

"Did you say Jack was at Orchard Field? I'll go see him as I'm here."

"Yes. I won't be long, so I'll see you up there. Got to go to Marshalls and pick up the part he's ordered. I don't even know what it is. Hope it fits in this thing!" I pat the beast; give Reggie a quick hug and we go our separate ways.

It looks like Jack has finally managed to tame the dinosaur that is the combine. The field may be burnt to a crisp, but at least he's caught up with the backlog elsewhere.

Dylan is off today, and as it happens, the diary is looking as empty as my bank account after a weekend online shopping with my new best friend, Vino. With music blasting through the speakers, "Born Slippy" by Underworld to be exact, I strut my way to the back rooms to tackle some much-needed cleaning.

Let me tell you, these rooms are filthier than a teenager's bedroom – Admittedly, I've only got Jack's old one to go on, full of old tractor parts, a once wild rabbit he caught injured and nursed back to good health but wouldn't release back, and many, many, smelly "Frankie says relax" T-shirts that he'd got at a bargain price down the market one day.

But, as the saying goes, cleanliness is next to godliness, so I roll up my sleeves (figuratively speaking) and get to work.

As I'm rummaging on my hands and knees, trying to sort through muck and dust, I hear the door chime. I rise up, only to realise that my hair is caught on the counter above me.

Great! just what I needed. After yanking and pulling at my hair like I'm in a tug-of-war match, I finally manage to break free, smooth down the knotted mess and flatten my clothing.

"Jim," he says, offering his hand for me to shake.

And there he is, standing before me like a silver fox in his dashing fire service uniform, with sparkling greying hair and piercing blue eyes that make me want to melt like butter on hot toast. Oh boy, this day just got a whole lot better.

My lip quivering, and my heart now racing, I can feel the butterflies in my stomach. I swear, I'd take him right there in the back office if I could! What is happening to me? It took me ages to work up the courage to ask Nate out, and now I'm ready to jump Jim's bones at the drop of a hat!

"Hello Jim. What can I do you for? Wait, that didn't come out right!" I stumble on my words, feeling like a bumbling idiot.

But Jim just smiles and pulls something out of my hair. "You're worth more than 17p surely?" he says, handing me an old stamp that was stuck amongst the knotted mat.

"I was just cleaning up the back by the post section," I explain, my cheeks turning redder than a rotten tomato with embarrassment.

"So, are you here to sell or buy something?"

"Neither, actually," the silver fox replies. "I'm here to do the annual safety inspection for the insurers. Didn't bother calling ahead since I heard you're open all the time. Is now a suitable time, or should I come back later? Perhaps, when it's a little darker maybe?"

"Fair enough. I did get the letter; it's somewhere on my desk, buried under a mountain of paperwork and empty mugs. Carry on, Inspector Gadget. Where do you want to start?"

Missing the hint completely, if it were a hint, I continue, "The fire extinguishers are sited over there, there, and two out there for the kitchen and back door area. Don't worry, they're not just for show, we're not planning on roasting marshmallows in the office anytime soon."

What the fuck?! I know I'm waffling but it's literally just flowing out my open gob and I can't seem to stop it!

"Inspector Gadget … haven't heard that for a while."

I put the "Sorry we're closed sign" on the door and lock up.

It will only be half hour or so. I leave Jim to carry out his inspection and go out the back again to "die" or to continue with the clean – whichever comes first.

It's only minutes until he is with me again, finding me up a step ladder attempting to clear the top shelves.

"Let me, Ms Doors. Want this all taken off?"

His arm, tanned with golden hairs, brushes past my face as his hand points to the items coated in two inches of dust. God, even his arm smells good!

As I stand on the steps, I realise that the Crew Manager is not as tall as I thought he would be. In fact, I'm pretty much at eye level with him. But what he lacks in height, he more than makes up for in other ways.

His face is weathered and shows signs of aging, but it only adds to his charm. There are little creases around his eyes that hint at a life filled with laughter, and a small scar on his cheek that only adds to his rugged good looks.

And of course, the uniform doesn't hurt either.

I try to focus on being professional, but it's hard when all I can think about is how turned on, I am by this man. There's just something about a man in uniform, you know? He could inspect me anytime he wants...

Wait, what am I thinking? This is not the time or place for such thoughts. I need to focus on the task at hand and try to ignore those darn butterflies in my stomach. But as he starts to speak, I find myself getting lost in his voice. It's deep and soothing, with, hang on... is that a hint of a Scottish accent? I try to keep my eyes focused on his face, but it's getting harder and harder to resist the urge to just dissolve in a puddle at his feet.

Okay, Diana, get a grip. You're a professional, and you're here running your hugely, successful, and somewhat fabulous business. But damn, it's hard when the man in front of you is so...distracting.

"Yes. Yes please. They've been up there so long I think I will probably throw them in next door's skip out in the courtyard. Do you want a cuppa?"

"Perfect. Milk, one sugar." He begins reaching up to start taking down the dusty items. "You're doing a wonderful job with the cleaning. I'm surprised no one has helped you with it before now."

I climb down the ladder, feeling slightly embarrassed.

"Well, it's been a busy summer with the farm and all. I've been neglecting this place a bit."

Handing me the first item he picks, it's a small wooden box that used to contain some very nice chocolates. Not sure why I kept it other than it being too nice to throw away. Don't even remember who gave them to me.

"I know what you mean. It's hard to keep up with everything sometimes. But you seem to be doing an excellent job anyway."

I can feel my cheeks flush again at his compliment.

"Thank you. That means a lot."

As Jim continues to take down the items, we make small talk about the shop and my life on the farm. I can't help but feel drawn to him. There's just something about him that makes me feel comfortable and at ease. Suddenly, remembering the promised cuppa, I disappear to the next room.

The kitchen, or rather kitchenette, is so small that it could pass for a dollhouse. Jim squeezes past me multiple times, giving me plenty of chances to ogle his pretty impressive glutes in those snug trousers. I mean, seriously, they should put his butt in a museum, it's a work of art! The only downside is that his uniform seems to be a size too small, but I'm not going to complain too loudly.

Whilst busy ogling him, I notice his top has dust and cobwebs all over it, hand him his cuppa and without thinking, start brushing the detritus away. As I do, I can feel his chest underneath the material. It feels incredible, and I find myself getting lost in the sensation. I realise what I'm doing and pull my hand away, feeling rather ashamed of myself.

But he just smiles and thanks me for the drink and the motherly touch! Great. I'm practically on fire with desire for this man, and I remind him of his mother!

Slowly taking a sip of his drink, I sense Jim is about to make a reason to leave and then... he leans in closer to me.

"You know, Diana, I've been doing these inspections for a long time, and I've never met anyone like you before."

"What do you mean?" Am I more shocked he didn't make his excuses and run, or the fact he may just be about to say something nice about me? Knowing my luck, he will be the king of all cheesy lines and I'm about to be hit with one... any moment... now.

"Well, you're just so... charming. And beautiful, of course."

And there is is.... full on Cheddar!

"I mean it. I think you are beautiful."

If it's even possible now, my cheeks burn up with the hottest of flushes, at his compliment and hear myself saying "Thank you. You're pretty charming yourself."

And then just like that it happens, he kisses me. It's a soft, gentle kiss at first, but then it becomes more passionate, and before I know it, we're lost in each other's wandering arms.

Grabbing his hand I move back into the post area,

push him against the back wall and go in for another full-on snog.

What do I do now? I know. I start to unbutton his shirt and swiftly move my hands onto his skin. Running my fingers through the hairs on his chest as we kiss harder. His hands are on my breasts, pummelling them through my dress. Easy tiger!

I pull away and begin to unbuckle his trousers, pulling them to his ankles, taking the waistband of his pants as I go. He's ready, erect, moist, and hard. Ironically, kind of reminds me of a fire hose ready for action!

I now lower myself and place his "everything" into my warm mouth and hold it there. He groans. The tip of my tongue explores, venturing and teasing around the small orifice, and when he groans further, I place my teeth around him, dragging them slowly over the skin as I move my head away, not quite to the point of withdrawing completely.

I move back into position and in slow motion take as much of the shaft as possible, encasing with my lips tightly. I begin to suck. With his hands, Jim pushes my head trying to get me to take more. My mouth is full. I want to gag. No Diana, not the time for gagging. Breathe for God's sake woman! It tastes so good. I really like the taste of a clean man's cock. I never thought I would, but I do. But now, it's me that needs more...

So, picture this: I'm standing there like a superhero ready to save the world, but instead of a cape, I've got a skirt on. And then, like a magician revealing a trick, I dramatically undo the skirt and watch it drop to the ground. Ta-dah! But the real magic happens when Jim steps in to help with my panties. Talk about teamwork! I mean, they're barely there to begin with, so it's not like it's a heavy lifting job or anything. But hey, a little assistance is always appreciated, am I right readers?

Now, I used to be self-conscious about my wobbly bits and extra curves. But I've reached a point where I just don't give a flying fig anymore. If a man wants to get jiggy with me, I'm all for it! I mean, who knows how many lives we've got? Gotta makes the most of every moment.

So, bring on the dance party, the wild nights, and the passionate romps! I'm making up for lost time, baby! And if that means embracing my wobbly bits and extra curves, so be it. Let's get this party started!

Inner voice is back. I think the carpet needs replacing. I can see it from here. I'm lying on my back; Jim is free of his uniform completely and currently about to slide his whopping great cock into me. I raise my legs, placing them either side of his head, on his shoulders, thrusting my crutch upwards for him to penetrate me. Glad that I remembered the Veet yesterday. I feel him enter and take a gulp of air as he goes deeper. Starting to build up rhythm he pounds into me like a jackhammer. My lower lips are swollen and wet. This feels so good!

Then, stopping to adjust his position, Jim rubs his knee. "I'm getting too old for these impromptu spur of the moment meetings me!"

"Want me to go on top?"

We exchange places, not sure if it's Jim's knees or my ankles cracking in doing the action.

I remove my top, unintentionally launching it over towards the kitchen, hitting him in the face as it goes.

"Oops! Soz!"

"Soz? Really?!"

"Too much? I do apologise for my incorrect English language skills!"

Not put off by my inadequate abilities to undress sexily, nor my poor choice of wording, he likes what he sees and takes hold of my bra, hoisting it over my mightily impressive, mammaries.

"I like to watch them if you don't mind." About as subtle as a train going past, I rub myself quickly between my legs, adjusting myself to take him. I crouch down and lower onto his shaft. From this position I can really feel the girth but more so the length. I clench my muscles together as I move up and down. Those years of crouching under machinery and my much detested, Kegel exercises, paying off right at this moment.

I then manoeuvre into a kneeling position and lean forward. My breasts touch his face. Jim opens his mouth, wanting to take my nipple. I tease and tempt but stay out of reach.

Moving down his body, my tongue contouring his pecks, ribs and past his navel, I continue until my mouth hovers back over his cock. I sit up, pinning him down, astride his thighs and begin to play.

Taking the shaft in my left hand firmly, I use my free fingers to pull the foreskin slowly down exposing the shiny head oozing pre-cum involuntarily. I move the foreskin up and down, still restricting the main shaft from joining in the motion. Further juices appear. Jim's arms are by his sides, his face tilted upwards, visibly trying to control himself from ejaculating too soon.

"Crikey Diana, what are you trying to do to me?"

I reposition again. Still kneeling, I feed myself back on to him. Fitting perfectly in me, a shock wave runs through my body as I enjoy the sensations, whilst the friction and momentum builds between us. Lifting his hips into me and thrusting from below, his piercing blue eyes aim straight at mine again.

Thrust, thrust, thrust, a quiet 'oh god" and he empties himself into my swollen, sodden inners. It feels so good.

I grab some fresh, blue roll off the countertop, left from the cleaning attempt earlier, lift myself off and, very un-lady-like, shove it between my legs. Was there ever a graceful way of doing these things?!

I hand another piece to Jim... the office clean up, not quite how I envisaged!

10 Sweet Heaven

It's still hot as I get into the beast. The mock leather seats burn the back of my thighs through my dress, enough that I get back out and lay my cardi down to sit on top of it. Changing the CD to 70's summer hits, the sound of Taste of Honey's 'Boogie, Oogie, Oogie' blasts out of three of the four speakers of the beast's quadraphonic sound system. On an early evening such as today it fits seemingly well for the start of the journey.

"What's the plan then mum?"

"I'm doing sheep. This blasted allergy business is making me quite knackered. Keep telling myself it's all in my head and to carry on going. Think I may need to get a prescription for stronger meds when I get the time. Can you take the trailer down to Baileys Field and collect the last of the bales? Only half a dozen or so were there. Stick them in the old stables for now."

"No problem (heart sinking about the on-coming fight with the trailer hitch once more). Good idea. When's Jack getting here?"

"He's not. Hasn't he told you? He is next door. Helping Veronica, clearing the barn. I've said he might as well finish the job. We can get on ourselves this evening."

Mum swills her mug out under the tap, cloth dries it and places it back in the cupboard before going out the back door, rubbing her lumber region as she strides across the yard. I make another mental note, this time to have a chat with Jack about the future plans for this place. Mum isn't young anymore and we need to come up with ideas on how to make the farm work for her and not, her work for the farm.

Before I head down to Baileys Field, I need to ditch my work clothes and transform into the ultimate trailer-hitching diva. I slip into a pair of daisy duke shorts that would make Daisy Duke herself blush and throw on one of Nate's old work shirts. To tame the excess material, I knot the shirt at my waist like a sailor on a sinking ship.

Looking in the mirror, I realise that I resemble a hot mess more than a hot mama's girl, so I scrunch up my hair into a messy bun that looks like a bird's nest on steroids, pop in my headphones and crank up the tunes, ready to tackle the Herculean task of trailer hitching like a boss!

As I swagger my way over to the beast, I can't help but feel a little spritely in my step. I'm ready to take on those bales like a champ.

Oh, for the love of...the engine won't start! It's not even giving me a courtesy turn-over. This situation calls for a change of plan. Where's a helpful Jim when you need him? Nope, that wouldn't work anyway. I'd be very distracted – especially if he turned up in that uniform again!

It looks like I'll have to bring out the big guns and use my grandad's tractor instead.

It's not all unwelcome news, though. This tractor is perfect for the job, and it's been a while since I've taken it for a spin. Plus, the old girl could use a bit of a run to stretch her legs. It's a win-win situation, really.

I make my way over to the tractor with a confident stride, ready to take on this new challenge. With a quick glance at the engine, I know exactly what to do. A few twists and turns later, and the tractor roars to life like a beast awoken from its slumber.

I hop on board, feeling like a seasoned farmer, and after a further half hour doing the tractor/trailer hitch dance, take off towards Baileys Field with a secret smile on my face. This little setback has turned into a mini-adventure, and I'm ready to tackle it head-on with my trusty International by my side.

Baileys Field, oh Baileys Field, the furthest corner of our little farm that edges onto the boundary with St Augustus's Church in Maybrook. It's probably my second favourite place on this farm, only behind the legendary Otters Brook Field. As a kid, I'd venture there with my dad, and we'd sit by the mini weir on the bank and watch the world go by.

Those were the good old days when the resident kingfisher would grace us with an appearance, or some other aquatic creature would put on a show. Sadly, no otters, not since the 1950s when the majority of them disappeared from the country. It's a tragedy, really.

Taking the most direct route across the farm will take me a good forty-five minutes to get there on the tractor. Settling on to the coldish metal seat I can feel "Rose" in place between my cheeks. This should be fun. I haven't used any of my toys since the cove visit. Partially due to lack of time, but mainly because I'm still trying to work out if I enjoyed being the complete submissive to that man, Bearsted Montague.

Don't get me wrong, he was the perfect gentleman and I really enjoyed it at the time, but I shocked myself that I put myself in that position and I'm definitely not keen on those nipple clamps. That's a no go from now on! The thought of using the toys has been reminding me of the holiday, but I gave myself a bit of a pep talk the other night and realised it's ok to like some things and not others -

and I like "Rose" ... now and again.

It feels a little bit naughty and a little bit nice, and it's my secret that nobody else knows is there. My shorts are probably a size too small nowadays, but I still fit in them, and it makes everything a little bit 'snugger.'

Now, anyone that has been on a tractor, modern or not, or even studied someone on one, will know that the ride is, um, a tad bouncy. Each time I bounce, "Rose" is giving me a little thrill of sensations. I stop, get off, open each gate, get back on, drive through, get back off, close the gate behind me, get back on and drive to the next. As I manoeuvre the little tractor, I get slightly more turned on.

My journey to Baileys is turning out to be surprisingly entertaining. I try to distract myself from my thoughts (mostly about "Rose") by admiring the scenic beauty around me. Suddenly, a group of deer run across Pond Field, reminding me of the time I had a threesome picnic.

I quickly snap out of it and try to focus on something less scandalous. But as I pass by Sycamore Field, I'm brought back round to reality seeing the charred remains. To make matters worse, I spot the new vicar bird watching on the public footpath near the church. I awkwardly wave and smile like a kid up to no good, hoping he won't suspect me of any immoral behaviour.

Just another day in the countryside!

My state of arousal is quite high by the time I reach the bales mum wanted to collect. I need "sorting." With nobody in sight I rearrange the bales into a horseshoe shape, more than mum recalled, grab a couple of fertiliser sacks off the trailer and lay them on the ground.

As that's all there is I take my shirt off, and along with my cardi use them for a softer covering.

My head is pounding from the unforgiving sun, and I can feel the heat radiating from my scalp. I reach up and grab the scrunchie, struggling to untangle it from my hair.

Finally, I manage to release it, and my thick locks tumble down past my shoulders, revealing themselves in all their glory.

As the slight breeze catches my hair, it creates a cascade of loose waves that dance around my face. I can feel the strands tickling my cheeks, and I can't help but smile at the sensation. It's moments like this, when the wind is in my hair and the sun is on my skin, which make me feel alive.

I shake my head, letting my hair fall back into place, and take a deep breath of the fresh country air. It smells of freshly mown grass, the sweet scent of wildflowers and cow poo. I close my eyes and just stand there for a moment, taking it all in.

Hate to admit it, but I am now in my happy place, where I can forget all my troubles and just be.

As I would, any other time doing my "mane" as grandma and grandad referred to it, I close my eyes and take a deep breath as I enjoy the tingling sensation of gently stroking the strands with my fingertips, feeling the texture of my hair between my fingers and the relaxing feeling it leaves me with.

It's funny how something as simple as running your fingers through your hair can make such an enormous difference. I settle into my little hidden den for pleasure. A lot of effort for what could be ten minutes of fun.

Shorts and pants down, ironically Marvin Gaye's "Let's get it on" starting to play in my ears, I move my hand down. Already quite moist, my fingers easily slip down the natural parting between my legs, either side of my excited bud.

The scorching sun is still beating down on me, making this summer the hottest on record. It's almost unbearable, and I let out a gasp.

Although I would never pleasure myself in public due to the risk of being seen, I feel safe where I am now. I'm nestled in a dip at the bottom of the field, surrounded by bales, which provide ample cover for me to indulge in my desires.

My eyes closed, music playing through my headphones, I'm in a state of hypnotic bliss as my fingers rub, tug, massage, and caress.

Suddenly I get a feeling I'm not alone. Grabbing my shorts to hide my modesty I sit bolt upright and scan through the gap between the bales. Shit! The vicar is in the field!

He's right there! He has his back to me now. Did he see what I was doing to myself? Grandad's tractor... he'll surely know I'm here somewhere.

After watching for a while, I finally start to relax as I realise that the new vicar is not paying any attention to me. Instead, he seems to be focused on something else - the rookery in the old woods. It's a spectacular sight, and I can understand why he's so engrossed in it.

I remember meeting him at the WI flower festival with my mum a few weeks ago. He's from a big town on the other side of the country and seems quite shy, often blushing at the slightest thing. I didn't purposely have my cleavage on show, just sort of happens.

I settle back down; I'm actually liking the idea of someone being so near. Diana of old would never do this!

I place my hand back into position and take a sneaky peak for the vicar. He's looking straight at me... with his binoculars!

I don't know why but it excites me, a vicar being one of those characters in life you take for granted, being innocent and trustworthy.

This one's staring right at me with my lady parts all on show. Sitting back up, I remove my bra and slip off my shorts and pants.

Completely naked I can give the chap a fun time without him knowing, that I know, he's looking!

The vicar can see all of me from where he stands, a quick flick of my eyes upwards confirms his focus is still this way.

What do I do now? How have I found myself here?

I'm not exactly one of life's showoffs! He seems to be curious, as he steps forward slightly. I pull my knees up to my chest and then open my legs wide. I don't know if he can see but I start to play once more.

Surprisingly, I become aroused very quickly, maybe this is just as much for me again as him. I close my eyes, forgetting I have an audience for a moment as I enjoy the sensations running through me.

My fingers sliding in my own juices, touching my lips, touching, and circling my bud. Handling my breasts, covering them in my own sweet nectar. I work myself up into an orgasmic frenzy relatively quickly. I haven't climaxed for days.

It's not about to happen now either. I open my eyes to see the vicar has moved closer still.

As he approaches, I can't help but feel a little nervous. I've never really flirted with a vicar before, or anyone in a religious profession for that matter. But something about this man's shyness and blushing cheeks intrigues me.

I take a deep breath, smile, and wave, trying to put him at ease.

It's a painful wait whilst the vicar heads towards me. His seems to be unsure about what he wants to do. As he gets closer, I can see there is an innocence to his face. His thick framed glasses hiding his eyes to me. His movements awkward and clumsy - unlike the person strolling along the road as I passed on grandad's tractor. He stops a few feet away, still looking a bit uneasy.

Acting as if sitting surrounded by bales naked was a normal thing to do around here...

"Evening Vicar" I say casually.

He nods.

"Hi there" I try again. "I'm sorry if I startled you.

I just couldn't resist waving."

He nods, still looking a bit awkward. "Yes, well, hello. Lovely day, isn't it?"

I nod back in agreement, looking up at the clear blue sky.

"It really is. I was just taking a break from work and enjoying the sunshine."

He glances around, as if looking for something else to say.

"What kind of work do you do?"

I hesitate for a moment, not sure if I should be completely honest. But something about this man makes me want to be real with him.

I introduce myself, "Diana Doors. We met briefly at the flower festival. Welcome to the new parish, vicar."

"I don't know where to look Ms Doors. I recall now. And thank you."

"I actually work on the family farm nearby, hence the tractor. I also have Doors Estate Agency in Richdore."

His eyebrows raise slightly. "A farm? That's quite different from what I'm used to. And estate agency, my sister would love that job. She really enjoys wandering around people's houses!"

I chuckle. "I bet it is. But I love it. There's something really satisfying about working with the land and animals, but the day job is what pays the bills; my little business is something I want to wake up to each day and do. Your sister should try it if it's something she would like to explore."

He nods again thoughtfully. "I can see how that would be fulfilling."

We stay in silence for a moment, both of us seeming a bit unsure of what to say next. Polite conversation already having covered the weather and career.

I decide to take a risk and see if he's interested in something more than just small talk. "So, do you come out here often? To bird watch, I mean."

He blushes again and shakes his head. "No, not really. I just moved to the area a few weeks ago and I've been trying to explore a bit."

I smile, feeling a glimmer of hope. "Well, if you ever need a guide, I'd be happy to show you around."

He looks up at me, his eyes meeting mine for the first time. There's a flicker of something there that I can't quite place.

"I would like that," he says softly, walking up the final slope towards me.

My heart skips a beat. Could it be that this shy, awkward vicar is possibly interested in me?

Now he is here I need to be calm and act naturally.

"Take a seat. Bale or fertiliser bag are the options for today. Sorry, no pews." I try to laugh. I got myself into this situation and now must work out what to do next.

As the vicar sits beside me, I can't help but observe his attire. Despite the sweltering heat, he is dressed in a thick shirt and a bird-watching waistcoat. His binoculars hang around his neck, and he has forgone his rigid clerical collar.

His shorts, with an abundance of pockets, reveal his hairy legs, while his tan-coloured socks and sandals complete the ensemble. His neat hair is parted to one side and tamed with wax, giving it a slight kink. He resembles a math teacher I had in my school days; he only needs leather elbow patches to complete the look.

As I take in his appearance, I notice the vicar is still blushing and fidgeting uncomfortably. I realise that my invitation may have come across as inappropriate, and I quickly try to put him at ease.

I make further small talk, asking about his

birdwatching and whether he's seen anything interesting in the area. He responds hesitantly at first, but as we continue to chat, he opens up, sharing his passion for birdwatching and the various species he's observed in the local woods.

As we talk, I notice his eyes lingering on me, and I can't help but feel a little flattered. Despite his initial reluctance, it seems he's warming up to the idea of spending time with me.

I find myself drawn to his shyness and his gentle demeanour, and I can't help but wonder what it would be like to explore a "deeper connection" shall we say, with him.

"Do you like what you see? I'm not the normal bird you'd be looking at!"

"Um... yes... no... yes... erm... I do but I shouldn't."

"What do you mean you shouldn't?"

 "I'm waiting for my wife."

"Your wife?! I didn't realise you are married."

"I'm ... erm...not. I... erm... erm... mean...um... I have been waiting for someone to...erm...be my wife."

"Oh, I get you. Not easy getting a wife as a vicar?"

"So far it has eluded me, yes."

"But you like what you see?"

"Yes."

"Do you want to touch?"

"Oh Ms Doors. I cannot! I cannot trust myself."

I take his hand and place it on my thigh. The vicar squeals like an excited piglet and quickly whips it back to a trusty pocket.

"Want to try again?"

Well, he starts nodding like he was about to audition for a bobblehead commercial, and then his hand decides to take a little joyride up to my upper thigh.

He checks for any lurking witnesses, and then pounces on me like a lion going in for the kill! I feel like I am back in senior school, having my first awkward kiss on the playground.

The vicar clearly has no clue what he is doing. His tongue flopping around like a fish out of water, and all I can think about is my laundry sloshing around in the washing machine once more! I have to break free before he suffocates me with his enthusiastic mouth-hugs.

I pull away, his face looks like he'd just seen a ghost, or maybe a math problem he couldn't solve.

"I'm so sorry Ms doors! I don't know what came over me! I've messed this up!"

"Let me show you. Take things slowly. Come here." I cup his face with both hands and pull him gently towards mine and kiss his lips. "Is this, okay?"

With yet another nod back, I kiss again.

"I like that. Thank you Ms Doors."

I kiss his lips again, and tease to part them with my tongue. It may not be a perfect kiss, but it's a good start. His hands begin to wander, accidentally meeting with my breast. He jumps.

"Oh! Oh! So sorry!"

"Its fine! Here..."

I take his hand and place it on my breast. The vicar just stares at it not knowing what to do.

"Play with it. Touch it. Tease it. You can even suck it and lick it if you want to."

Looking at me his eyes are wide, just as a child's would be in their favourite sweet shop. His fingers touch gently the darker skin around my nipple.

I'm resisting the urge to touch him back, although I can see his erection pushing taut his shorts. The innocence of his actions is an incredible turn on for me. As he explores my breasts, he repeatedly checks he is not hurting me, but the fact is reader, I'm getting quite worked up – in a good way. And don't want him to stop!

"I think we may need to remove the binoculars and some of your clothing. You're looking quite warm vicar!"

"Oh... yes... right...absolutely." The vicar stands and carefully removes the binoculars, placing them on the ground out of the way, followed by his waistcoat, neatly folded next to it.

"You may want to take your shirt off too."

I watch as his hands slowly undo each and every button, getting glimpses of a six-pack underneath. Well, I wasn't expecting that!

"Sit astride me and let's try another kiss." Still in his shorts, socks and sandals, the vicar stands over me before kneeling awkwardly on either side of my waist. He leans in. This man is a fast learner. The kiss is perfect(ish) in a kind of innocent, cute type of way.

I find myself staring into his eyes, mesmerized by their beauty. (Is it obvious I have a thing for eyes?!) The specks of green and outer ring of darker brown are so striking, and I can't help but admire the tanned complexion of his skin.

It's clear that he spends time outdoors, perhaps birdwatching or exploring the countryside, maybe walking to parishioners – although, this year everyone is sporting at least sun kissed skin. His glasses, slightly askew from our impromptu make-out session, add to his adorableness.

I realise that I've been staring for too long and quickly look away, feeling my own blush rising in my cheeks. But when I steal another glance, I notice that he's looking at me with a softness in his gaze that I haven't seen before. It's as if he's seeing me for the first time, really seeing me.

We sit there in quiet for a moment, the heat of the day starting to dissipate as the sun dips lower in the sky. I can hear the distant sound of cows mooing and the occasional rustling of the nearby trees. It's peaceful and quiet, and I find myself feeling oddly content.

The vicar clears his throat, breaking the silence.

"I'm sorry," he says, his voice slightly hoarse.

"I don't know what came over me."

I smile reassuringly at him. "It's okay," I say. "We're both consenting adults. And, if I'm being honest, I did kind of beckon you over."

He nods, looking relieved. "Yes, you did," he says.

"But I shouldn't have taken it as an invitation to...well, to kiss you like that."

I shrug. "It's not a big deal. It was just a kiss."

He looks at me with a mixture of uncertainty and curiosity. "But do you want to do it again?" he asks tentatively.

I ponder his question for a moment, like a philosopher contemplating the meaning of life. The truth is, I'm not entirely sure. Kissing him was...nice, I guess? It didn't exactly light a fire in my loins, but it was better than a root canal. Still, there's something about him that's drawing me in faster than a child full of E numbers.

Maybe it's the fact that he's a walking contradiction - a bird-watching vicar who wears socks with sandals but has abs that could rival Michelangelo's David. Or maybe it's the way he gazes at me like I'm the last slice of pizza at a party. Either way, I'm intrigued.

"I'm not sure," I say finally. "But I'm willing to find out."

He smiles at me, a genuine smile that crinkles the corners of his eyes. "Okay." he says. "Let's find out."

And with that, we kiss again, slower, and more tentatively this time. It's not fireworks or passion, but it's nice. It feels comfortable and safe and... right, somehow.

As we pull away, I decide I'm looking forward to finding out more about this mysterious vicar and what else he might have to offer. I touch his bare abs - the first time he has felt my hand on him. He tips his head backwards.

"I like that."

"I haven't done anything .... yet!" I lightly run my nails over his chest and down along his V-line. Adonis belt they call that bit. I can see why. Why did I think a vicar would be less sexy than the average person? This is like Clark Kent versus his superman character! I start to undo the top button of his shorts.

"Wait! I've got my everyday boxers on that my aunt got me! This isn't right! I planned this in my head years ago. I should have nicer ones on, not these!"

I carry on, four buttons later and I have an almost full frontal of a vicar's crutch, complete with happy face emoji boxers....

My headphones are on top of the bales at this point, still loud enough to hear Bobby McFerrin's "Don't worry, be happy" aptly playing. I refocus, having gotten over the amusement of perfecting timing.

"What would you like to do with me or to me? Or would you like me to suggest something?"

"I would like to lay next to you and cuddle. I've never cuddled a woman. Only my mother."

"Really?" I'm taken slightly aback by this confession.

The vicar looks at me. "Oh! Not in that way!"

"Thank heavens for that! Naked or as you are?"

The vicar answers by removing his sandals, socks, and shorts, again placing them neatly next to his binoculars.

"How do you want to do this? Spoons or on top?"

"If I can cuddle you from behind, I can smell your hair too."

In the spoon position now, and a very tight spoon at that, we lay there. The sun is beginning to lower and cool but it's still warm. I feel his breath on my shoulder, cutting over to my face.

"It smells nice. Coconut, is it?"

"Yes, still working my way through last

Christmas's box sets."

"I'm trying to stay calm but my ... erm... 'thing' ...um... keeps twitching. Sorry if its digging in."

"It's telling you something." I roll on to the other hip so that we're facing. "It wants to play."

I kiss the vicar with a firm, hard kiss, put my arm around his back and pull myself into him. He has no choice but to grab my behind to steady himself. He groans and pushes into me instinctively.

"That's it. Do that again. I want to feel you against me. In fact, soon I want to feel you in me."

The vicar continues to dry hump. He has good rhythm - must be all that time singing on the job (so to speak).

"Oh! Something's happening!"

I look down and the front of his boxers are a tad wet.

"Nothing I can't handle!"

I slide down until I'm level with his crutch, trapped behind the smiley faces.

Guiding him to lay on his back I then "rescue" the semi flaccid cock through the boxers and place it into my mouth. I hold it there listening to the vicar as he makes whimper noises and takes deep breaths.

The shaft is long enough I can settle my head on his groin and still have it in my mouth whilst lying next to him rubbing his legs gently and suckling at the same time. I move up from his legs and start to stroke his balls, cupping them and pushing them up, into the base of his shaft, as I start to suck a little harder.

When life has reignited between his legs I straddle him, directly placing my moist and swollen hole above him. I slide on, all the time watching the vicar's face. Holding his hips, I move up and down, back, and forth. His eyes never stray from mine.

With a slightly louder than normal groan the vicar comes. No thrusts or pounding. Just the release. Some would say I did all the work; I would say it was his moment to enjoy.

If this was his first time, he did alright. A little quick maybe...

I stay sat over him for a moment, eventually placing myself next to him again.

"Was that okay for you vicar?"

"It was. I liked it." He looks down at my breasts. "Can I try those please?"

I feel a wave of pleasure wash over me as the vicar continues, pleasuring me with his mouth. His lack of experience shows, but there's something endearing about it.

I let out a small moan as he switches to my other breast, his hands exploring my body as he goes. As he continues, I can't help but wonder what led him to this moment. Was he always curious but too afraid to act on it? Or did something in his life recently trigger this newfound desire? For now, I focus on the sensations coursing through my body. The vicar's attention to my breasts is sending electric shocks down to my core, and "Rose" - I feel myself growing wet with desire.

But just as I'm about to suggest moving on to something else, the vicar abruptly stops and looks up at me with a concerned expression.

"Ms Doors, I'm sorry. I'm not sure I'm ready for more. You may need to wait a bit."

I smile and stroke his hair reassuringly. "It's okay. We can take it slow. There's no rush."

He nods, visibly relieved. "Absolutely. Thank you. You're very kind."

Now suckling like a baby, the vicar murmurs "Sweet heaven Ms Doors. Sweet heaven!"

11 Decision Time

Oh, October! How I love thee. The crisp air, the stunning colours of the trees as they change, and the first log fire of the season. It's a time for harvesting the fruits of our labour, bundling up in cosy sweaters, and enjoying all the delights that autumn brings.

As I breathe in the cool air, I can't help but smile at the thought of what's to come. I can already taste the hot chocolate, feel the warmth of the fire, and see the leaves crunching beneath my feet.

And let's not forget about the upcoming holiday season, with Christmas just around the corner. Even though the farm work won't stop, it's still a time for taking a break from the office and enjoying some proper time away with loved ones.

Yes, autumn truly is a magical time, full of endless possibilities and cherished traditions. It's a season that reminds us to slow down, take a deep breath, and appreciate all the wonders that life has to offer.

However, so far, it's been pants!

Two long and challenging weeks have passed since the day when Mum was called next door to help out Veronica. She found Reg Braye lying unresponsive, and the medics rushed him to the general hospital. Unfortunately, that's where he's been ever since, as they discovered that he has cancer. The news hit us like a ton of bricks, and the weight of it has been almost unbearable.

It's been a difficult and emotional time, as we've watched Reg's condition deteriorate day by day, feeling powerless and helpless in the face of his illness. We're all praying for a miracle, but the reality was that every passing day brought us one step closer to saying goodbye to a dear friend and neighbour.

Today, we received that news. The news that we had been dreading - it's time to prepare for the inevitable. Mum, Jack, Veronica, and I are all making the journey to the hospital to see him for what will likely be, the last time.

As we travel to the hospital, the weight of the situation hangs heavy on all of us. We're all lost in our own thoughts, knowing that there are no words that can ease the pain we're all feeling.

Reg's son is also on his way, but he won't be here for some time yet. So, for now, it's just us - united in our love for Reg and our shared grief at the thought of losing him. We don't know what the future holds, but we do know that we'll be there for each other every step of the way as always.

Losing Reg will be like losing another beloved family member. He's been such an integral part of our lives, especially for Mum and Jack, who have built a close-knit working relationship with him over the years to manage our farm businesses. Mum is doing her best to keep Veronica occupied, but with her own emotions still raw from losing dad not too long ago, it's a struggle.

The Brayes have been friends of our family for as long as I can remember. Mum and Veronica first met at a mother-toddler group in Richdore, and they hit it off right away. Veronica was one of the few people who accepted mum, being German, with open arms.

When dad's parents needed to sell their property next door, Reg jumped at the opportunity, having come from a farming background himself. In a gentleman's agreement, Grandad and Reg shook hands, and a symbolic £1 note was exchanged. After the paperwork was completed, the farm was theirs, and my grandparents moved in with mum and dad.

Reg has been an important part of our lives ever since. He's been a constant presence, always willing to lend a helping hand and offering his sage advice whenever we needed it. We're all feeling the weight of the impending loss, but we're determined to stay strong and support each other through this difficult time.

As I wait, looking at Reg, my mind starts to wander to memories of him. I remember how he would always be the first to volunteer for any job that needed doing, no matter how big or small. He was always the life of the party, telling jokes and making everyone laugh.

And now, he's lying in this bed, barely responsive, barely even there.

Veronica breaks the silence, her voice shaking as she speaks softly to Reg, telling him how much she loves him and how much he means to her. Mum nods her head in agreement, tears welling up in her eyes. I can see how hard it is for her to keep it together, but she's doing her best to be strong for Veronica.

I start to think about how fleeting life is. How we take so much for granted and how we never really appreciate what we have until it's gone. Reg's illness has reminded me of this, and I feel a sudden urge to make the most of every moment, to live life to the fullest.

As we sit there, holding Reg's hands, I feel a sense of peace wash over me. And even though we know that Reg's time is coming to an end, we're here for him, and that's what matters.

As the hours drag on, I can feel the weight of the

stifling atmosphere in the room growing increasingly heavy. My heart is heaving with sadness and grief as I watch Reg's condition deteriorate. It's painful to see him like this, frail and weak, struggling for each breath.

Suddenly, there's stillness in the air.

Reg takes his last breath and passes away at 15:08pm.

A deep sense of loss and mourning washes over me, and I sit there in silence, struggling to come to terms with what has just happened. Despite the sadness, I feel a sense of relief knowing that Reg is now at peace and no longer suffering. It's a small comfort, but it helps to ease the pain just a little.

"You get one?"

My current thoughts about bales of hay, virgin vicars and wondering what is next on the "Diana Doors Sexual Liberation" tour are broken momentarily.

"One what?"

"The grand invite to the manor of course!" Dylan was struggling to contain his excitement.

I throw an imaginary dagger his way with a side

eye.

"Oh shit! Sorry. Forgot. I'll put the shovel down before I dig the hole any bigger, shall I?!"

Every year, the grand manor house perched atop the hill - you know the one reader, the one Richdore is infamously named after?

Well, that one throws open its doors to the local townspeople and villagers for an annual Halloween celebration. It used to be a harvest festival for the mere paupers and pheasants that grafted away on behalf of the rich, but nowadays the crops are harvested year-round by all and everyone, so the festivities have shifted to an All-Hallows' Eve experience instead.

The event is a massive affair, with almost everyone in town and nearby invited, and most people making an appearance.

If you ever get the chance to go dear reader, prepare to be spooked out of your socks at the country club, located in the spine-tingling basement of the original manor house. The place is transformed into a creepy wonderland, with cobwebs, skulls, and pumpkins adorning every visible surface. The lighting is perfectly matched to the eerie decor, adding to the creepy ambiance.

They go all out every year with a hugely expensive, professional decorating team, sparing no expense to bring the frightful atmosphere to life. You won't be left thirsty either, with a full bar in every corner, offering everything from the usual beer and wine to exotic cocktails.

And don't forget the central dance area, complete with the world's largest disco ball, comfy corner seating, and scattered tables for resting your trembling bones.

As if the free-flowing drinks and food weren't enough to entice attendees, the manor house's lush gardens, filled with winding paths and hidden alcoves, provide the perfect backdrop for those looking to take a break from the party and steal a quiet moment with a new flame or old friend.

Overall, it's an enjoyable way to spend a spooky evening with a mix of familiar faces and new acquaintances and a highlight of the year.

Having said all that... for me there's a slight problem. Just an itsy, bitsy, teeny, tiny one ...

Nate's family, who happen to own the manor, are the ones behind the invites, and they'll all be there on the night. And you guessed it, that means Nate's going to be there too – it being the ancestral family pile. The cherry on top? According to Alex, Nate has a girlfriend. And a young one at that!

Last year I managed to avoid the whole palaver, but oh boy, if I decide to go, this Halloween could be spicier than a ghost pepper.

"I got one."

I pull the invite from my jacket pocket, picked out of the mouth of The Dick, before leaving earlier.

"Not sure what I want to do really. If I go, I'll see Nate and Elizabeth and if I don't go, I look like I wimped out."

Richdore Manor Country Club
cordially invites:
Diana Doors
to step back in time
on
ALL HALLOWS EVE
31st October 7pm"
(1970's attire a must – <u>adults only</u>)

"Go, you old tart! You have as much right there as she does. At least if you go you can suss out the competition!"

"If he's seeing her, there seems no point in even being in the competition, does there?!"

"There's every point. You dress to the nines, and you knock him dead!"

"You and James are going I assume?"

"Why of course! He's already picked out the outfits in his head. It's our first big bash as a couple. Can't say thank you enough for arranging that fire safety course for me to attend. You know how much I like an older man, and in uniform, well, what can I say?!"

"That was fluke, and you know it! How was I supposed to know it was a mass group hug for the LBGT community?!"

I give Dylan a big smile. He's not been this happy for a long time. This James chap must be pretty darn special. The door chime goes and Christa walks in.

"Hey you! What are you doing here?"

"Need your help. The landlord is chucking us out. Says there are too many of us in the house, and that he didn't really know how many kids we've got etc. Usual excuses to get rid I suppose. Nice top. Like the tractor motif."

She looks totally disheartened. She and her family love next door. I mean, I don't know how many kids she's got, and the landlord does have a point, but she pays on time each month and never caused any problems as far as I am aware.

"Thanks. Sale at Marshalls. What do you want to do? Look for somewhere else to rent?"

"Nah. We only rent because we like that place so much. Been saving for years, that's why I work in dad's card shop. Had our eye on the Coburn place but then you sold it."

"Christa! Why didn't you say? I think it's going to fall through. I've been speaking with the solicitors early this morning and neither side are convinced it's going to happen."

"How many kids do you have?" Dylan's woken up ... it's been an on-going joke between us that, no matter how hard I try, I cannot get the names right of any of her kids.

"Not many. I have two sets of twins. Two boys and two girls. They wind everyone up by renaming themselves. It's been going on since they were small, and for some reason, they find it hilarious. We've gotten so used to it that we don't even bat an eye anymore."

That makes sense now...

"I'll be calling the buyer later. Can't yet until they finish their shift but will ask them what's going on. I'll text you. On a side note, want to do my hair and makeup for the manor do in exchange for a bottle or two?"

"Can do. You're going then? Thought you may want to avoid it?"

"I'm coming around to the idea."

What do I know about the Seventies? I've made a special trip out to "the big town" to trawl around the vintage clothing shops. I'm still undecided as to whether to go or not.

As I stand outside "Reusable Vintage," I peer through the window to see a sea of beige and brown clothing hanging on the racks. I ponder for a moment and decide that if I'm going to put myself through this ordeal, I'll do it in style with bold and vibrant colours. It's crystal clear that this shop is not my cup of tea, and I venture on to the next one.

"Vintage Clothes 4 U" looks more hopeful. I walked in there, brave as can be, ready to find some amazing threads. But then, BAM! The smell of grandma's bathroom smacks me right in the nose! I swear, I could practically see the mothballs flying through the air.

And the music? Forget about it. "Monster Mash" by Bobby Pickett and the Crypt Kickers was blasting so loud from the ceiling speaker, I thought I was gonna get spooked right outta there! But I soldiered on, determined to find some vintage treasures to wear.

But alas dear reader, it is not meant to be.

Everything on the rails looks tiny, like it is made for elves or something! There is no way I am gonna be able to squeeze my ample booty into any of these clothes!

Feeling slightly deflated I move on to the men's section. But even then, I am having a tough time finding anything that would make me look or feel fabulous. I mean, I don't want to wear some ratty old shirt that looks like it's been through the wash a million times! I'm getting my inner confidence on and that needs to show!

Just as I am about to give up and head out, an elderly gentleman appears from the back room. He reminds me of Mr. Benn, you know, that old-school kids show with the magical costume shop. I half-expected him to send me off behind the curtain only to come back as a vintage fashionista!

"Afternoon miss. Anything I can help you with?"

It's been a while since someone addressed me as "miss," but I appreciate the politeness.

"Actually, I'm looking for a 1970s outfit for a Halloween party at Richdore Manor, but I'm not sure if you have anything that would fit me."

The man looks me up and down, and I can tell he's not so sure either. "Ah, they used to eat less in those days."

Well, that's rude!

He continues "I've been to that country club a few times myself, but I don't get invited anymore. You know, there's some wild shenanigans that happen in that place. Got myself into lots of scrapes in my time. Changed my ways now. Are you sure you want to go? You might be getting into more than you bargained for!"

"Oh, you mean the naughty stuff that happens behind closed doors. I think that's just rumours and gossip." I reply with a chuckle.

The elderly gentleman shakes his head. "Not from what I've seen. But I won't say more than that, miss. Anyway, if you're looking for a '70s outfit for a Halloween do, I suggest you check out 'Seventy Seconds' on Rope Street. They'll have just what you need. They cater for the larger woman."

"Oh, okay, I think, and thank you. Not heard of 'Seventy Seconds'."

A few streets later and I'm stood in front of said "Seventy Seconds." I think that gentleman might be having a laugh with me... I walk in.

A "lady" strolls over to me in full drag. "Well hello darling! Welcome to 'Seventy Seconds'!"

She grabs my arm and pulls me further on to the shop floor. "They look so real! And your hair and makeup ... amazeballs!"

"I think there's some mistake."

"They all say that darling! Born wrong at birth, born into the wrong body ...I've heard it all before!"

"No, seriously. I think there is some kind of mistake. I was sent here from 'Vintage Clothes 4 U' to get a seventies outfit for a Halloween do."

"That'll be George. Does it all the time. But honestly, they (looking at my ample bosom) look fantastic. Where did you get them from?"

"Is that 'Un bel di" from Madame Butterfly?" I try to change the subject.

"It is darling. One of my most favourite operas. Where did you get them from?"

"I was born with them! My name is Diana. Diana Doors. Born a girl. Always have been a girl and always will be a girl!"

"Diana Dors?"

"D.O.O.R.S as in the wooden things between rooms. A dad joke."

"He has a humour."

Patting me on my shoulder as if I were a sweet little puppy, she takes my hand again.

"Elganzia Bush at your service. I do apologise darling. I'm just on the lookout for a decent pair myself. You lucky thing you! Only need them in here – rest of the time I'm Harold, a part time plumber for the family business. Let's sort you an outfit."

"I can't see anything seventies(ish) in here. I'm looking for an outfit to knock the socks off my husband ... ex-husband... erm... possibly ex-husband... oh, I don't know. It's complicated!"

"I'm taking you in the side room. I'm sure, in fact I know, I'll have something in there to fit you."

We head towards a drawn curtain. I presumed a dressing room. But then, with a flick of her wrist and a manly shove, she pushes the curtain aside to reveal another room full of clothes! I swear, it was like stepping into Narnia or something. And let me tell you, Elganzia Bush has some serious fashion game hiding away back here.

"I'm presuming you want something girly. Sucking in and displaying those beauties? Are you going maxi or mini?"

"Who knows. Right now, I'll be happy to find

something that fits! Then there's the shoes... I inherited dad's big feet..."

Elganzia laughs "Big feet are our specialty dear! You've forgotten what type of shop we're in!"

"Interesting name for a shop that doesn't specialise in the 1970's."

"Oh, my dear child! It's not the decade dearie, it's the average length of time a man lasts with me! I thought it rather amusing myself."

Two and a half hours later, I have an outfit I feel "amazeballs" in, paired with some knee-high boots made for strutting my stuff.

Well, would you believe it? Nate's nowhere to be found at the damn zoom meeting again. The counsellor and I have become quite the duo with our one-on-one sessions – if being told by a complete stranger about her conversation with your ex-husband means being "quite the duo."

But here we go again, Nate's come up with yet another excuse. This time, he's apparently somewhere in the country dealing with family money matters. Yeah right, I bet he's just holed up somewhere with his new squeeze "Elizabeth."

And to top it all off, we've already paid for two

more sessions until the end of the year. I mean, what's the point? If he's going to keep playing these games, I might as well just use the sessions to talk to myself. I mean, I'm a great listener, and at least that way, I won't have to deal with any more of his flimsy excuses.

I'm trying to get into the spirit for tonight. Margaret has been playing seventies music all day from the kitchen. The pups have been walked to the sounds of Cliff's "Devil Woman" Kate Bush's "Hammer Horror" and "Black Magic Woman" by Santana. There's also been the Carpenters, The Bee Gees and Chic "La Freak," but I'm still not feeling "it."

Plans are falling into place now. Christa will be here soon to do hair and makeup. I'm meeting Dylan and James at the office. Dylan can leave his car there in the market car park overnight safely. I'll chauffeur the three of us in the trusty beast, as I am absolutely adamant I will not be passing any alcohol through my lips this evening.

As I ogle at the outrageous ensemble, I can't help but feel a mixture of excitement and trepidation. Who wouldn't be thrilled to strut their stuff in a groovy skater dress and towering platform boots? But at the same time, I know I'm going to have to squeeze my middle-aged bod into that all-in-one lace body suit laying there, and I have a feeling it won't be a walk in the park.

I take a deep breath and start the ordeal of getting dressed. It's like trying to push a watermelon through a keyhole. I squirm and wiggle and tug, but that cursed suit just won't co-operate. I'm sweating buckets and swearing like a trooper, and I can hear Christa cackling outside the dressing room.

After wrestling with that cursed lace body suit for what seems like a lifetime, I finally emerge from the bedroom, feeling like I've been shrink-wrapped. I take a peek in the full-length mirror on the landing, and I must say, I look stunning! My curves are hugged in all the right places by that psychedelic skater dress, and those platform boots make me feel like a runway model giving me extra height as a bonus.

I twirl around, feeling like I'm on top of the world, and suddenly there's a loud clatter and crash around me.

Or should I say, I make a loud clatter and crash as I trip over my own two left feet and nearly face-plant into the wall. I'm pretty sure I just scared the living daylights out of the pups, who are now cowering in a corner wondering what kind of wild creature just stumbled out of the bedroom.

As Christa attacks my hair, I feel like a victim in a medieval torture chamber. The heat from the curling iron is singeing my scalp, and the spray she's using smells like it could take down an elephant. But despite my discomfort, I have to admit that the end result is impressive.

My hair is a curly mess of tangles, but it somehow looks intentional, and the makeup she's applied to my face is downright spooky. I'm not sure what I was expecting, but I certainly won't be walking around looking like a predictable corpse bride tonight – she made no promises.

Oh well, at least it's a conversation starter.

"Have a fabulous time, Diana! You're going to be the talk of the town!"

Christa gives me a hug that nearly knocks me off my platforms, grabs her things (and the promised wine), and scurries out the door.

As for me, I'm starting to get the jitters. The dress barely covers my rear, but the boots are sky-high. If I need to crouch down, I might give everyone an eyeful. I'm only planning to pop in for a bit, say hello to the in-laws, and then make a swift exit.

Dylan's arranged for a taxi to take him and James home, so I won't have to worry about that. Anyway, I need to be up early tomorrow to tend to the sheep at the farm. Mum's feeling a bit down about Reg still.

"Ziggy Stardust" and "Twiggy" are stood waiting for me at the office. It turns out Dylan has quite shapely legs and the twiggy look suits him well. James is hidden behind the make-up but stands a good few inches taller than him. You can see he's the older one in the relationship, but he appears to look after himself. Both clamber into the back of the beast laughing.

"Zombie Butterfly. That's different."

"Leave it out. Turns out Christa only does kids face painting. Specialties being butterflies, tigers, and a little blue train with eyes on it. I thought cats and steam trains a bit too much, what with the orange dress too."

"I don't know...think it would have been tangerine-tantastic!"

"Sweet Mary, save me now from these two!"

As we get closer to the front gates of the manor, I start to feel like I'm about to enter a scene from a Gothic horror movie. The gates are massive, towering over us at least twenty feet tall, and are made of dark, twisted wrought iron. The intricate scrollwork and twisted design send shivers down my spine – always have done. The torches that line the driveway flicker and dance in the breeze, casting eerie shadows on the gravel path.

The drive itself is impressive, stretching out in front of us like a long, black ribbon climbing up the hill. It's flanked on either side by perfectly manicured lawns, with ornate fountains and topiary hedges adding a splash of formality to the landscape.

As we make our way up the drive, the cars already parked are a wild assortment of colours and makes, like a kid's toy box spilled out onto the tarmac. There's a bright yellow Lamborghini parked next to a sleek black Jaguar, and a vintage red Corvette with a gleaming paint job. I even spot a neon green Mini Cooper that looks like it's straight out of a cartoon. It's like a gathering of cars from every decade and country, all brought together for this one event. The beast feels ever so slightly out of place, yet it knows here better than any of its fellow four wheels that have arrived before us.

The parking zones are marked out with white lines, and parking marshals in bright yellow vests, like human sized minions, wave us into our designated spot. It's a tight squeeze, but I manage to manoeuvre the beast into the bay without hitting any of the other cars. We all pile out, ready to make our grand entrance into the manor…or not, in my case.

As we start walking towards the building, I can feel my knees wobbling and my palms getting sweaty. I take a deep breath and try to steady myself. "Come on, Diana" I tell myself, "You can do this."

Dylan and James link arms and walk ahead of me, looking like they own the place – or is it Dorothy and the Tin Man from the Wizard of Oz?! I trail behind them, feeling like a country mouse in a city of peacocks.

Approaching the entrance, I can hear the thumping beat of the music and the excited chatter of the guests. My heart starts racing, and I can feel my face flushing with nerves.

There are people everywhere. Hundreds of them, all dressed in fancy costumes.

Unsurprisingly, no zombie butterflies to be immediately spotted.

Many garish make-ups, masks, and hoods. This was the highlight of the Richdore calendar for a lot of the locals. We all walk at a snail's pace into the grand doors of Richdore Manor.

The entrance hall, with floors of marble, the statues, busts of family relatives no more, huge paintings and drapes - I've always thought it reminiscent of school trip museum visits. There's a slight pang of loss in me. This has been a place of incredibly happy memories of Nate and me. We had our wedding breakfast here in the orangery, wed in the garden in one of the larger follies and had our wedding reception in the grand hall – where we all head now for pre-drinks.

The decorations are incredible. There are spider webs draped over the chandeliers, pumpkins and bats hanging from the ceiling, and a giant cobweb covering the grand fireplace. The guests are all in high spirits, and I can feel the excitement building in the air for everyone else.

I spot some familiar faces, including Dylan's cousin Lucy, who is dressed predictably as a wicked witch, not having inherited the same enthusiastic outlook in life as he, and there's Nate's aunt, who is dressed as a mummy - because she is a mummy (on social media anyway – the nanny does most of the work away from the camera.)

As we make our way further into the room, I can't help but notice the food table, which is overflowing with delicious looking treats. There are bowls of Halloween inspired sweets, trays of mini burgers, hot dogs made to look like dissected fingers and a towering red chocolate fountain perhaps meant to be dripping blood perhaps.

I grab a glass of champagne from a passing waiter (bang goes the theory about not drinking), and we all begin to mingle with the other guests. The night is young, and I have a feeling it's going to be one to remember one way or another. Let's hope, in a good way.

I nod to the in-laws in acknowledgement of everything going on. Well, I think it's the in-laws.

There's a scream across the room as Alex flies towards me.

"Di you made it! I thought you wouldn't get here thanks to that fucker over there! Rescue me, another fucker in that direction won't leave me alone!"

I turn to my right.

Leaning against the oversized fire mantle, ever so tall, strong, and handsome, despite the homage to the prince of darkness himself, Ozzy Osbourne (Ironic as "Sabbath Bloody Sabbath" resounds around the room.) stands Nate, and he's looking straight at me.

To his side a petite woman dressed as "Morticia" from the Adams Family. I watch as he places his goblet down and makes his way across the room. The little woman follows, tripping on her long gown. She is very pretty.

Then I turn my sight to where Alex is pointing.

She moves in closer, her voice dropping to a bare whisper.

"The one dressed as a giant chicken. He's been trying to get with me all night. I'm about ready to pluck his fucking feathers out."

I chuckle and take a sip of my champagne, scanning the crowd for the offending chicken.

"Well, just steer clear of him then. I don't think I'm in the mood for any poultry-based drama tonight."

Alex grins and links her arm through mine. "Agreed."

It's clear that Nate hasn't lost his charm as he approaches me with a smile on his face. Morticia stays a few steps behind, watching our interaction with a hint of curiosity.

"Well, well, if it isn't the lovely Di," he says, his voice low and smooth. "You look stunning as always."

Like a horse jumping hurdles, I feel a shiver run through my body at full speed, as the sound of his voice filters through all the now white noise around me. It's been a long time since I've seen him, and I'm surprised at how much my body still responds to him.

"Nate," I try to keep my voice as steady as possible in the circumstances. "It's good to see you."

He steps closer, his eyes locking onto mine. "It's good to see you too," he says, his breath warm on my face. "It's been too long."

I try to keep my composure, but I can feel my heart racing in my chest.

"Yes, it has," I manage to say.

Nate leans in, his lips brushing against my ear. "I've missed you." he whispers.

I pull back, trying to regain my composure. "Nate, we need to talk." (I sound more matron than wife.)

He raises an eyebrow, a hint of a smirk on his lips. "Is that so? Well, we have all night, don't we?"

I can feel Morticia's stare, and I know I need to extricate myself from this situation.

"Excuse me," I say, turning away from him. "I need to go find my friends."

As I walk away, I can feel his eyes on me, and I know that this conversation is far from over.

"Nigella!"

Reggie's voice is easily recognisable anywhere.

He and Jack appear dressed as the blues brothers with added gruesomeness.

"Nice outfit's lads. Good to see last year's 1980's theme recycled for tonight. Bit tenuous though don't you think?"

"Ah, well, actually the film was based on the act from 1978 so I think we can get away with it for another year." Jack replies confidently.

"That will be three years in a row! Two years ago, it was the remake!"

I glance back over my shoulder hoping to see my husband pining for me. Nate is back at the fireside with the delightful Morticia. I note he doesn't look particularly happy, that's good enough and tough!

I'm beginning to enjoy myself.

"Psycho Killer" Talking Heads plays as we all make our way down into the country club itself. Many locals have filtered out into the garden already with their buffet plates stacked full. The staff are walking around topping up glasses and others with trays laden down with crudités and dips in tiny pots.

I'm conscious not to take any alcohol on offer. I purposely chose to be driver - even if one direction only. I really can't have any more. The champagne will wear off by the time I need to drive home plus, that way, I can't make a fool of myself either.

The lads are making their way around the room chatting up all the girls. Reggie looks hot in his suit, as in sexy, not sweaty – Jack, well Jack is Jack, failing to get anywhere other than a quick smile.

I know my brother Jack wouldn't want to meet anyone here. He's just enjoying himself. No drink for him either. Driving the 360° tomorrow clearing the drainage ditches.

Alex is draped over some poor soul who looks like they'd rather be anywhere but here. You can practically see the "help me" plea in their eyes. And why is Alex latched onto this person like a koala bear? Well, it seems she's making attempts to console them, bless her heart.

But here's the thing: she's dressed like a scary clown. I mean, the whole getup - oversized shoes, red nose, rainbow wig, the whole shebang. And let's not forget the pièce de résistance: the Pierrot tear on her cheek. It's like she's a mix between a circus performer and a mime, with a dash of nightmare fuel thrown in for good measure!

Honestly, it's hard to tell if her efforts at consoling are actually working, because the poor sod she's clinging onto probably can't even tell what emotions she's trying to convey through all that clown makeup. I mean, how do you even comfort someone when you look like a demented Ronald McDonald?

All in all, it's quite a sight to behold. Alex, the clown/mime hybrid, trying to comfort a reluctant party guest. Sorry reader, I digress once more but who wouldn't, confronted with that scene?!

No sign of Nate. Perhaps he's still upstairs.

I scan the room again and as I peer through the patio doors; I'm greeted with the sight of...well, not much. Just a bunch of people mingling and chit-chatting like they're at a knitting circle. I mean, where's the excitement? The drama? The possibility of someone falling into the pool after a few too many drinks?

It's like everyone at this party is content with just standing around and making small talk, instead of doing something truly wild and memorable. As I continue to observe the crowd, I can't help but wonder if this is what adulting is all about. Standing around at a fancy shindig, pretending to care about other people's lives, and trying to stave off the creeping feeling of existential dread that comes with realising you're not getting any younger and have very little in common and then questioning how many more of these blasted do's one has to attend before saying "no thanks" when the invite falls through the letter box.

As the evening moves onwards, the dance floor

livens as the alcohol kicks in. Dylan and James are an unlikely duo underneath the disco lights - or should I say Ziggy and Twiggy! Holding hands and twirling away, not quite Saturday Night Fever or Grease but the moves are in there somewhere. Who'd have thought Dylan would get his dream firefighter partner? Let's hope it lasts.

Feeling a cold breeze from the open doors, I pull the hem of my dress in a pointless exercise of trying to make the material cover up a bit more leg.

"I wouldn't bother if I were you. You look lovely as you are." Alex has re-joined me.

"Have confidence in yourself. You look bloody amazing!"

And then she's gone again. Waltzing across to the opposite corner, helping herself behind the bar, leaving me stood like Billy no mates.

The DJ plays some cracking tunes as the night progresses. I've decided to take Alex up on her offer of crashing at the gatehouse with her and a few others later. Christa has had the text to help with the pups and cat with attitude. She said she would earlier, but I still feel guilty asking her. First glass of alcohol down and I'm on to my second...

Reggie comes over. "Will you stop looking for him. He's with her now."

"Is that a certain? Is that a certain Reggie?" My heart sinks.

"So, I hear. It's been a bit of a shock to the family I gather. They all thought you and him would be back together by now. They know it's him too as to why it hasn't worked out with you. He's a workaholic and that's never going to change."

My heart sinks to the bottom of the ocean like a lead balloon. I don't know what I thought would happen tonight, but I know I didn't want to hear that.

"I'm going outside. Coming?" Reggie grabs my arm and drags me onto the veranda.

"Let's go sit at the ha-ha. Why is called that anyway?"

Obviously, the estate agent in me can't resist a question like that.

"It's a hidden sunken boundary wall normally to contain grazing animals. The ha-ha part is when the gentry fall over into the lower section and everyone else piss themselves laughing."

My friend raises an eyebrow. "Really? I always thought it was called the ha-ha because it was like dangling your feet into water - except there wasn't any."

I have to admit, I like his version better. It's like a poetic, almost childlike interpretation of something that's actually pretty mundane. But of course, leave it to the fancy gentry to make everything sound far more sophisticated than it needs to be.

As we settle onto the ha-ha and dangle our feet over the edge, I can't help but chuckle at the thought of some pompous nobleman taking a tumble and getting a face full of grass.

We must have been here for quite a while now. Reggie has his arm around me, and I'm relishing the comfort of his presence. As we discuss the night's events, I glance around and conclude that a great many people have already left.

Checking my watch, I see that it's already past midnight.

Time sure does fly when you're having fun, doesn't it reader?

Despite the hour, I'm not quite ready to go home yet. There's still something magical about the night air and the way the stars twinkle overhead.

Reggie seems to read my mind, and we both agree to take a leisurely stroll before heading back in.

I do another search for Nate and this time I spot him and Morticia frantically waving hands in the air with each other. Not all rosy now, is it?!

Nate looks in my direction, he's just not the Nate I knew. I give him a small wave, smile, then turn back to Reggie.

"Let's go to the bar. Time to catch up with the rest!"

"Not a good idea Di. You've told me a hundred times tonight that you're at the farm tomorrow."

"Sod the farm! I need alcohol..."

Reggie signals for a staff member to bring me a glass of milk. Milk! Can you believe it? Who drinks milk at a party? But hey, it's Reggie, and he's always looking out for me.

Surprisingly, the milk goes down well, and I feel a sudden burst of energy. I'm not sure if it's the milk or just the excitement of being with Reggie, but I'm feeling good.

We're now nestled into a cosy corner sofa, tucked next to one of the bars. It's the perfect spot - we can people-watch to our heart's content while still being able to grab a drink if we need one.

Suddenly, the lights dim, and a hush falls over the crowd. Ooh, this is exciting! What's about to happen? Is it a surprise performance? A magic show? A celebrity appearance?

Reggie leans in close, and I can feel his breath tickling the hairs on the back of my neck.

"Hold on tight," he whispers "This is when it gets interesting around here. But you know that?"

Nope. Haven't a clue what he's on about, but I get the feeling I'm about to find out!

The room is much darker now. The lighting has changed to a moodier feel compared to the disco balls before. The staff are clearing away and gradually finishing for the night, other than the bar staff. The last of the partygoers, not staying, are dispersing. Jack must have already gone. I can see Alex straddled a person made up to look like a chucky doll. Yet again, I'm not sure the attention is reciprocated.

"How long have we got before they throw us out too?"

"No chucking out from now on Di. This is where the fun really begins."

He tips my chin up towards his face and leans in to kiss me. His hand on my breast.

"I've wanted to do that all evening."

"Have you?! Why? What on earth for?!"

I'm flattered and flustered at the same time. I didn't realise Reggie was actually attracted to me; just thought he quite liked me.

I quickly gather my senses and look for Nate. Nowhere to be seen. Why should I be even bothered? He's got the ever so lovely Morticia now. Alex is occupied with one of the waitressing staff, snogging her against the eighteenth-century wall tapestry depicting the manor grounds.

So, this is the "after-party" is it?

Well, this is quite an unexpected turn of events. It seems as if I'm in a bad movie that I didn't sign up for. I mean, I knew Nate's family are known for being a little eccentric, but I didn't think they were into this kind of thing.

I appear to have strayed into a late night swinging session where anything goes. I'm noticing there are pairings scattered throughout the room.

As I look around, I can't help but feel like I'm in the middle of a scene from a crazy seventies top of the shelf video. There are people making out on the sofas, others getting frisky on the dancefloor, and a few just watching from the sidelines like it's some sort of spectator sport. I'm just waiting for the plumber to arrive to complete the combo.

From the corner of my eye, I catch a glimpse of Dylan being led out on to the patio by James, followed by a "Twiggy" wig, flying through the air.

This is not what I planned. I haven't even had any sort of proper conversation with Nate, let alone "knock him dead" in my outfit. How can I if I have my brother's best friend attached to me, and a husband that's disappeared out of sight with his new and ever so gorgeous, fresh faced, perfect skinned, just out of school, girlfriend?

Talking of which... Morticia suddenly appears from outside, hastily followed by Nate, trying to grab her arm.

"Get off me!"

"You've got it wrong. That's all!"

"Get off me Nate! You've led me on! I want to go home."

"Elizabeth! I never said anything! It's you that's made conclusions!"

"Just arrange for my car to be brought round to the front. I'm going!"

Nate stands, holding his head in his hands. He turns and looks straight at me, mouthing "I'm sorry." before dashing out the room after Morticia.

Reggie and I continue to stay seated. "Do you think I should go after him Reggie?"

"Nope. He's made his bed."

"True. I feel I've made a lot of effort for no reason tonight."

"You look amazing Di. And I'm not the first to have said so, am I?"

Reggie hugs me tighter. It feels nice. To coin a phrase from the vicar... I like it.

David Bowies "We are the dead" plays, as a tear rolls down my cheek. It's truly over, it has to be. Why else would Nate have said he was sorry.

"Kiss me again Reggie." I move out of the hug and sit over his lap.

"Are you sure Di?"

"I'm sure."

I feel his hands on my bare cheeks, hidden by my dress. I grind against his semi-firm erection.

"No. This is wrong." He pulls away. "Our friendship means more to me than a meaningless kiss and shag."

I can feel anger in me. I've not felt like this since

dad died. Holding back the emotions, I remove myself from his lap and ungainly stumble in my 1970's platforms back out on to the veranda.

I'm not angry with Reggie. I'm not even angry with Nate. I'm angry with myself for wanting...no... needing sex right now. I'm confused.

Do I like Reggie in that way more than I realise? Is that why Nate and I failed? Is that why we never got intimate for years? Or is it just the atmosphere in that room right now where everyone is either doing it or watching others doing it?

I seek out my favourite tree in the grounds, the one with the poppy petals cast in the ironwork of the seating that wraps around the old and gnarly trunk.

I need time to take breath. Time to restock my thoughts.

◆◆◆

Reggie now sits beside me, holding my hands, forever the gentleman.

"I'm not leaving you until I know you are in the right frame of mind Di. Nate is a twat. No, that's actually a bit harsh. I mean, he has all this money around him and he cares little for it so he's not that much of a pregnant goldfish, but right now it's questionable whether he cares even less about his marriage."

"Oh, that makes me feel really good! Thanks for that!"

I know Reggie means well, and he's right, Nate is, not quite, the black sheep of the clan, but has gone off to do his own thing, to earn his way, rather than rely on the family farming empire to bring him his wage. Thankfully, he is good with his hands because right now, some would say he isn't good at using his head!

"I don't feel like staying with Alex. Can you drive the beast and me back to mine? Crash out with me if you want to."

"Jack's gone anyway. Might as well. Won't be the first time."

With his hand on my thigh, we head back to mine in silence, it only breaking when The Dick and the digging one greet us loudly at the door. Cat with attitude climbs my bare leg just to let me know he's starving, fading away in fact, and Reggie puts the kettle on for a cuppa.

Animals settled, tear-stained zombie butterfly removed at the kitchen sink after some serious scrubbing, tea drunk, we head to bed. It's been a long day and we're both tired. Fully clothed and me still with my boots on, we crash out on top of the duvet, looking out at the night sky through the sash window.

"It was a good night tonight. Despite me losing my blues brother glasses ... and Nate of course."

"It's time to move on Reggie. I think he already has."

I reach for a reassuring hand. It's there waiting. Reggie, the one, solid friend. Reliable Reggie. My schoolgirl crush.

Will I regret what I am about to do...

"Reggie?"

"What's up?"

"I need you to fuck me hard. I was thinking about it all the way home."

"Wait! What?!"

"Can you fuck me hard Reggie? I need to know."

"Know what?!"

"I need to know if I still love Nate."

"How's fucking me going to tell you that?!"

"Because I trust you and I know it won't go any further. Just fuck me please." I get off the bed to undress.

"Wait!" Reggie looks at me "I'll fuck you hard if that's what you want me to do, but a favour, don't strip off. Let me have my little fantasy if I'm going to be used in this way!"

He's grinning at me like the Cheshire cat. "Skater dress and knee-high boots...most blokes can only dream of this opportunity!"

He chuckles, grins at me even more, grabs hold of my hips and spins my body around.

"Bend over."

Reggie lifts my dress to reveal my 'G' string body suit. Pulling what little material there is to one side and holding my cheeks apart, he shoves his tongue wildly into my ass and down into my lips.

Sweet Mary, oh, that feels good. He repeatedly penetrates both holes with his tongue. I wobble on my platform boots and take hold of the metal frame at the foot of my bed for support. Reggie has slipped his fingers into me, moving them in and out, in and out. I don't think I need that much foreplay to turn me on right now – I just need sex – but this is pretty enjoyable I have to say. In fact, very enjoyable indeed. I can feel my eyes almost going to the back of my head as I relish the sensations right now.

"Still want me to fuck you hard?" Reggie's voice is rasping. "I'm rock hard. All you got to do is say 'yes'."

"Yes Reggie! Yes! I want you to."

In a matter of moments, he is sliding into me, all of him. It's got to be the biggest and widest girth I have felt. I didn't have the pleasure with Daniel and him that time. It didn't feel right, but tonight, oh god, tonight, this is exactly what I need.

He pumps in between my wet, moist lips, his rugby thighs smashing against mine. I'm receiving everything I just asked for. The full force of being fucked so hard, by something so large... I gasp with each in-stroke of his cock.

Reggie moves his hands from my hips and onto my breasts, taking hold of them unintentionally firmly, whilst still slamming me. He's a fitness freak. It shows as pounding, after pounding, keep coming with equal momentum.

"Let me try something." Reggie withdraws and takes me towards the wall "I've always wanted to fuck someone hard against the wall." I place my forearms up on to the flock wallpaper.

Reggie lifts my dress out the way, shoving his rigid cock straight into me. I feel him grab my hip with one hand and pull my hair hard with the other, he's fucking me as hard as he physically can. Back and forth, back, and forth, again pound after pound coming. My head yanked back towards him,

Reggie lets out a loud groan as he removes himself quickly, spurting as he comes over the floor, before collapsing against my back.

I got my answer. I still love Nate...

12 Crying In The Rain

November chills... Ah, another day in the glamorous life of a real estate agent – as in, a real one and not a pretend one. I'm suited up in my trusty hat and coat, ready to take on the next viewing. Today's mission: measure up Coburn's house with the ever lovely, Christa and her rather rowdy family. The sale is in full swing, and we need to make sure everything is in order.

As I stand there waiting for Christa to arrive, my thoughts of Reggie are still fresh in my mind. What the hell was I thinking? I know, I know... I'm on a year-long "free break" as that bloody woman, Melanie, keeps on reminding me at each zoom session. Does she have that same conversation with Nate? I can hear it now "Yes Nate, of course you can shag the ever so lovely Beth...remember, you are on a get out of here free pass of a whole year!" I really struggle to understand why after all this time that woman hasn't concentrated on anything other than sex.

Although, the fact she was recommended by my

ex-husbands' swinging family, I shouldn't be surprised should I.

The not so faint sound of "Love Cats" by The Cure can be heard in the distance now. Ah, Christa must be on her way, or perhaps she's around the corner and just got an eclectic taste in loud ringtones.

Typical of my luck though, the sky above me looks like a grim reminder of my love life - dark and ominous. And to make matters worse, I've got a trip out to Dalebank after this. I mean, could this day get any better?

And just as I'm cursing my luck, an ancient minibus screeches to a halt in front of me. I'm half expecting a troop of clowns to come pouring out, but instead, it's Christa's family. They emerge from every nook and cranny of the vehicle, like some sort of human Tetris game.

"School run." Christa has the look of a hassled mum "Line up you lot. One, two, three, four, five, six, seven ... where's eight?"

"Still in the bus, mum."

"Thought you said you had two sets of twins Christa?"

"I do. The rest were all single births." She smiles "Just all very close together. Eight! Get out here now!"

I assume the final child has appeared and I can now unlock the front door without fear of leaving anyone out in the cold.

As soon as I turn that key, it's like a stampede of wild animals racing towards their prey, each of them desperate to claim their own personal kingdom, also known as a bedroom.

It's a free-for-all, with elbows and knees flying in every direction, as they jostle for position and try to gain an advantage over their siblings. It's like watching a scene from The Hunger Games, only instead of fighting to the death, they're fighting for the best and biggest bedroom.

But eventually, they all manage to stake their claim and settle into their respective rooms, like a pack of wolves finding their den.

"Heard from twat features yet?"

"No. Nate's been quiet since the do. Not even been two weeks yet to be fair to him."

"True. Still, he's being more of a dick than your dog."

"Where do you want to start? Kitchen?" If I left Christa to her own devices, she'd be here all afternoon. I give her an hour and send her on her way.

I need to get to Dalebank before the merchants close. It's the start of tupping season. Mum needs a fresh stock of raddle powders, as the two tups (uncastrated rams) brought in will be going into the ewe field tomorrow. She ordered last week but had to wait for the stock to arrive back in, or so she says.

I have had an inkling for some time now, that the income is right down from the farm, and she is struggling to make ends meet. I can see she's not eating well, not being much of her anyway, the slightest weight loss is very visible.

"Here you go." I place the last of the bags of yellow and green raddle onto the kitchen table. "Thirty-nine quid each! Can't believe how much it costs these days. Don't worry about paying it back. What's happening next door mum? When's the funeral?"

"We've been told late November/early December. Even though he was in hospital she's got to wait for the coroner's report. Bloody daft if you ask me."

"Fair enough. Weather looks awful for the whole of next week and into the following. Jack fixed the sheep shelter, didn't he?"

"Ja. All done. I don't know what I'd do without you two, now dad isn't here. It's a worry for the future. You two have your own businesses. I can't rely on you all the time."

"Relax, mum. We've got this. We do it because we love you, and because we know how much this place means to you. As soon as we have a spare moment, Jack and I will sit down and brainstorm some killer ideas to take this place to the next level. But for now, I better go. Dad's dogs probably have their legs crossed by now, and I don't think they can hold it much longer. Love you loads, and I'll call in on Sunday."

As I trundle my beast of a vehicle through the rural lanes on my way home, the sky opens up and releases a deluge of rain upon me. The drops pelt against the windshield like a thousand tiny fists, and the sound of the water splashing up from the surface water is like a symphony of percussion instruments.

The puddles have built up to epic proportions, as many of these roads used to be mere tracks in a bygone era. Now, they are riddled with massive dips that catch unsuspecting townies and visitors, often ripping off their exhausts or catalytic converters.

But I am undeterred. I'm a big girl now, and with David Gray's "White Ladder" album blasting from my speakers, I am homeward bound. Music is my refuge, my shelter from the storm. The melancholic notes of the track, "Sail Away" seem to mirror the rain pounding against my windshield, as if the universe is trying to tell me something – that if I carry on it might be me that "sails away." And yet, I push on, determined to make it home despite the odds.

And as I drive, the water continues to splash up from the puddles, coating my vehicle in a not so fine mist of rainwater. But I am at peace, content to let the rain wash away the worries of the day and cleanse my soul. For even in the midst of a storm, there is beauty to be found, if only we are willing to see it.

Pulling up to the words of "Say Hello, Wave Goodbye" I see The Dick hanging from the net curtain in the bay window.

You'd have thought they would be growing out of their pup-hood by now. I open the front door and quickly grab an envelope from the letter box – who, in their right mind, would put a letter box at the bottom of the door. Not only must it be a pain for the post staff, but it's also ideally placed for anything shoved through to go straight in the mouth of the family dog.

As normal, it goes in my coat pocket, to be forgotten about until my hand finds it in there, whenever.

The weekend passes without much happening. I spent Saturday working, followed by a day on the farm on Sunday. Now, I'm back to my usual routine of a lunchtime chicken salad sandwich and fizz from Bob in the bakery and giving a nod to Dave the butcher on the way.

Dylan had his lunch before me – he meets James, now he has formally retired from the fire service, and they go off to the local for food most days. Things are looking up and promising for them. Dylan's even talking about James moving in already! Oh, to be in the throes of early love once more.

"It's pissing down out there now!"

"I hadn't noticed. You back from Mill Lane already? That was quick."

"They didn't turn up. Could have called and let me know. People don't give two hoots these days about manners. I rang them, and then I had to explain to Mr Jarvis that it was them and not us messing him about again. Why can't people see his place is in the middle of nowhere before they book a viewing?! I'm soaked down to my undies!"

"Do you want to go home and change? Got nothing else in the diary. People are already winding down for Christmas. Could even have a half day off if you want to. I'm in a good mood!"

"Can I? We want to go choose wallpaper for the front room. Just been talking about it over steak earlier. Could do that."

"Take your sou'westers and wellies with you, looks like it's set in for the long haul."

"I have no idea what a 'sow estra' is but okay."

"James will know...It's a generation thing!"

"Oi!"

Dylan grabs his bag and dashes out the door before I change my mind.

The phone rings. Veronica is on the other end.

"Sorry to bother you Diana, I don't want to disturb your mum as she's always busy this time of day, and it might be a bit tough for her anyway, what I need help with."

"What's up Veronica?"

"You know I move out the farm next month, well, after whenever the funeral is."

I didn't know. All I was aware of was the clearing of the yard and bits, that Jack had been doing recently. Hadn't even crossed my mind the Brayes would ever leave the farm, except as Reg has done, via a box, so to speak.

"That soon? Gosh! How can I assist?"

"There's still a lot of things that belonged to your grandparents here. Do you have time to look and decide what you want to keep? Reg gave Jack all the hand tools and kit from the workshop. He didn't want owt else. Said you may need it."

Thanks Jack! What will I need with duplicate farming equipment?

"Shall I pop over now? The diary is empty, and I have a good four hours to fill before I go home."

"It's been playing on my mind for a bit, so yes, that would be helpful indeed."

I lock up the shop and head towards my car, the "Back Soon!" sign swaying against the glass of the door. I might just be exaggerating a little bit, but this must be the hundred and thirty ninth storm of the week, just as forecasted.

The rain hits my face like ice, and despite my fully buttoned coat, it seeps through and soaks my clothes underneath. I look completely dishevelled by the time I reach my car. I can't show up like this to see Veronica. Bless her, she would be concerned and worry about me getting sick. I'll stop by my mum's house first and borrow some dry clothes. At least my jeans are still there.

I arrive at Veronica's wearing my mum's bib and braces, with knitted jumper below. Turns out my jeans weren't there. The familiarity of the property, Reg's photographs on the hallway walls, his chair where he sat for many a year in the back room – same room as my grandparents.

The smells, oh wow the smells. This is going to be an assault on all my senses and emotions. I've spent more time here in the past year than I did in the previous three decades.

"Where are you going to go, after the farm?"

"What do you mean?"

"If you're leaving the farm, where are you going to live?"

"Hasn't your mum said?"

"No. Does she even know?"

"I'm staying local. It's all sorted. I found somewhere near here."

"Oh, that's good. I wasn't aware anything was for sale?"

"Private agreement. Shall we do the loft? There are loads of boxes and stuff in there still from your grandparents. Or do you want to work through the furniture first?"

Veronica looks tired. In fact, she looks totally drained. These past few weeks must have been pretty foul for her.

"How about a cuppa first? I'll put the kettle on." I head to the little copper kettle, sat ready to go, on the hob."

Having both decided not even to attempt to work through anything, let Veronica take what she wants when she moves out and then leave me to sort what's left, I head back home to the cottage and pups.

The rain has been relentless all afternoon and into the evening but has died down now. I have loose plans to meet Dylan and James at the Walnut Tree for an evening drink and after changing, put my long coat and hat back on and begin my walk into the village. A small bit of alcohol would finish the day off nicely.

Putting my hand into my pocket for my gloves, I come across the envelope I shoved in there the other day. No stamp. It's Nate's handwriting. Nate never writes. He hardly texts, let alone sit and write anything down. My hands shake as I open it up and pull the note out from inside...

Di,

Where did it all go wrong?

I'd watch you from the stairs at night, sat at the kitchen table crying, and it would break my heart. You wouldn't let me hold you. You wouldn't let me console you. I get you were angry. I get that you were hurt. I don't get how we got there though. No matter how much I pull apart those last few years together, I don't understand what happened.

You looked amazing at the party. I wanted to come to you. I wanted to hold you, to smell the coconut in your hair, to touch your face. I wanted to say I love you so much I cannot think of my world without you in it. There is nobody I want to be with, but you, my beloved wife. I'm sorry. I hope it is not too late.

Please call me.

N x

Shit! Didn't need to read or "hear" that! How can somebody claim to love me so much but can't even be bothered to turn up for the counselling sessions? It's like trying to train a dog to drive a car - pointless and frustrating.

I mean, seriously, what's the point of him saying all these things when he doesn't even follow through with his actions? It's not like I'm asking for much, just a little effort, a little commitment. And if he loves me so much, why bring a girlfriend to parade in front of me – and a much younger one at that! The beginning of the year was promising. We're at the end now and have very little to show for it.

I walk into the pub and see Dylan and James being the life and soul of the party at the bar. I turn around and walk back out again, doubting they had noticed my arrival. I don't feel up to jollities now. It's been a long day anyway.

The full moon hangs high in the sky, casting an eerie silver light across the landscape. The rain has cleared the clouds, leaving a sparkling display of stars that twinkle above.

I decide to take the scenic route home, back past the church and through the woods.

St. Mary's Church is a majestic sight, illuminated by the moon's soft light. I pause, captivated by its beauty, and breathe in the peace and tranquillity that surrounds it.

As I wander through the churchyard, my heart heaving with sorrow, or is it self-pity? Hard to tell the difference if I'm honest right now with myself. I come across a child's grave with a doll's pram and dolly engraved on it. The sight breaks my heart, and I am left feeling an even deeper sense of sadness. I don't stop for long. Life is cruel.

Further along, I come across another grave, listing the names of several family members who have passed away over the years. As I read the inscriptions, my eyes fill with tears and my throat tightens with emotion. The weight of life's fragility there in front of me. Perhaps I shouldn't have come this way after all reader.

Then, I arrive at Jack's friend's final resting place, a stark reminder that life can be taken too soon. And yet, a random Nerine, still in its vivid pink bloom, stares right back at me. New life next to late life.

Reg will join them here soon, in the same churchyard where he was christened, married, and will now be laid to rest. The thought is almost too much to bear, and I can feel the tears streaming down my face again.

As I make my way into the woods, a chill runs down my back. My father's words, warning me never to venture here at night, echo in my mind. But I can't resist the pull of the moonlight filtering through the leaves, casting strange shadows on the forest floor. The trees rustle in the breeze, and I can almost hear them whispering secrets amongst each other.

The silence is oppressive, punctuated only by the sound of twigs snapping beneath my feet. The silver birch trees glow with such delicate, almost unearthly light, casting a ghostly aura around me. The darker trees loom like ominous shadows, and I sense a shudder run through my torso.

As I walk, Nate's note in my pocket feels like a lead weight, a constant reminder of the pain and confusion that haunts me. I try not to dwell on it, instead hurrying through the woods and emerging back onto the lane, relieved to be out of that dark, foreboding place. The moonlight guides me home, a beacon of hope in the midst of all the darkness.

The rain begins again. Head down I increase my pace back towards my porch.

As I reach the cottage I look up and instantly recognise a familiar vehicle parked next to the beast. The five-bar gate to my drive has been neatly pulled too. For once, there is no music in my ears. The beat is of my heart I can hear, and now it is deafening and only getting louder. The truck door opens as I get closer.

"You didn't call."

"I've only just read it."

"Can I come in?"

Fighting with the keys, I say nothing but unlock the door.

The pups are just as shocked as me to see Nate standing here. He passes me the Barefoot Cellars Sweet Red brought with him.

"From mum. Left over from the do."

Normally I'd quip about it being a good call or similar but not tonight.

After rolling on the floor with The Dick and the digging one, he picks the cat with attitude up and gives him a stroke behind the ears. Flopped over his shoulder, Attitude purrs contentedly.

I'm struggling to stay composed. I hold the bottle of wine tightly in my hand not knowing whether to open it or not. I want to see what he has to say but I feel like I want to hit him or push him out the door with it.

"I'm useless with words Di. You know I am. I didn't know what to write but I didn't want to write nothing at all. I need you to know is how I feel."

"How's Elizabeth?"

"Beth? What about her?"

"How is she? Seemed a tad upset at the party."

"You know who she is... don't you Di?"

"Yes. Your girlfriend. Alex told me."

"My girlfriend?!"

"Yes. Girlfriend."

"I don't have a girlfriend. You really don't know who she is?"

Why is he looking at me like that?

"You haven't worked it out, have you?"

"Worked out what? I saw with my own eyes her trailing behind you everywhere. Getting upset when you two had some kind of lover's tiff!"

"That's Beth. Beth. As in Reg and Veronica's Elizabeth, their granddaughter. Their son's eldest. She's doing an apprenticeship with me!"

Gobsmacked. That's what I am. Totally and utterly gobsmacked.

"Wait. Hang on, Elizabeth is Beth Braye? She's still at school! You're going out with a child Nate?!"

"She finished school nearly ten years ago Di! She wanted to retrain and has ended up with me. And no. I am not going out with her for heavens' sake."

"So why are you having sex with her?"

"Really?! Do you think I want Beth? Or anyone

else? I'm married to you for Christ's sake. That's all that matters to me. Besides, it would be like shagging a doll, a woman that size compared to me."

"So, you have thought about it then? I don't know what I think about any of this. You don't turn up, always making excuses. Work, work, work. Always bloody work with you. So, wanting to prove to your family that you can make it on your own. Well, you've done that now. What next Nate? What next?!"

I realise I need to take a breath dear reader but wanted to get that all out before my brain decided to have a late evening siesta and forget all the words.

"Don't be angry Di. I'm trying! Why do you think I am here?"

The tears are back. Wiping my eyes with my coat sleeve, they continue to build. Conscious I'm now doing the dreaded snot, sniff, manoeuvre in front of him, and not wanting it to turn into the even less flattering snot, sniff, random snort, I head towards the back of the kitchen.

"I'm going outside. Need some fresh air. Just go home Nate." I close the stable door behind me, leaving him and the pups inside.

As the rain continues to pelt down on me, I feel as

though I'm being beaten down by the forces of nature itself. The wind is picking up, making my hair whip around my face, stinging my cheeks. I lean back against the damp brick wall of the cottage, seeking shelter from the elements. My breathing is heavy, ragged gasps that I can barely control as I try to make sense of the jumble of emotions inside me.

With one hand, I fumble with my ear pods, my frozen fingers shaking uncontrollably as I try to get my playlist started. I need something to distract me, to help me sort through the mess in my head. The flattened notes of Gary Jules' version of "Mad World" fill my ears, a perfect reflection of the despair and confusion I feel. But even as the music washes over me, I hear Nate's voice calling out my name from behind the door.

Part of me wants to ignore him, to shut out the world and curl up in my misery. But another part of me is filled with a desperate hope that maybe, just maybe, he can fix this. I cling to that hope even as I feel the tears start to flow, mixing with the rain as they course down my cheeks.

Not realising it came out with me, I clutch the wine bottle tightly, my fingers white-knuckled as I try to make sense of my conflicting emotions. I love Nate, of that there is no doubt. But the pain and anger that he has caused me is almost unbearable. I don't know how to forgive him for walking out on me, for throwing away everything we had built together.

As I sink to the ground, the cold, wet of the ground seeping through my clothes, I feel as though I'm drowning in my own despair. The world around me is a blur of rain and tears, and I can't tell up from down.

I don't even know how long I've been sitting here until Nate takes the wine bottle from my shaking fingers. He's soaked to the skin, his hair plastered to his forehead, his teeth chattering uncontrollably.

Despite my anger and pain, I can't help but feel a twinge of concern for him. But I know that I can't let him back in, not yet. We have so much to work through, so much pain and betrayal to confront.

"Why haven't you got a coat on?"

"I didn't bring one. I also didn't expect to be stood out here for what feels like an hour watching you cry. Come back inside Di."

He holds his hand out to me.

"Go home Nate. I don't think you should be here."

I put my ear pods into my coat pocket. The note is still there. The words are still in my head.

"No. Not yet. Let me get you inside. I need to know you are alright first."

He continues to hold his hand out for me. The inner stubbornness within refuses to be helped but he grabs my elbow anyway and pulls me up.

I find myself with my face in his chest. At six foot seven, he stands literally head and shoulders above me. I remember how I used to feel with him around me. His presence always made me feel protected, looked after, secure. I felt tiny against him, especially when we made love.

He was the man I needed and the only man I wanted ... when he was there.

Nate holds both my hands in his now.

"You're shaking Di."

He puts his arms around me and brings me close. Automatically, my arms go around his waist. There's a comfort there that I have missed. His head lays on mine. The rain continues to fall as we stand there holding each other. I feel his chest raise and lower as his breathing slows, he kisses my hair and holds me tight. Time has stopped momentarily.

As the heavens open even more, we have no choice other than to make our way indoors.

"Where are your towels?"

"There are dog towels just inside the hallway. In

that cupboard where the battery lamps are kept."

With a small hand towel, I wipe my face.

"I look a mess, don't I?"

"You look lovely to me. I don't care about smudged makeup or perfect hair Di. You know me."

It's true. I fell in love with this man because he liked me.

He liked the fact we were both from "farming stock" as he referred to us and, I got messy, hands on, and just got on with the job – which he found incredibly sexy apparently.

Nate's rugged good looks and charm were enough to make any woman swoon, but as far as I know, he never cheated on me during our marriage. He was always too focused on work, too dedicated to build his business.

Despite his busy schedule, he was a beloved figure in our small community. Whenever he was back in town, he'd be called upon by farmers to help with carpentry and repairs, and he never charged a thing of course. He had a heart of gold, and it was one of the things that drew me to him in the first place.

Nate's reputation as a local hero didn't come as a surprise to anyone who knew him well. Especially me. I mean, who else would have the patience and endurance to deal with stubborn cows, noisy tractors, leaky roofs, or anything else he could turn his capable hand to?

He was like a real-life superhero; except he didn't wear a cape and had a taste for cheap beer instead of expensive wine (just don't tell his parents.)

I used to tease him that he had a secret lair somewhere in the woods, where he kept his tools, his collection of sawdust, and his stash of old Carry-On movies. He'd just chuckle and say that I had an overactive imagination, which was probably true.

Maybe it was his devilish smile, or his rugged physique, or his ability to fix anything with duct tape and a prayer.

Or maybe it was the fact that he never seemed to age, even though he'd been working in the sun and rain for decades alongside the day job. I swear he once had a portrait in our attic that aged instead of him.

But regardless of his secrets and quirks, I knew one thing for sure: Nate was the kind of man most women dream of, one who made you feel safe and cherished, even if he wasn't perfect. And that was worth more than all the riches and fame in the world.

Even after our separation, I couldn't help but feel a sense of pride knowing that he was my husband (once) and that he wouldn't stop at anything to help someone out whatever their dilemma was.

"You're saturated. I've got some of your old shirts here still. May still even have your lucky paint trousers under the stairs in a cardboard box there."

I go off to hunt some of his clothing down after convincing him to go for a shower to warm himself up.

In the bedroom I place the garments at the end of the bed, then quickly get undressed out of my wet clothes into something more comfortable - a camisole, thong (top of the pile), and dressing gown.

I'm mid hair brushing when Nate comes out of the bathroom with a towel around his waist.

Well, fuckadoodle doo! Wasn't expecting that and nearly pee myself in response to the Adonis stood before me – well, reflecting in the mirror anyway. He's been working out and looks amazing. I try to act as if I haven't seen him and start to brush my hair again. I feel a pang of jealousy, wondering if he's been working out for someone else.

But then I remind myself that it doesn't matter

anymore. We're over, and I need to move on.

He walks over... bugger! Act cool.

"Can I do that? Can I brush your hair Di? Let me."

We're looking at our reflection in the dressing table mirror. It's been years since we've been here. Same mirror. Same dresser. Same positions. Different house. Different life.

As Nate takes the brush from my hand and stands behind me, running it through my hair and smoothing it with his hand, I feel myself melting into him. It's such an intimate act, and as he does it, I'm reminded of my parents.

They had a similar routine, with my father brushing my mother's hair every night before bed. He was a quiet man, but his actions spoke volumes. He adored my mother and brushing her hair was his way of showing it. It was a way of saying, "I love you. You are important to me." And my mother knew it without him ever having to say a word.

My eyes open when the brushing stops. I see that same love and appreciation in Nate's eyes, and I know that I have been lucky to have him in my life despite where we are now with each other.

"I need to get dressed. I should head back." He starts to look for the dry clothes I've put out for him.

"Okay. I'll go downstairs." Can't lie. I'm pretty disappointed the moment had to end.

"It's fine. Sit on the bed if you want. Not like you haven't seen it before, is it?"

"I know. Just doesn't feel right, Nate. The counsellor made a point of stressing to us not to end up in this scenario. That we had to work on the other parts first."

"What scenario? Being in a room together? We're husband and wife Di. Husband and wife."

"*Separated* husband and wife. There's a really big difference. This is wrong."

I sit on the edge of the bed. Nate sits next to me. It feels reassuringly nice, despite the conversation.

"Does this feel wrong to you?" Nate turns towards me, moving a strand of hair from in front of my eye.

"No."

"Does this feel wrong to you?" He places his hand on mine.

"No."

"How about this?"

He places his hands gently either side of my face and leans in for the lightest touch of his lips on mine. He pulls away and removes his hands.

"Did that feel wrong?"

"No."

He leans in again and we kiss. I'm not familiar with the feelings I'm getting right now. I don't remember it.

This is gentle and caring. Was it always like this and I just don't recall? Why did we stop being intimate? What actually happened to us?

As we break the kiss, I look into Nate's eyes, searching for answers to questions I haven't voiced. He holds my gaze, as if he knows what I'm thinking. His fingers trace gentle patterns on my cheek, and I feel a warmth spreading through me that I can't explain.

"I've missed you," he says softly, and I can see the sincerity in his eyes.

"I've missed you too," I whisper back, surprised by the emotion in my own voice.

In that moment, everything else fades away, and it's just the two of us, there in the quiet of the bedroom.

The memories of our past life together swirl around us, and I realise how much I've missed the feeling of being close to Nate, of being loved by Nate.

As my husband leans in again, I know that I want this - whatever this is - more than anything. And for the first time in a long time, I feel hopeful that we can find a way to make it work.

"I want to make love to you Di. I've missed you so much."

Wow, I didn't expect to see water pooling in his eyes. Is he actually showing this much emotion for me? I feel so confused right now, and I want this moment to last forever. I'm not sure what I should be doing, but I know that I don't want to mess things up between us.

As I lean in to kiss his cheek and wipe away the single tear slowly falling, I feel an overwhelming urge to kiss him on the lips. Before I know it, I'm kissing him passionately and running my lips down to his neck. It seems like my heart has made the decision for me, and I don't want to let this moment go.

I'm not sure what the future holds, but for now, I'm going to enjoy the right now and let my heart guide me.

"Are you sure Di? Do you want to do this?"

After hesitating for a few moments, I finally gather up the courage to stand up and reveal my naked (well, almost) body to Nate. As I shed my dressing gown, I can feel my heart pounding in my chest.

It's been years since I've been this exposed – the last time was when I accidentally walked naked into the wrong shower block at the gym on my one and only visit there. Mortified, I never went back. Christa found it hilarious though but then she would; she was the one who told me the shower was that way.

But I know I need to do this. It's time to show Nate what he's been missing out on. I take a deep breath and strike a pose, trying to look as confident and sexy as possible.

I peek at Nate through my fringe, watching as his gaze travels from my face to my body. Those eyes of his are absolutely captivating. I can't help but feel weak in the knees just looking at him. But why isn't he touching me? Is he repulsed by the way I look now that he's seen me with all my added curves and crevices? Is my body a turn off?

My insecurities start to take over, and I begin to second-guess myself. But then I remind myself that this is Nate, the man who used to love every inch of me. I take a deep breath and try to push away my doubts, waiting for him to make the next move.

Nate's reaction is immediate. He jumps up from the bed and covers his eyes, yelling, "Oh my God, my eyes! They're burning!" then falls back onto the bed.

I can't help but laugh at his over-the-top reaction. "Come on, Nate, it's not that bad."

Nate peeks through his fingers and shakes his head. "I don't know, I think I need some bleach for my peepers after that."

I roll my eyes and playfully swat at him. "You're such a drama queen."

Nate grins and finally lowers his hands. "Okay, okay, I'm sorry. I just wasn't expecting the full Monty."

I smirk at him. "Well, you're getting it now, buddy."

We both burst out laughing, and suddenly the tension is gone. It feels good to be able to joke around with Nate like this again. Who knew getting naked could actually be fun?

"You look bloody hot Di." Standing, Nate drops the towel from his waist. Fuck! Fuck! Fuck! I've waited for this moment for so long. And now it's here I feel so inadequate with all my wobbly bits and he's throwing compliments at me.

Again, he holds my face and kisses me softly before scooping me up and laying me on the bed. Wow! That's a new move!

Lying next to me, propped up on one elbow, he traces my body with his free hand. The tingling sensation pulses through every part of me. I've longed for Nate's touch...I close my eyes and enjoy the moment.

"I've missed this Di. I've missed this, you, the pups, even the cat with attitude, I've just missed so much and don't know how to make it up to you."

"I've missed you too. Life, marriage, its more than just this though, Nate."

"I know."

He lifts my camisole and places his hand directly on my skin. The warmth of his hand filtering through into me.

"This is my favourite bit of you. I love your belly. I don't know why it is, but I love it! It's so soft and squishy, like a little pillow! Womanly, so unlike those washboard stomachs and skin 'n' bone females of today. Other's may like that, but it's not for me. I like a woman to be a woman, feminine, soft to the touch. It's just so much sexier too."

Wait! He likes my belly. The bit I, and probably half the female population, detest more than anything else on our bodies? And he likes it?! What about my ample bosom, or my gorgeous bum, plenty to grab there. I like to think my strongest physical asset is my hair or maybe my eyes, not my belly, or come to think about it, my biceps like a brickies or my non-existent ankles. Nate moves to kiss his favourite part ...

"Mmmm, coconut and... what is that?"

"Well, if you're down there, then it's probably Veet, from this morning."

Bang goes the romance.

"Hang on! Does that mean what I think it means?" he continues his kisses a few inches further down, over my lace thong, pulling it down slightly.

"Hello there! Haven't seen you for a while my friend."

Then moves back to propping himself up next to me, kissing me on the lips once more, before straddling me and sitting back on his knees.

"I'm so nervous. I've wanted this for so long."

Nate nervous? He certainly wasn't coming across that way right now. Fair enough, his hands are shaking as his fingers trace over my bustline and down my torso - reminding me of the early days, getting to know each other. Although, his tanned chest and honed abs, right now in front of me, haven't changed in all these years. If anything, they are even more a turn on now than ever. But nervous? Nate doesn't seem nervous.

"Kiss me please." I pull him awkwardly back towards me. The new bed frame isn't built for someone his height but was all I could fit in the room. His legs lay at an awkward, uncomfortable angle; he doesn't seem to notice. We kiss, more confidence building that it's okay to do this.

His hands firmly rubbing the length of me, my hands around his neck holding him there as the heat grows between us.

Legs either side of me again, he grabs hold of the silk covering me and rips the camisole apart. Fleetingly the price of the item flashes past my eyes before I refocus on him cupping my naked breasts, placing the nipples in his mouth, and gently biting them. He moves, trailing his tongue lightly over my skin, around my navel and down again.

"Sorry to ruin the moment, I need to rearrange things. My legs are killing me."

Beaming back up at me, this was something we were both familiar with. After a quick rethink, I position myself, laid back, with my legs over the edge of the bed, Nate carefully removes my thong before kneeling between my thighs.

"I'm going in!"

As he nuzzles his mouth and nose into me, I realise all the things I've been missing about not having Nate. All these other "liaisons" from the past few months felt nothing like this. It feels so good, the tip of his tongue tenderly caressing my swollen bud, his strong hands gripping my thighs as he pushes into my lips, searching for my womanly juices before delving his fingers deep inside my wet, sodden hole.

I'd forgotten how good he was, how thoughtful he was, to me, when we did make love.

"I'm about to explode Di. Can we try doggy?"

As he slides his rock-solid shaft in, hands firmly on my hips pulling me on to him, I gasp. He's the perfect fit to me. I can feel the sides of him moving against the sides of me, back and forth, as he pumps his hips and groin on me.

There's a sense of a further rigidity before Nate rams into me hard, releasing everything as he does, then again and again and again, before stopping and holding himself in me.

Moments later he has flipped me over and is back right between my legs. This time he concentrates on my bud only. His fingers wet from his own bodily fluids mixed with mine, he slowly moves them either side, massaging me, teasing me, stretching me, pulling me, then I feel his mouth envelope me, sucking gently at first, just a slight tug and release motion.

The familiar feeling of electricity running through from my ankles into my calves, up through my thighs as the muscles tense.

The tugging, sucking sensation is increasing both in strength and urgency, He doesn't stop as he senses my thighs clamp around his head, my hips bucking and my vicelike grip on his shoulders as I reach peak sexual arousal, climaxing with a great spurt of juices on to him and the bed.

"Oh God! I'm so sorry Nate!" The embarrassment of my body's actions overtaking the opportunity of relishing in the aftermath of an eye-watering orgasm.

His face has a massive smile. "I can't help it if I'm really good at the job now, can I?!"

"Twat!" We both laugh.

After a quick tidy up, we crash into bed, me cuddling Nate from behind, spoon style, just like the old days when deeply in love. But tonight - is it just because the bed is too small?

"What do we tell the counsellor next month?"

"I don't know Nate...I really don't know. A lot has happened this year that we need to talk about first."

But Nate is already asleep, his breathing slow and steady.

In the darkness, I reach for his hand, feeling his fingers and intertwining them with mine. It's a natural and familiar, one that brings me comfort and a sense of hope.

13 Your Wallet's Here Santa Xx

December. It's hard to believe how fast time has flown by - it feels like just yesterday that I moved into the cottage. Yet here we are, and the 27th is right around the corner.

Today is a sombre day, as it's the day of Reg's service. My mum and Jack are going to be there to support dear Veronica and accompany her for the funeral cortege from the farm. As is tradition, the cortege will pass through Richdore market square, giving anyone who wishes to pay their respects the opportunity to do so. From there, the procession will continue on to St. Mary's at Malthay for the service and burial.

"Oi! Earth calling Dylan!"

"Sorry. It's a dog carrying a duck in its mouth. So cute!" Dylan puts his phone back in the desk drawer. "These mini videos can be so addictive. Not good."

"I noticed." Rolling my eyes at him with a smile.

I nod towards the fake fir tree in the bay window.

"Thought you said you had sorted those lights out? Bright red and so many of them. Looks like we should be on a street in Amsterdam advertising a different kind of service! We'll have the parish council here soon if we don't get back to the obligatory white light theme."

"It did say on the box 'vintage white.' Promise you! I'll go back to Christa's later and see what else she has in the shop."

"Probably best to keep them off whilst Reg goes past."

Dylan will be staying in the office for the afternoon. I have arranged to meet Nate at the church. I've seen very little of him in the past few weeks since our evening together. Work for him, farm for me, when not in the office here. Yet again he didn't join the counselling session as he was at solicitors in Dalebank sorting out a business issue.

My mobile pings with a message from Jack.

"Bernard and Beth have broken down – I'm off to find them." Bernard, being Reg and Veronica's son.

I reply with the standard response "X."

Apparently, Beth has gotten over whatever she had to get over, according to Nate.

"Right, I'm off. At least it's not raining today."

Back at the cottage I've asked Margaret to play Christmas tunes while I sort myself out. I'm trying to take my mind off the next few hours. Letting the pups out the back to the dulcet tones of Noddy Holder, I take note of the changes in the garden. No leaves left on the trees; the only seasonal colours are coming from the pine right at the end and a few scattered conifers. The grass, yellowing and too long and wet to mow, has taken over some of the borders as well as the lawn itself, and then there's mud. Plenty of mud from the digging one enjoying himself. It just looks a mess really.

The dress code for the service – as per Veronica's request – bright and cheerful. I toyed with the idea of wearing the red all in one jumpsuit but decided against it, due to the toilet access issues and the fact, with little time for error, I will be back at the adjoining church hall to assist with the Christmas tree competition later this evening.

Then there was the floral skirt I wore throughout the summer, which Reg loved seeing me wear (as did Lawrence Barker), but in the end I have chosen a 1950's inspired pencil suit in emerald-green – hopefully bright enough for the service, but festive enough for this evening. A pair of comfortable Mary Jane shoes finish the outfit, high enough heel to look elegant, low enough heel to keep my knees happy for the next twelve hours or so!

Well, I've done it. I've squeezed into my suck-it-all-in underwear, and now I can barely breathe. But hey, beauty is pain is it not? My hair is perfectly coiffed, and my makeup is on point. I'm looking sharp in my suit, even if I can't feel my legs. It's time to face the world and hope that my lack of oxygen doesn't make me pass out before the day is done.

I walk to the church along the main footpath, not wanting to get muddy through the woods. I've been keeping the pathway clear of brambles and things, just as dad used to, but it's a welly boot walk not formal footwear. I'm plugged in, presently listening to "Live It Up" Mental as Anything, as I make my way past the Walnut Tree pub where the wake will be afterwards. Probably a bit too upbeat a tune for the occasion but a song I have always found to put a smile on my face.

I haven't heard from Jack since this morning's text. I can see Bernard, a short, stocky man with his pinstripe suit on, stood next to the massive yew tree talking to the new vicar – not that he's that new now. Covers both here and St Augustus and been in the locality for about a year. Bernard's parents were so proud when he became a solicitor in the big city, although sad it meant he lived so far away with his family.

My brother and Beth must be here somewhere. I can't see Nate either. Why doesn't that surprise me? I finish listening to "Birdhouse in your soul" by They Might Be Giants and place my ear pods into my pocket.

"Hi Bernard, sorry about your dad. Are Jack and Beth with you?"

"Hi Diana, separate cars. Jack got mine going and I made my way here. Beth needed the loo, so he took her back to use his first."

"Okay. Quite the congregation gathering now for your dad, don't you think?"

"Indeed. Indeed."

Oh, here they are. What kept you? Where did you park?" Jack and Beth appear from the far side of the church.

They looked a bit flushed.

"Thought we were going to miss it. I've parked at yours; no space out the front here. Mum is just around the corner, waiting to turn in. Too many people. Oh, and Nate's down at the old post office, trying to direct the traffic with Mr Hooper."

After another ten minutes or so, I see Nate's head

above the hedgerow surrounding the church. Soon he's standing next to me as we wait for Veronica, mum, and Reg's immediate family to make their way into St Marys.

The service is lovely. Very fitting for such a well-known, full of life character. Nate and I are sat two rows back from mum, Jack and the Braye family, Nate's legs sticking out into the aisle.

It's a beautiful service, and I can feel myself getting emotional as Veronica delivers her eulogy. Reg was a wonderful man, and it's clear many loved him. As we wait for the family to pay their respects at the coffin, it is the opportunity for Nate and me to speak, albeit in whispers.

"Sorry Di about the other day. I had to go to the solicitors to sign some papers. Took longer than I expected. Had to be done though."

"You could have dialled in off your mobile Nate. Not really an excuse, is it?"

"Dialled in?! What era is your world?! And, please, don't be like that. It was important."

"And our marriage isn't?"

"Of course, it is. I promised the family I'd deal with it, and I couldn't break that promise."

"Of course... the family! It's always 'the family' Nate!"

"Not..."

"Shush! They're coming. Stand."

There's a silence, before the organist begins to play "All Things Bright and Beautiful." Veronica, mum, and the family make their way towards the doors.

As they pass, Veronica stops and turns towards us.

"Thank you, Daniel. Thank you for everything you've done for me this week. It's made life a little easier."

Nate smiles graciously. "Not a problem. Honestly. Least I could do."

As they move on, Nate looks at me and jokingly face palms his forehead. "It's Nathanial! Bloody Nathanial!"

"I don't know... you're quite sexy as a "Daniel"."

"You see my car keys anywhere? My wallet's in the truck."

Wake finished, the four of us, me, Jack, Nate, and

Beth, are back at the cottage.

Jack's not feeling great and is impromptu pup sitting as there will be fireworks later after the Christmas Tree competition – anyone and everyone had the opportunity to sponsor and decorate a tree in aid of the church repair fund. Tonight, it's the winner trophy giving ceremony. I'm helping with the tea, coffee, and cakes. Nate has been dragged in to assist with Santa's Grotto for the kids.

"Are you walking or driving?"

"I'll let Nate decide. I'm happy to walk back up there, but he may not be."

"My keys... where are they?" A six foot seven Santa walks into the kitchen.

"Yes, I know. You can all stop laughing. Joys of owning a costume company I suppose. Bound to happen eventually. Are you sure you're feeling unwell Jack? This isn't your way of getting back at me?"

"Nah, I really don't feel well, and poor Beth is stuck with me until I drive her back later." My brother didn't think I noticed the sly wink at Beth.

I scan around the kitchen until I see Nate's keys hanging up with mine. The matching "his" and "her" fobs sat side-by-side. The penny I gave him, that time at the beach, still threaded on to the ring itself - dull now where he rubs it between his fingertips when it's in his trouser pocket.

"Behind you. Your keys are on the hook."

"I don't even remember doing that! I'll get my wallet.

Fancy a walk Mrs Marlowe?"

We head out the door together, leaving behind my brother and Beth to probably finish what they had started earlier.

With a heavy frost forecast for the morning, the air feels crisp and clear right now as we walk. We get a few odd looks from passing vehicles but generally the people that are out and about are all heading in the same direction as us.

"I've been meaning to ask what Veronica meant earlier, at the church."

"Don't you know? She's moving in with your mum isn't she."

"She is? When was this decided? I have no knowledge of this whatsoever!" I stop in my tracks staring at Nate.

"Hang on, is this what Veronica meant when she said she was staying local? I'm not mad. Not at all.

I think it's a lovely idea that they, being lifelong friends, will be living together. Mum could really do with the company. Bernard and his family will have the farm to themselves, and mum and Veronica will be next door. That's a nice set up."

"Come on, we've got about half hour before doors open."

Nate grabs my hand and pulls me onwards. Still wearing my pencil skirt, I can't move as quickly as him so hitch it up to give me a bigger stride.

"Nice!"

"Stop it, Santa! Not here in front of the kids!"

Nate quickly looks around, notes no kids in sight, and seizes the chance to pinch my backside.

Finally, the moment of truth arrives – I get to meet the infamous Mabel Wainwright.

As the unofficial head of the Malthay Women's Institute type of club, she's known for running the refreshments from the church kitchen with military precision. But as it turns out, she's also the vicar's wife and genuinely a nice person. I must admit, I was a bit apprehensive at first, expecting her to be a bit overbearing and imposing, but she's surprisingly pleasant. Sure, she does have a tendency to be a bit too organised and officious, but that's just a part of her charm.

The awards ceremony is a smashing success, and even the appearance of a towering Santa Claus fails to faze the kids. In fact, the jolly old fellow is probably now sporting the most selfies he's ever taken with kids and their mothers!

The evening is capped off with a stunning fireworks display, bringing an end to an exhaustingly long but satisfying day.

After finishing the tiresome task of stowing away the trestle tables and chairs, cleaning up an enormous amount of dishes, and saying goodbye to everyone, Nate and I start heading back to the cottage. Despite all the work, the evening turned out to be quite pleasant.

It seems like Jack and Beth have flown the coop, leaving behind only the remnants of their saucy soirée - two empty wine glasses on the drainer and a rogue condom wrapper that missed its target.

"Looks like your brother's been up to some hanky-panky," Nate quips, winking mischievously.

"That's Jack for you. Cuppa?"

"Lovely. I'll go get changed out of this."

There is a homely feel having Nate here with me. Him fleeting in and out isn't a marriage, isn't what either of us wanted when we said our vows.

Dressed in jeans and a lumberjack shirt, Nate downs his drink before a quick peck on the cheek and disappearing out the front door.

As he heads out, I can't help but admire his rugged, outdoorsy look. The lumberjack shirt is doing wonders for his broad shoulders, and those jeans...well, let's just say they're fitting him like a glove. I may have said "I do" to a suited-up version of Nate, but this casual yet manly look, definitely grew on me instantly.

The quickness of him leaving was surprising even for me. I can't help but feel a twinge of disappointment. I mean, I know we agreed he wouldn't be staying over, but a girl can still dream? But alas, the night is over, and it's time for me to tend to my furry roommates.

As I leash up the pups and head out into the crisp night air of my midnight garden, I can't help but chuckle to myself. It's funny how even after all these years, dogs still insist on marking their territory at the most inconvenient times.

Once we're all back inside and settled, I make my way to bed. As I lay there, listening to the gentle snoring of my canine companions, I can't help but wonder what tomorrow will bring.

I wake up earlier than my usual routine, feeling a bit groggy after a restless night. But there's no time to waste, I need to catch up with my mum and get the latest update on Veronica's situation. So, I quickly send a text to Dylan informing him of my plans, get ready for work, gather my furry companions into the beast, and hit the road.

The Dick and the digging one love the farm. They've obviously known it their whole lives. They smell the frosted air as we head up past the Brayes farm and on towards mum.

As I get closer, I see Nate's truck down the lane, heading off in the other direction. There's a sudden wave of disappointment in me, that I've missed him. It's still early enough that he's probably just left for work from his place. Plus, he wouldn't have known I was coming this way before the office. I haven't asked him what he thinks about having Bernard as a landlord now, must be a concern for him.

"What's this I hear about Veronica moving in mum? Did you forget to tell me?!"

"Of course, not darling. I wanted it to be a surprise. Hopefully, a nice surprise for you. Jack's been clearing everything out and she's coming over from next week - in time for the festivities. It will be nice having her here for Christmas dinner, rather than be on her own down the road."

"I'm really pleased for you, for both of you."

Giving mum a hug, I'm reminded how small she is against me now. Once upon a time we stood eye to eye. She seems so happy I won't pry and rib her further. Why upset the apple cart and all that.

Jack walks in at this point, followed by both pups and his sheep dog "Twig."

"Feeling better I see! How's Beth?" I push the dogs and their muddy paws down from my suit.

"Beth's good ... very good!" Jack has the beaming smile of a naughty child across his face.

"Seeing her again?"

"Maybe..."

Back in the office, Dylan has been busy playing Christmas elf. He's replaced the "prostitutes available here" lights on the tree with twinkling ones and transformed the windows with an excessive layer of fake snow spray. He's obviously been on a mission to make the place look "a bit more Christmassy."

The phones are as dead as a doornail and there's

not a single appointment in the diary. Both of us have our faces in our mobiles when the door opens; I'm catching up with today's news online. I expect Dylan is probably watching more dogs with ducks videos.

"James!" Dylan runs over, giving him a massive bear hug and smacker on the lips.

Once stripped of his Ziggy Stardust persona, James' rugged features become apparent, revealing a face that has seen more of life than the average person. Reggie had mentioned that James, or Jim as he's known to them, had spent his entire career in the fire service, earning the respect of all those who worked alongside him for his expertise and extensive experience. His countenance exudes an air of wisdom and maturity, a face that can only be earned through years of life's trials and tribulations, as my grandmother would often remark.

"Lunch?" He takes Dylan's hand. "Hello Diana, good day so far?"

"It's been quiet. Not unexpected, so close to Christmas. Take him please ... and his fake snow canister!"

My mobile pings. It's Nate. "Do you still finish early on Saturdays?"

"4. Why?"

"Busy?"

"Rushed off my feet. What's up?"

"Look out the window?"

"At what? There's nothing there."

"The other one."

Nate's peering through the smallest of holes left clear of Dylan's spraying - he's literally gone around every property picture and most of the glass but Nate, at his height, can still see in above the whiteness of the once clean panes.

"What are you doing here?"

"Shall I come in? Or shall we continue texting?!"

"Can do."

"Cuppa?"

We both head into the kitchenette.

"Shall we talk here or later? We need a catch up before the counselling session. Melanie will want to know what our plans are."

"Dylan will come back in about an hour. He's lunching with James across the square."

"Shame. Later then. I've got something to show you anyway."

"Shall I come to yours on way to get the pups from mum? I can call and see if she's happy with them for a bit longer."

"Perfect. Nice outfit. Like the paw print on the back. Adds a touch of class."

"Wait! What paw print?!"

"Got ya!"

"Twat!"

As the clock strikes four, time seems to drag on at a snail's pace. I make my way towards the beast while Dylan stays behind to lock up. Meanwhile, Christa is parked next to me, frantically shoving last-minute presents into the back of her minibus.

"Who did you forget to buy presents for this year?!" I ask with a friendly smirk.

"Only my bloody husband!" she exclaims.

"With the house purchase, school finishing two days earlier than planned, and the shop being so busy, I totally forgot."

"Why did school close early?" I inquire.

"They didn't. I just wrote it down wrong on the blasted calendar. Damn dyscalculia strikes again. The kids don't care though. They spent the extra two days making crap paintings and clay pots made from plasticine to stick on the fridge at home. They're rubbish, but you have to pretend to like them because the kids made them. Do the teachers do it just to annoy us parents?!"

I can't help but chuckle. "You love it all really."

"Yeah... I do. Just don't tell anyone ...you seen twat features lately?"

"On my way now as it happens. Still don't know what to do. Love him and all that. Can't lie, he still makes my heart jump when I see him, but really, can I really see us back together? I'm struggling to answer that."

"What's meant to be ... Best leave you to get on your way. Good luck!"

For some reason I'm quite anxious about this meet up. I've been sat opposite, in the lay-by, for fifteen minutes pretending to do something on my mobile.

"Flip! What did you do that for?! You've set off the dogs now!"

The Dick and the digging one bark joyously

behind me. I didn't realise mum had plans this evening to help Veronica move a few more things across.

"You weren't coming in, so I thought I'd come check you were alright. Didn't mean to make you jump. Hi pups. You joining us too?"

"I just had to send off an email. That was all."

Nate opens the beast's door, creaking on its hinges. "I'm surprised this thing is still going really. Been a steady old bird, hasn't she? Any sign of my wallet at yours?"

"I always thought of it as male...stops and starts but not much else goes on under the bonnet. No. I haven't seen it, but then wasn't looking either."

"Now! Now! We can't help how we are wired! Fair enough. Right, shall we get this over with?"

With our furry companions in tow, we make our way into the cosy cottage that has always felt like home.

The name, "The Nap" has a certain charm to it, conjuring up images of warmth and comfort. I've been told that it was named after a painting from the 1800s.

Nate helps me remove my hat and coat before hanging them up above the row of wellies, just as he always did. As we step into the snug, welcoming kitchen, I can't help but feel a sense of contentment wash over me.

"Shall we do this at the table. How formal do we need to be?"

"I don't think Melanie will need a transcript Nate! She just wants to know how we have gotten on over the past twelve months with her assignment."

"I wasn't sure about it at first. What about you?"

"What? The fact the only thing she focused on was our lack of sex life. Or that she thinks fixing that, will fix you being a workaholic or never being here or any of the other stuff. The bigger stuff?"

"Harsh but true."

I settle myself down at the table with my favourite mug. Why I left it with him I don't recall. I thought I'd be back by now I suppose.

Nate joins me moments later with biscuits "January... thoughts?"

"Hold your horses...I can't get my phone to respond. I'll have to use the note app on yours."

"Ready? Let me just put down the whole point of this..."

As I tap the screen keyboard I speak out-loud as really I don't want there to be any misunderstandings between us."

"To think creatively, try new sexual situations, to live out at least one sexual fantasy each, to not judge, just do, and remember what happens this year is acceptable to, and agreed by both of you. That was it wasn't it?"

"Sounds about right. I liked January. Why didn't you tell me you liked milkmen? I'd have pulled out the costume long before, had I of known!"

"It's not about the milkman Nate! It's about the spontaneity!"

"Oh, okay. What did you like about the act itself? I really liked walking in and seeing you leaning over the stable door, knowing what I was about to do. That gown you purchased was just the right length too. I could see your cheeks through the material and just poking out the bottom of it. That was a real turn on."

"Feeling you against me, feeling you being hard and rubbing against me. I hadn't felt that for so long. Your voice got me too. It had been a year since I physically saw you last. Oh, and when you turned me around and I saw those damn eyes and long lashes. You know what they do to me!"

"What about the table? Being on the table? I've

always wanted to try that position."

"Can't say it did much for me. I felt really exposed and it was hard! But I realised I like having my arms above my head and then when you went down on me...I was so nervous but sweet Mary, you were spot on with your tongue and everything. How did you learn to do that?!"

"I thought it was the same way as I've always done it. I have spent the last two years watching porn I suppose. Must have picked up a few tips on the way. What about February, here?"

"That didn't quite go to plan, did it?! Me ending up arse over tit under the beast! Instead of it being all for you, you had to make sure I wasn't broken first!"

"That was a classic moment, watching you slip and slide your way down from Veronica and Reg in the ice and snow. I felt like a helpless spectator, but it was worth it just to see your head disappear at lightning speed below the hedgerow. It was like one of those viral videos on 'Clickclack'. You know the ones that make you laugh and question humanity at the same time?"

"Is that what it's called? Never knew... I was lucky I didn't hurt myself really. Back to 'Daniel'... Did you like what I did to 'him'?"

"Did I like what you did?" Was it not evident?

When you held your mouth down there, over my jeans... I could feel the warmth of your breath on my cock. I was trying not to come right there and then! You've never done that before."

"I asked Dylan what he liked. Thought I'd try it on you."

"Wow! Does he know?"

"No. We have conversations like that sometimes."

"Right...I liked the dance beforehand. Ah, yes. The performance prior to the main event was quite...what's the word I'm looking for... enchanting. Being in your embrace, the aroma of your luscious locks and delicate skin. It's delightful to know that your fondness for coconut still lingers."

"You did go over the top on the box sets last year..."

"Sorry. I was just so pleased you had agreed to speak to the counsellor that I wanted to show you, but you said not to spend loads."

"March..."

"Remind me..."

"My pussy needs attention too."

"Yes! The dog walker advert! The community admin team really helped us on that one! Did they not realise how the advert read after they had 'assisted'?!"

"It was freezing. Why did you want to do it outside in bloody March! My boobs didn't recover for ages after leaning over that bench!"

"When I put that down on paper I forgot about the time of year. It was fun though..."

"Maybe for you. You were the one standing up! I feel the alcohol may have made it better than it was."

"April?"

"April! I've been meaning to ask where you got that flipping name from? I nearly choked when you rang through to the office with that fake voice. Lawrence Barker? I mean... really?"

"Lawrence Barker... named after The Dick of course... hey Larry?"

"I was shagging the dog's namesake?! Oh, and now I get it... Bearsted Montague...that's you Monty Bear, isn't it?"

I pat the digging one on his rump. "April has to be one of my favourites but then it would be, I chose the theme."

"I'll admit, I loved that one! I have to say, that was one of my favourite experiences with you! The anticipation leading up to it was so intense. I mean, following you up the stairs and seeing you with nothing on underneath was a major turn on. And then the whole plan around the house, it was thrilling. But I have to ask, when did you come up with the idea of heading to the barn? I thought we were just going for a quick, tied hands encounter in the straw."

"Hay fever – thought better of it. Before you arrived, I did the other viewings and saw the meat hook on the back of the door. When you turned up, wearing that belt ordered off the bondage site I'd mentioned, I just knew I wanted to be stretched out and finger fucked that way. The rest was down to you!"

"I like this language you're using these days. It's kind of dirty Diana rather than the polite Di I'm used to. It's making me slightly aroused just sat here."

Nate re-adjusts himself in the chair, before continuing

"I think about that session a lot. You looked so feminine in the full skirt and blouse – sorry about the buttons by the way – and your breasts, your breasts all on show like that. Did you like the way you weren't able to do anything? That I had full control?"

"I loved it to be honest. I've concluded that I like being restricted. I think the visit to the cove proved that to me, but we will get on to that one soon. How you grabbed me from underneath and rubbed my bud whilst your fingers were up inside me, how you lifted me and penetrated me whilst I was still tied."

I can feel even now, just the thought of that barn visit makes me aroused. It really was a good session.

"May – That one was rather spur of the moment, wasn't it?! I really did just go to help Reggie out with the fencing that afternoon. You know, when Pete couldn't help; but darn, you looked so sexy in that tight jumper and jeans. Who wouldn't want to fuck you?!"

"I think that ended up being a collaboration of both our fantasies. The get out of jail card of being able to do it without any comeback. Thankfully, Reggie sussed out quickly to join in with us. Trying to explain afterwards was the difficult part bless him! It helped that he was my childhood crush and I fancied him... once, and the fact he is such a free spirit when it comes to sex – he was the ideal person for a threesome."

"That moment when you have my solid cock in you and Reggie is sucking you right there as well. I could feel you tighten around my shaft, and I just had the perfect view of your cheeks as you slid up and down on me.... I'm getting quite stiff thinking about it... moving on... June?"

"Birthday month. I just had to try it didn't I? You know I've been curious about girl-on-girl, but you, providing toys and then watching from the landing... that was one hell of a birthday present! Trust Alex to be up for it. Should have guessed it would have been her. Three bi-cousins, at least you didn't convince your first cousins to do it! Although ... twins...Mmmm... I joke! I joke! Third cousin it was."

"You liked the butt plug. Watching her insert it into you and then teasing you with it. I know you had mentioned trying one years ago but didn't know whether I was pushing my luck?"

"Hell no! I've got four different ones now! Love! Love! Love being plugged – but only now and again! What else did you like about that one?"

"I liked watching you enjoying it. I didn't see it as Alex, just two beautiful women making love. The application of the oil was full-on arousing. Her hands on you, oh, and when she sat on your face, and you tasted her for the first time..."

"July – that's one hell of a rental property. New to your parent's portfolio, is it?"

"Got it last year. Bought off one of dad's swinging mates. They lost loads of money during the pandemic and decided to sell up. Dad had the cash. Made sense. I had to do a few trips to set that one up for us."

"I've never really understood how your whole family are into that sort of thing, one way or another – although I was more enlightened at the annual do this year, and yet you, well personally I think you must have been adopted!"

"What can I say?! I just like one woman at a time me...now back to July. Since when did you become the submissive? You literally took everything I gave to you, from being strung from a beam, the ball gag, nipple clamps – yes, I know you didn't like them – and the spreader bar and makeup brush – where did that idea come from?"

"I began looking into submission sex after the barn. Saw a video where a woman was spread out like that, and it made me a little excited. I watched it a few times, actually. The makeup brush thought came to me that morning when I was putting "Rose" in. The brush was just there, staring at me, and I like how it feels when it touches my skin. I won't ask whose vibrator wand it was, that you used. Hope it wasn't your mothers!"

"I bought that in the sex shop, you know the one we have to drive past on the main road after the city. Again, back to the porn videos for inspiration!"

"August – Thank the skies I hadn't met Jim at that point! Reggie mentioning his colleague, in full uniform, so distinguished and older, gave me that idea. Little did I know he was more into Dylan that he would have been me! How did you get the silver fox look? If that's what you'll be like in a decade's time I'll be well happy in the bedroom!"

"My office job - box of wigs, fake hair pieces and temporary hair colours. The blue eye contact lenses took some getting used to. I wasn't keen on those; now I know why they all complain backstage about them! That was intense and quick that one. All that effort in the costume department and you had me done and dusted in twenty minutes! I do love it when you give me a blow job though Di, especially when you drag your teeth over me."

"I like giving head. You just never made me feel like you were interested in anything to do with sex. Not after 'that' conversation."

"It was years ago. I've apologised Di! Thousands of times. I just didn't think!"

"Are you kidding me?! After all the pain and struggle we went through for over a decade, and the huge amount of money we spent on IVF, all you had to say about our lost child was how hot I looked when I was pregnant? What kind of insensitive remark is that?! Millie is no longer with us, and all you cared about was my physical appearance. Every time I visit her gravestone, that conversation replays in my mind, reminding me of your callousness. Your complete and utter thoughtless words. It's like you don't even care that our child is gone."

"Sexy as in mother of my child and an amazing thing to have happened! Not that you're not sexy any other time! I was trying to make you feel better, not worse about yourself! I was grieving too! I still am. I will never, ever forget Millie! You completely shut down on me and we were never the same again, not until this year. It was easier to switch the bedroom light off and pretend to be asleep, then speak with you and get silence back. Shall we talk about September and the virgin vicar?"

"Yes. Let's move on." We haven't spoken about Millie in what feels like forever. I try to refocus. It's hard.

"Again, that was my idea. You were always so confident with sex from when I met you, I kind of wanted to see what it would be like if I were the femme fatal for a change. I felt so daft trying to put a display on for you and the binoculars. Really not my thing being a showoff. I'm so conscious of my body; having to stand there naked, because I had committed to that roleplay for the month. I really hoped the actual vicar didn't venture into the field."

"When I drove past him, so close to where we'd agreed to meet at Baileys Field, I was secretly hoping he'd watch! I thought you were extremely sweet to 'the vicar' and how you managed his nerdiness and innocence."

"October and your parents infamous parties – is that why we never stayed after hours? That's when the swinging and dogging activities begin. Is it only me locally that didn't know it happened here, on our doorstep?!"

"Sounds like it is. Ah, that one really wound me up. Beth had totally convinced herself we were going to be future husband and wife and then seeing you with Reggie, astride his lap..."

"You saw that? But you weren't in the room! I looked for you."

"It wasn't part of the agreement. That hurt. Beth was distracting. She was acting like a child – better off with Jack – no offence to your brother – but she's too immature for me and I'm not interested anyway."

"Remember, don't judge, just do. That was the rule. I was upset. You were all over her and then Alex saying she was your girlfriend...what was I supposed to think?"

"I wasn't all over her. She was tagging me. I just wanted to come over and speak with you, admire your butterfly zombie face paint and ..."

"Piss off about the face paint! I honestly didn't know Christa could only do that kind of makeup! I felt like a five-year-old child, turning up there. I certainly didn't look or feel sexy, and Dylan told me if I were to go, I had to knock you dead with my outfit! I couldn't walk in my platforms – much prefer my black leather boots, those ones with the laces up the back – and Beth looked so pretty in her Morticia outfit."

"I thought she was the one that looked like a child, not you. Must be her baby-face. Seeing you in your mini dress, head scarf and boots did all sorts of things for me. Shame it went to waste."

"But it didn't..." I stop myself. Taking Reggie back to mine wasn't part of the plan. Nate doesn't need to know about that one, yet. "If it had the right response on you... down below... then it was worth it."

"November, last month – my favourite month this year. You and me. Just us being us. It was like the early days. I mean, I didn't like seeing you so upset. When you were there in the rain, just on the floor hugging the bottle. I didn't know what to do. It reminded me of those nights wanting to hug you at the kitchen table but feeling unable to do so. But after, afterwards when we warmed up. That was just us and I have wanted that for so long Di. I didn't want it to end. I hope you feel the same?"

"I have hated you throughout the year for not coming to the counselling sessions. Speaking with Melanie separately, always being away when those times were important. Never putting me first anymore. Then you wrote that note and that shook me. That was the Nate I know, the one I love, the one I want to be with. I was upset. I wanted answers and all I got was a note. I still have it. It's only been a matter of days, but I read it differently now. I see you are there. I see you have been hurting too. Then, when you made love with me it reminded me how good it was and how good it can be again. I've enjoyed you being around these past weeks. Even last night when you came down the stairs dressed as Santa, my legs wobbled, and my heart fluttered. My own Santa, no-one else's. You are my husband and I want you to be with me. We just need to work that bit harder together."

Nate stands up from the table. "I agree. That's why Jack is taking over the lease for The Nap and I'm moving on to ..."

I cut Nate short.

"Moving? What do you mean moving?" I have that sinking feeling.

"Next door Di. Next Door. I've bought the farm and here...for us...for our future."

I'm dumbfounded. Totally blindsided, and not for the first time in the past twenty-four hours.

"What do you mean you've bought the Brayes? What about Bernard? Why hasn't anyone said anything to me? Why hasn't Jack told me?"

"It's why I had to go to the city the other day – to sign the paperwork at the solicitors and finalise everything. I spoke with your mum and suggested buying the farm for you and me – bring it back into the family – and from there it snowballed with Veronica moving in with her, and Jack taking this place on. He can live here on a lifetime lease if he helps with the two farms as he already is. Bernard is happy where he is and not interested in farming."

"What do you mean us? We're not together. We haven't made that decision yet. What about the cottage? What happens to that?"

I feel overwhelmed right now. So many thoughts going through my head.

"I've got the keys. Shall we have a look? I'm moving there anyway. I love you Di and want us to be together. I just want you to be happy... with me. We've been through so much and I thought...hoped... you feel the same way. I can work from home more as Beth and the lads take on more jobs. That's the plan anyway."

"I do! I do feel the same way! It's a lot to take on board right now and I don't know what to say or do."

Without thought, I put Nate's phone in my pocket, just like the old days, settle the pups and head out and on to the flint lane.

The sight of the old wrought iron gate hanging off its hinge, with the remains of the clematis plant woven through, fills me with nostalgia and joy.

Wincing once more at the doorbell "Can you change that awful thing? Those camera ones aren't exactly in keeping with the age of the property."

Nate smiles and turns the key in the lock. We step inside, and instantly the familiar smells of the house wash over me. The hallway is dimly lit, and the many photographs of the Brayes, the retirement newspaper announcement, and the picture of Reg at the bar in the east end pub are all gone. The sun-faded paper is all that remains, marking the places where they once hung.

As I wander through the rooms, alone with my thoughts, I realise that this could work. Nate and I could make a life here together, with Jack taking on The Nap and mum and Veronica just up the lane. Even Reggie, who's looking for a more permanent home after relocating, might be interested in renting the cottage from me.

I turn to Nate, a broad smile spreading across my face.

"I want to do this. I want to make a life here with you."

Nate's eyes light up, and he takes me in his arms. As we embrace, I know that this is where I belong. This is where I'll find happiness – we just have to work hard at everything.

Together, we explore every nook and cranny of the old farmhouse, planning our future together – even where the next Christmas tree will reside. As we stand back in the hallway, taking in the moment, I feel a sense of peace wash over me.

This is where I'm meant to be. I can feel my grandparents here, probably watching over with dad at their side who'd be shouting down at me "About bloody time Di. About bloody time!" - or similar.

The vibrating from my pocket breaks my thoughts. Forgetting it's Nate's mobile for a second, I place it on the little telephone table.

"At this time of night, it won't be important. I'm not ruining this moment, this one right now - bound to be work anyway."

The screen fades to black. Hiding the words…

"Your wallet's here, Santa! M Xx"

The End

ABOUT THE AUTHOR

Born in Kent, in the middle of nowhere, the youngest of four daughters, I was blessed to have amazing parents, who fought against the odds of having very little, working hard to provide everything and leave us wanting nothing.

A childhood full of colour and wonderment, surrounded by mother nature. A time often referred to as the "halcyon days of youth" where everything was so much simpler.

Now, with children, animals, and a husband too, I try to lead a less complicated life than the world around me tries to dictate.

Veg growing, flower planting and digging ponds – that's where you will find me, if not writing the next book.

Printed in Great Britain
by Amazon